To All a Good Night

To All a Good Night

DONNA KAUFFMAN
JILL SHALVIS
HELENKAY DIMON

BRAVA

KENSINGTON PUBLISHING CORP.
www.kensingtonbooks.com

BRAVA BOOKS are published by

Kensington Publishing Corp.
850 Third Avenue
New York, NY 10022

All Kensington titles, imprints and distributed lines are available at special quantity discounts for bulk purchases for sales promotion, premiums, fund-raising, educational or institutional use.

Special book excerpts or customized printings can also be created to fit specific needs. For details, write or phone the office of the Kensington Special Sales Manager: Kensington Publishing Corp., 850 Third Avenue, New York, NY 10022. Attn. Special Sales Department. Phone: 1-800-221-2647.

Brava and the B logo are Reg. U.S. Pat. & TM Off.

ISBN-13: 978-0-7582-2849-9
ISBN-10: 0-7582-2849-X

First Kensington Trade Paperback Printing: October 2008

10 9 8 7 6 5 4 3 2 1

Printed in the United States of America

CONTENTS

UNLEASHED

1

Emma Lafferty's life had gone to the dogs. Literally. And to the cats. And the parakeets, goldfish, hamsters, even the occasional potbelly pig. What it and her fledgling pet-sitting service hadn't gone to was her bank account. Not enough, anyway.

She glanced quickly—again—at the Google map printout she'd made based on the reams of detailed information she'd gotten from Lionel Hamilton's assistant. She'd always done better with a visual map rather than the go-south-on-route-whatever type instructions. Who knew which way south was? As luck would have it—her luck anyway—the aerial route had looked a lot simpler online. Of course, online, she hadn't been trying to find a strange house in the middle of the night, in the middle of nowhere, during a surprise winter ice storm.

"Happy holidays to me," she muttered, squinting through the permanently fogged windshield of her beloved, but beat-up Land Rover.

She cracked the windows a bit farther, hoping in vain that would help clear the view a bit more, then rolled her side window down enough to reach out and slap the wiper against the windshield. Again. The rapidly building crust didn't even budge.

Her headlights barely penetrated the sheet of dense gray in front of her. Regardless, she couldn't risk getting out on such a narrow, winding road. One oncoming vehicle and she'd be toast.

She slowed as she reached the peak of yet another long hill, bracing herself for the drive down the other side. Actually, a controlled slide was probably the best she could hope for at this point. "Why," she muttered through chattering teeth. "Why did I agree to this?"

She knew why. Chelsea, her best friend and cohort since their days together at Tech, had sold her on what had, admittedly, sounded like a pretty sweet deal. Chelsea was in Human Resources at Hamilton Industries, and she'd heard through the grapevine that the grand poobah himself, Lionel Hamilton, was looking for someone to take care of his home and assorted pets over the holidays. A sudden change in dates for a scheduled business trip to the Far East had, apparently, thrown a last-minute wrench into his holiday plans.

Emma had thought it odd that one of Lionel's many household staffers hadn't taken on the job, but Chelsea explained that he'd already surprised them with an extended vacation for the two weeks over Christmas and New Year's and didn't want to rescind the offer.

The dilemma for Emma had been that the job required her to live on premises as both house sitter and pet sitter, and, being that he housed his pets at his weekend residence, said premises was a good two hours outside of town. Which meant she'd have to turn her regular clients down. During one of the busiest seasons of the year. But the pay was ridiculously good, and while she certainly wanted to make her newly established client base happy, Chelsea had also pointed out that doing a good job for Lionel Hamilton might be her ticket to building the kind of clientele any business would love to have. The kind with deep pockets and no time to manage their own lives, much less their own pets. So, Emma had crossed her fingers . . . and taken the deal.

Hamilton Industries was a conglomerate that owned most

of Randolph County, Virginia, and employed pretty much everyone in it. Everyone except Emma. She'd removed herself from
their payroll seven months earlier when a small inheritance
had given her the gumption to do what she'd always wanted
to do—open her own business.

Emma's former job in accounting would have led to a nice,
stable career. She was good at her job, and it was a dependable
source of income. The only problem was it bored her to tears.
In fact, she'd hated it. The idea of toting up long columns of
numbers for the rest of her natural days left her feeling numb
inside. She didn't want to be numb. At twenty-nine, she was
too young to be numb.

She smacked the dashboard, trying to beat the heater into
functioning, not missing the irony as her teeth chattered so hard
her jaw hurt. "So, I open my own business, and I'm still numb.
Just literally, now."

Three treacherous hills and numerous Hail Mary's later,
Emma finally spied the huge wrought iron gate, announcing
the entrance to Lionel Hamilton's mountain getaway. As she
made her way slowly up the immense circular drive, she found
herself wondering, if this was the weekend house, what did his
everyday house looked like?

It was amazing even beyond what she and Chelsea had
imagined during the hours of animated discussion they'd in-
dulged in since she'd agreed to take the job. The massive marble pillars and soaring double-door entrance alone would have
sent her best friend into gossip nirvana, Emma thought as she
navigated her way around to the separate garage in the rear.
Not that she wasn't goggling over the place herself. In fact, she
could hardly wait to get settled in so she could call Chelsea
and share every detail.

She used the garage door opener that had been messengered
to her, along with a small, bound notebook containing the most
anal-retentive, detailed list of instructions, notes, and maps
she'd ever seen in her life—and was profoundly grateful to
have, as she'd accepted the job without ever directly speaking

to Mr. Hamilton. She'd gotten a handful of his assistants instead, over the phone, via e-mail, and text message, all of them borderline frantic to make certain she followed the notebook to the letter. Emma had assured the seemingly harried crew that she'd be fine, privately wondering what the hell she'd really signed on for. Then the notebook had arrived. And she'd been a little worried ever since. Maybe more than a little.

Hamilton apparently micromanaged his pets and his home the way he did his assistants. It was no wonder his employees sounded like they needed antacid chasers with every meal. She was close to that herself, and she hadn't even officially started the job yet.

Reminding herself how great the payday was going to be, plus the potential future clients the job would nab, Emma took a deep breath and eased her Land Rover into the ten-car garage. She then spent the next several minutes jaw-dropped as she stared at the half dozen or so very shiny, very expensive cars. She pulled in next to a midnight-blue Maserati and parked, then patted the dash of her Land Rover. "Don't let them make you feel bad. You have character."

She turned on the overhead light, sighing in relief when it didn't flicker back off, then consulted the first of the many detailed house maps in the addendum section of the notebook. After making sure the garage door was closed behind her and the alarm light activated, she grabbed two of her lighter bags, and made her way to the main house through an enclosed passageway. Once she made sure she could get in and move around without setting off the alarm system, she'd unpack the rest. But first she wanted to go introduce herself to her charges.

They didn't come to meet her at the door, but her notebook had explained that they would be penned up off the kitchen in the back, awaiting her arrival. She just followed the barking. And a voice shouting, "Welcome! Right this way!"

She wound her way through the expansive foyer, around the central staircase, then down one long hallway before finally coming to the double swinging doors that led to the kitchen. If you wanted to call it that. It did, indeed, have kitchen appliances and a large workstation in the center of one part of the immense room. That was the smaller part, though there was nothing small about it. Martha Stewart would weep for such a well-appointed kitchen space. But Emma's attention was drawn to the rest of the room, starting with the overlarge, low, round table, patterned in beautiful detailed mosaic tiles. The chairs surrounding it were cushioned with heavy brown and burgundy pillows and the whole thing was framed with an immense stone fireplace.

"Welcome! Right this way!"

Smiling, she went over to the huge wrought iron aviary and smiled at the rather imperious African Grey perched inside. "You must be Cicero."

"Cicero!" he repeated. "Welcome!" Then he whistled a beautiful tune that Emma didn't know the title of, but couldn't help laughing at, as she enjoyed his little show. She then turned her attention to the series of French doors leading to the enclosed, equally impressive, sunroom off the back of the kitchen. Most of her one-bedroom apartment would fit in that space. Behind the doors waited a tail-thumping basset hound named Jack, and Martha, a Harlequin Great Dane.

"Hi, guys," she said, accepting their enthusiastic welcome with a sincere smile and open arms. They made quick friends, then she found their leads and specially tailored doggie jackets right where the notebook said they would be. Thankfully, they were both used to wearing their Burberry plaid winter-wear and didn't struggle too much as she slid on the lined pieces and strapped them and their leads into place.

She led them both out into the cold, damp of the night as the ice and snow continued to pelt down. "Sorry, critters. I know this isn't the best of situations, here." As she carefully led them across the patio, lights sprang on in the trees, illuminating the immediate area, which was mostly wooded and slanted immediately uphill. The dogs were obviously used to the topography as they easily led her up a snow- and ice-covered path. The heavy layer of leaves and pine needles beneath the slippery surface provided much needed traction as their feet broke through the crusty surface. Still, she was huffing a little as they finally made it to a clearing at the top of the rise. The lighting cast an eerie glow through the mixture of snowflakes and slanted streaks of ice pellets, making her wonder what it must be like up here on a clear night. She spied two stone benches and evenly spaced mounds around the circumference, which were probably gardens or landscaped areas around the edges of the clearing, before becoming wooded once again.

Fortunately, the dogs made quick work of the business at hand, and they were soon heading back down the path and into the house. Where, just as the book noted, there were towels and a brush to loosen leaves and burrs, and chunks of ice, in this case, if needed. She quickly removed their leads and jackets, and rubbed them both down. Jack especially seemed to love this part of the deal, and squirmed in rhapsodic delight, while Martha spent most of the time sniffing Emma and trying to give her a dog-tongue facial. At least they were going to be easy to get along with.

"Welcome!" Cicero greeted them as Emma let all three of them into the kitchen area. "Right this way!"

She found the dogs' water dishes and topped them off, cleaned Cicero's as well, then rubbed her hands as she decided what to do next. First, she placed a quick call to her parents, letting them know she'd arrived safely, and once again assured them she would be fine, and yes, she was definitely going to miss seeing them for the holidays. She hung up, feeling a bit homesick. Christmas was her favorite time of year to go home to Connecticut. And though disappointed at not seeing their only daughter over the holidays, her mom and dad understood about the business decision she'd made and had supported her, for which she was very grateful. She thought about calling Chelsea, but decided to put that off until she'd settled in and seen more of the place. Which was, admittedly, calling to her. So, she also put off the plan of heading back out to the garage to get the rest of her things in favor of exploring. Otherwise known as snooping around.

She dug a bag of pretzels and a bottle of water out of one of the satchels she had carried in, and crunched on a few while she consulted the maps in the addendum section of the notebook.

"Snack time for Cicero! Snack time. I'm the pretty bird. Pretty bird!" There was a repeat performance of the whistled song, with a new flourish at the end.

She laughed and shook her finger at the Grey. "I've been well warned about your charming ways, mister. You're not going to wheedle junk food from me. You'll get your bedtime piece of mango, and that's it."

In response, Cicero gave her a wolf whistle, then laughed, quite impressed with himself.

Shaking her head and smiling, Emma balanced the notebook, the pretzels, and her water bottle, and wandered back to the main foyer, trying to decide where to explore first. Jack and Martha followed, quite happy to be off on another trek. She'd been informed that as long as she was in residence, they had the run of the house, but were to be put out in the Florida room if she had to leave for any reason. So she waved a hand toward the stairs. "Shall we?"

Martha loped easily up the wide marble staircase, while Jack took his time as his stubby little legs required a bit more effort to heave his long body from one riser to the next. But his tail was wagging the whole time, so she left him to his labors and went back to consulting the maps as she climbed to the second floor landing.

An hour later, she was quite thankful for the addendum maps, as she'd be hopelessly lost without them. Actually, even with them she'd gotten herself somewhat turned around, out at the end of the west wing—at least she was pretty sure it was west. Even the dogs had given up on the adventure and trotted off after some time, to God knew where. She was sure they'd find her when they got hungry or wanted to go out, so she wasn't too concerned about that. But she was getting hungry herself and she had no idea how to get back to the kitchen, much less the garage, or the rooms she'd been assigned to stay in.

She was stumbling down a dark corridor, unable to find the hall light switch, when a very deep male voice said, "If you're a burglar, then might I direct your attention downstairs to the formal dining room. The silver tea set alone would keep you in much better stealth gear for at least the next decade. At the very least, you'd be able to afford a flashlight."

Emma let out a strangled yelp as her heart leapt straight to her throat, then she froze in the darkness. Except for the animals, she was supposed to be completely alone. Not so much as a valet or sous chef was to be on the premises for the next twelve days. Of course, the notebook did say that Cicero had a lengthy and amazing vocabulary. But he was at least two floors away. And she doubted he knew how to use the house speaker system. Armed with the notebook and not much else, Emma decided offense was the best defense. "Please state who you are and how you got in here. Security has already been alerted, so you'd best—"

Rich male laughter cut her off. "You must be the sitter."

"Which must make you the burglar, then," she shot back, nerves getting the better of her.

More laughter. Which, despite being sexy as all hell, did little to calm her down. Because, though she'd been joking, the idea that she'd been on the job for less than two hours and had already allowed a thief into the house was just a perverse enough thing that it would actually happen to her.

The large shadow moved closer and she was deep into the fight-or-flight debate when a soft click sounded and the hallway was illuminated with a series of crystal wall sconces. Emma's first glance at her unexpected guest did little to balance her equilibrium.

Whoever he was, he beat her five-foot-nine height by a good half foot, which made the fight thing rather moot. Flight probably wasn't going to get her very far, either. He had the kind of broad shoulders, tapered waist and well-built legs her defensive line coach dad would recruit in a blink, and charming rascal dimples topped by twinkling blue eyes her Irish mother would swoon over as she served him beef stew and biscuits.

Emma, on the other hand, had absolutely no idea what to do with him.

2

Trevor Hamilton took in the unexpected sight before him. She was tall and quite capable-looking. Certainly looked up to the task of riding herd over the ungainly Martha, while staring down Cicero even on his most demanding days. She was doing a pretty damn good job of staring him down, and he knew that to be a challenge. When he wanted it to be, anyway. He wondered where Lionel had found her. Despite her quite capable demeanor, she didn't look nearly stressed out enough to be on his regular payroll.

"Lionel Hamilton is my uncle," he told her. "My great uncle, that is. His younger brother, Aloysius, was my grandfather. He passed on when I was little, so Lionel was sort of my substitute grandpa."

If his family cred did him any justice in her eyes, it was hard to tell from her steady regard. She was attractive, in an unconventional way, he decided. She had a head of thick, very unruly russet curls that tumbled over her shoulders and down her back and made a man want to bury his hands fist-deep. Her cheekbones were sharp, probably more so due to the set of her jaw at the moment. Her eyes, so far as he could tell, were a nondescript hazel, and yet easily held his own in a way that, admittedly, intrigued him. Her mouth . . . now there's where he got tripped up just a little. It was wide, with a deep bottom lip that begged to be nipped at while being kissed. He'd bet big money they were as soft as they were lush.

Her lips were so diverting, in fact, that it took him an extra moment to take in the rest of her. She wasn't slender, but not heavy either. Sturdy was the word that came to mind. And curvy. Strong shoulders and legs were offset by breasts that would more than fill a man's hands, and the kind of hips that would likely draw attention when she walked away.

And he should know. He'd had a lot of experience watching women walk away. Most often per his request.

Being decent, relatively attractive, and ridiculously wealthy should have been the trifecta of good fortune where meeting women were concerned. But he hadn't found that to be the case, so much. The ridiculous wealth attracted all sorts, as did the good looks, which made it hard to tell if any of them were there for the decent person part.

Which made the irony of this particular night all the more perverse. Because, in truth, he was behaving quite indecently at the moment. He despised golddiggers, and yet here he was, stealing from the Hamilton family trove. Or hoping to, anyway.

He'd been waiting a long time to get back into this house, but Lionel was always here, or some brown-nosing assistant who worked for him. This was the first time in five years his uncle had given the entire staff off for the holidays and had left town himself, to boot. Trevor had jumped on the opportunity, despite the chaos it had caused in his own life. Thanks to their somewhat shared grapevine, he'd even known about the hired sitter, and had planned to get what he'd come for and be gone before she'd arrived. Then the storm had delayed his flight to Virginia, and he'd had to rely on luck to get up the mountain before she did.

Apparently luck wasn't going to be on his side. But he was here now, and he wasn't leaving empty-handed.

"I'm guessing you haven't worked for Lionel before," he said, nodding at the small notebook in her hands that she'd clearly been referencing as she'd snooped about. "Anything I can help you find? I make a pretty good tour guide. I'll even throw in a few colorful family stories, if you'd like. We've had more than our fair share."

"Why are you here?" was her only response.

He didn't mind the bluntness. "I was going to surprise Lionel with a holiday visit, but apparently the surprise is on me." Which was true enough, just not in the way she'd interpret it. He lifted a hand to stall her response. "I already called. I know he's in Japan." He smiled, walked closer. "Must be tough taking on a live-in assignment during the holidays." He lifted his hands in the universal gesture of peace. "Since I'm here, I'd be more than happy to take on the sitter duties. I was planning on staying, anyway." Not for two weeks, he mentally added, but if he could get her out of here, he'd have free reign to dig to his heart's content, then he could always find someone else to come finish up the pet- and house-sitting jobs. It didn't really matter what Lionel would think about coming home to find a new sitter with his beloved pets. If Trevor took what he'd come for, his great uncle would have a lot more on his mind than a replacement sitter.

"There's a storm raging outside," she said, "in case you hadn't noticed."

"I didn't mean you needed to leave this exact instant, just that—"

"I do the job I'm paid for, Mr. Hamilton."

"Oh, I'd pay you your full fee. It's not your fault I showed up."

Her scowl didn't go away as he'd hoped. For most people, money solved everything. He was admittedly a little intrigued when it didn't seem to be an immediate attraction for her.

"I start a job, I finish a job. Unless Mr. Hamilton—Lionel Hamilton—requests that I hand the sitting duties over to you, then I'm here for the duration."

He wished he didn't admire her integrity, as it would make things a lot easier, but he did. "Fair enough. For now." He allowed his smile to spread when she arched a brow. "I'll have to figure out the time difference between here and Japan, and check his schedule before I bother my uncle, but we'll get it all sorted out. Unless you have a pre-planned time to communicate?"

She regarded him silently for a moment, then shook her head. "But I have contact information, so I certainly could, if I chose to," she added, clearly still wary of his presence.

Smart woman.

He stepped back and turned, sweeping his hand out in front of him. "Why don't we go downstairs? I don't know about you, but I'm hungry, and I'm sure the beasts are ready for their supper."

A stricken look flashed across her face as she darted a quick glance at her watch. "It's not—wait a minute." She looked back up, slightly accusatory. "It's almost ten o'clock at night. They don't get fed until the morning."

"Treats then," he said, completely unrepentant. It was nice to know she could be rattled, at least a little. And that she did, truly, seem to take her job seriously. He waved her forward. "Come on. The dogs might be on a strict dietary regimen, but that doesn't mean you and I can't raid the fridge."

She consulted her notebook again, but he wasn't sure she was really looking at anything meaningful, given he was pretty sure she was lost anyway.

He stepped forward to take a peek and she all but slapped the book shut in his face. "Fine," she said. "But you're on your own in the kitchen."

"Not much of a cook?"

She stepped around him. "I'm a great cook. But I'm not your cook." She walked away.

Stalked might have been a more accurate term, he thought, grinning as he watched her staunch retreat. He'd been right, he noticed. Quite a nice swing on that back porch of hers.

"Right, then down the steps, then left," he told her, when he caught up to her at the end of the hall in time to see her pondering which direction to take next.

"I can find my way," she told him sharply, then seemed to realize she was being overly tense about the situation, and relented slightly. "But thank you for the assistance." She started down the short hall, but paused at the top of the steps and looked back at him. "I'm going to settle the animals in for the night, then get my things and settle in as well. We can figure out how to handle . . . everything else in the morning."

She turned to go, but he put a hand gently on her arm. "I know my visit isn't in your little notebook, but I'm sure we can figure out how to stay under the same roof without all the tension. It's a big house. It shouldn't be too hard to stay out of each other's way. If we want to, that is."

Her gaze darted from his hand on her arm to his face. "Meaning what, exactly?"

He couldn't help it. He smiled. He hadn't meant that to sound as suggestive as it had. In fact, he wasn't sure why he'd tacked that little part on. It was to his advantage to have her want to steer as far clear of him as she could during his, hopefully very brief, stay. In fact, as soon as she tucked herself in, he planned to resume his hunt. If his luck changed, he'd be gone as soon as the sun came up and he could get off the mountain.

He lifted his hand, palm out. "Just that we're both here, we both have a right to be here, so we might as well make the best of it. Most people find me a relatively decent sort of chap, charming, even. So I just thought—"

"I'm here to take care of the animals' needs, not—"

"I wasn't asking for that. In any capacity."

Pink bloomed on her cheeks then, and she ducked her chin. "I'm . . . I apologize. You're right, it was silly to think—my mistake."

"No worries," he said, tilting his head just slightly as he continued to regard her. The sitter was turning out to be quite the puzzle. He already had one mystery to solve, however. No time to take on another.

When she didn't turn to leave, he gestured to the stairs. "Ladies first."

She jerked her gaze away, as if unaware she'd been staring. The pink still in her cheeks, she started down in front of him, then abruptly stopped on the next landing. She almost plowed into him when she suddenly swung around. "Oops, sorry. I didn't know you were so close."

It's your hair, he could have told her. He'd had to curl his hands into his palms to keep from reaching out to touch it. Even now he found himself wondering what scent of shampoo she used. "What?" He cleared his throat. "What's the problem?"

"No—no problem. But, can I see some identification? No insult, it's just—"

"No, no," he said, reaching into his back pocket. He smiled. "Lionel was smart to hire you. I'll be glad to put in a good word for the thorough job you're doing." Not that Lionel would have any interest in his great nephew's opinion, but she didn't have to know that. "Make up for scaring ten years off your life up there in the hallway."

"That's all right," she said, peering at the driver's license he flashed at her. "Chapel Hill?" she said, looking up.

He nodded. "Went to college in North Carolina and stayed there. Go Tarheels." He got the tiniest flicker of a smile from her then.

"You're speaking to a Hokie, here, so don't expect any enthusiasm on that score from me."

He made the sign of the cross with two of his fingers. "An ACC rival. However will we survive under one roof?"

"As long as that roof isn't the one covering Cassell Coliseum, you—and your Tarheels—are probably safe."

The stubborn had been replaced by smug. It was a damn cute smug, too. He really had no business noticing. "Very amusing.

It won't be so funny when your boys are at the Dean Dome this weekend."

Her smile went from smug to downright insouciant. "Big talk. Care to make a wager on that, Mr. Hamilton?"

He smiled, pleasantly surprised by the sudden shift to what could be described—almost—as easy banter between them. Amazing what college rivalries could do to lower defenses. Or at least distract them for a short time. "A betting woman, huh? And it's Trevor. Please."

"Okay, Trevor Please, I'll wager twenty and spot you the spread."

"Very generous. Why don't we go double or nothing? Seeing as you're so sure and all."

"I'm a loyal alumni, but I'm also a new business owner, so—"

"Say no more. I understand the fiscal fears there." She smiled, but her eyes said she didn't believe for one second he understood what it was like to lose sleep, sweat bullets, and yank out your hair over the start-up of a new company. He was a Hamilton, after all. They had piles of money just lying around. Which, was not altogether untrue. He'd just never once happened to touch his own pile, that was all. But why bother explaining?

"I'll tell you what," he offered. "Skip the monetary bet. We can wager food."

Her eyebrow edged up until it was lost beneath the cascade of curls. "Food?"

"You said you were a great cook. I win, and you're my cook. For one meal. Your pick which one."

"And, if I were to agree to this bet, and win, which I probably will, what would I get out of the deal?"

He gave her a mock affronted look. "I'll have you know the chicken Marsala I personally prepared for my last dinner party is still talked about in certain circles."

"As long as those circling weren't standing in the emergency room at the time, then I suppose I can agree to that. Except, how do you propose one of us collects on this bet? FedEx the ingredients?"

"Still trying to get rid of me?" He pushed open the doors to the kitchen, where they were both enthusiastically greeted by Martha, Jack, and Cicero.

"Welcome! Right this way!"

It wasn't until she moved past him as she crouched down to scratch Jack's head that he finally got a whiff of those softly scented curls, and he realized . . . "I don't know your name."

She stood but misjudged her footing, and he had to make a quick grab for her arms to keep her from stumbling backwards and falling over Martha. Which had the added benefit of bringing her flush into his personal space. They were, indeed, hazel, he thought, looking into her startled eyes, leaning toward green when her pupils dilated, as they were now. He discovered he was in no hurry to let her go.

"Emma," she managed, the word hardly more than a whisper. "Lafferty."

"Pleasure to meet you, Emma Lafferty." He smiled. "So, what are you going to cook for me?"

3

"Awfully sure of yourself, Mr. Hamilton."

"I thought we'd progressed to Trevor. Please."

Her lips curved a little at that, but she stepped back, breaking his hold. "Trevor, please let me know when you're done in the kitchen. I'm going to go unpack and settle in, and I don't want to be in your way."

"We haven't settled the terms of the bet."

"Why don't we leave it at this: If you're still here on game night and you win, I'll cook you the meal of your choice the following day. I win, I get your infamous chicken Marsala."

"So, I have to be present to win." He grinned and was entirely too charming about it. "Are you encouraging me to stay now?"

Emma picked up her satchels and slung the straps over her shoulder. Not that she didn't trust him, leaving them there while she hiked back out to the garage, but she suddenly felt like she needed to do something, anything, with her hands. Mostly because she couldn't stop thinking about his. On her. All warm and broad and strong and— "We'll work out the shipping details later if it comes to that. I'm sure you're good for it."

His grin only broadened at that, which she took as her sign

to skedaddle. The low chuckle as she scooted toward the door leading to the enclosed passageway didn't help much, either. Lord, but he was one very fine-looking man, with far too much charm and the kind of confidence that naturally came along with it.

"And, he's richer than Croesus," she muttered beneath her breath, feeling the heat bloom in her cheeks all over again as she recalled her bold assumption that he'd been suggesting some kind of intimate arrangement between the two of them. Not that she lacked at least a basic level of self-esteem—she loved dogs, but didn't consider herself one—however, a supermodel she was clearly not. And Trevor Hamilton could easily score in that range and probably did every damn day of the week. She cleaned up okay, but she wasn't, and never would be, in that range. She chalked up the flirting to what was likely his natural condition around women of any age, size, and flavor.

"The multimillionaire and the pet sitter," she muttered. "Yeah. That would happen." She dug out her phone. Chelsea would flip out when she described the place. And it would help take her mind off of her unexpected houseguest. Only, there was no way she was going to be able to keep from telling her best friend about that part, too, and Chelsea had a much higher opinion of their collective worth on the dating market than Emma did. But then, Emma was a realist. She pocketed the phone and went into the garage. Looking over the gleaming cars, she wondered which one belonged to Trevor, then immediately rolled her eyes at her continued interest in the man. "Eye on the goal, head in the game," she said through gritted teeth as she fought with the tailgate window of her Land Rover. "And Trevor Hamilton is not, I repeat, not, the goal. Nor are you even in the game."

"Need some help?"

She spun around, hand clutched to heart, to find Trevor leaning against a shiny black Mercedes. Cheeks hot—again— she tossed her hair back and prayed he hadn't overheard her little self-lecture. "If one of us is supposed to be a burglar, I'm thinking you're definitely the one with the stealth skills."

He shrugged and pushed away from the car. "Just thought you might need a hand. No need to get prickly."

"You could help by not handing me a heart attack every five seconds. And I'm never prickly. I'm cheerful and sunny." Even she had to smile a little at that acerbically delivered statement. "Animals love me for my warmth," she added, dryly.

Grinning, he said, "I'm sure they do." He stepped closer and nudged her out of the way, then popped the back door of her Land Rover with an easy twist of the handle. At her little huff, he turned to her. "I had this problem with mine, you just have to tug the handle down a little as you turn it. Here." He closed it again, then took her hand and put it on the handle.

She was so flustered by his assertiveness, and maybe a little by his hands being on her again, that she let him.

"Pull down a little, like this, and—" The door popped open quite easily. "See?"

She was too happy to have a solution to any of the myriad problems her ancient Land Rover gave her to give him a hard time about being so pushy. But she did slide her hand out from under his. "Thank you. I really appreciate that."

He peered inside. "Where're all the bags?"

"What bags?"

"You're staying for a few weeks, right?" He hefted out an old canvas army bag and a smaller gym bag. "Where's the rest?"

He'd hefted the strap of the canvas bag over his shoulder and slung the red nylon gym bag under his arm like they weighed nothing, when Emma knew damn well the canvas bag alone felt like it weighed three tons when she'd loaded it into the car. "Remind me to call you when I need a Pyrenees or a Newfie loaded into the back of this thing."

He just laughed. "In the front?"

"Dogs go in the back."

"No, I mean the rest of your stuff."

"You're carrying pretty much my entire wardrobe, which

probably says everything about me you never needed to know. Essentials are in the red bag."

"Essentials?" His confusion cleared. "Oh, you mean all the girl gear. Potions, lotions, magic makeup."

"Uh, sure." Let him think that. It was far more flattering than the truth. And she wasn't about to tell him that her idea of essentials had more to do with reading material, her glasses, and, yes, her retainer, than eyeliner and manicure supplies. "Some snacks I packed are in the front. I'll get those. If you're sure you don't mind." She nodded toward the load he was carrying. She still had the satchels to carry in. Again.

"This? No, not at all." He poked along behind her, like a nosy puppy, when she moved around to the passenger-side door. "What kind of snacks?"

She grinned as she turned and opened the plastic supermarket bag. "Dental bones and liver treats. Your pick. Or, maybe you're more a millet seed guy."

He looked in the bag, and back at her, pity clear on his face. "You need remedial road trip lessons. Where are the chips, sodas, and cookies?"

She'd felt his hands on her, and though his clothes hung a bit loosely on his frame, there was doubtful a spare ounce of fat to be found on the man. It wasn't fair that he could look like that and talk about cookies. "Right where they need to be," she said. "Out of my undisciplined reach."

He lifted his free hand up, and for a split second, she thought he was going to touch her face, but he just snagged the strap of one of the satchels, which doubled as her laptop bag. "You need help," he said, as he straightened, his face having come far too close to hers. He smelled good. Really good. So unfair. What had she and her perfectly innocent hormones done to deserve this kind of torture, anyway?

"Well," she said, sliding out from between him and the car and stepping back out into the open area of the garage. "I guess I'm lucky you're here, then. I really appreciate you lugging that stuff in for me." She should take at least the laptop off his hands, but decided retreat was the better part of saving herself from doing something really embarrassing, and all but fled back to the kitchen.

Trevor entered a minute later. "You're sure this is it?"

"Yep," she said, busy putting on the dogs' jackets and leads again for their last trip out for the night.

"Could you do me a favor, then?"

She looked up warily.

"I was going to pull my rental into the garage to keep it out of the storm. You'll need to set the alarm code for it anyway. I don't know the current one. Anyway, if you'll go out there and open the doors so I can pull in, then we can set it for the night."

Emma didn't want to think about spending the night with Trevor Hamilton. Well, not *with* Trevor Hamilton. But under the same roof. Even one as big as this one. "Uh, sure. But, can it wait until I get back in? They're all ready to go and—"

"No, no problem. I'll just pop this stuff in your room. Where are you set up?"

It was silly, because, in the big scheme of things, who cared? But she didn't want him in her bedroom. If she knew where it happened to be. Which she didn't. "I'm—actually, can you just wait for me to get back in? Don't worry about my stuff. I'll take my own bags up." Or over. Or wherever they were supposed to go in this rambling monstrosity of a mountaintop mansion.

She glanced back as she led the dogs through the French doors into the Florida room in time to see him lift those broad shoulders and shrug her bags gently to the floor, then wander over to the massive fridge instead.

Sighing in relief, for the moment, anyway, Emma turned and opened the door to the backyard, only to be met by a wall of stinging sleet and pellets of ice. She started to retreat back into the closed-in porch, but Martha was already pulling her out into the now blistering storm. Jack wasn't as enthusiastic, but trudged along, head ducked. Emma flipped the hood up on her fleece-lined canvas coat and kept her head ducked, too, as she led them to the edge of the trees. "Here, guys," she said, having to raise her voice over the cracking sound of the storm as the ice and sleet pummeled the trees and ground. "Not going up that hill in this." She had her good hiking boots on, and they had great traction, but ice was ice. She'd have to look in the addendum section to see if there was a note about where she might find a bag of gravel or something to throw around, at least in the backyard.

Maybe Trevor knows, she thought. No. If she was lucky, he'd have already fixed a sandwich or something and gone to bed. Wherever that was. A vicious gust drove the ice pellets sideways, hitting her cheek as she tried to corral the dogs back toward the house. And even that didn't stop her from picturing Trevor in bed. Getting ready to get in bed. Possibly taking a shower before going to bed.

"Come on," she shouted to the dogs, perhaps a bit more loudly than absolutely necessary, then all but dragged them back inside. "My God, it's nasty out there, isn't it?" she said, talking to them as she took their jackets and leashes off and toweled them down. Poor Jack was trembling, not enjoying the rubdown nearly as much as he had last time. She crouched in front of him and worked the ice from his paws. "I'm sorry, little guy. It sucks to be a small dog in a big storm, I know."

Martha was licking at the ice clumps in her paws, but otherwise didn't seem to be all that adversely affected.

"Wow, check that out," came a male voice almost directly overhead. "The storm's really picked up."

She prided herself in not even glancing up as Trevor's jean-clad legs passed by her lower line of vision. A mere tip of the chin would have put her eyes right in line with his— "Sorry, fella," she told Jack, forcing her attention to stay exclusively on finishing up with Jack's ice-clumped feet. "I know it hurts."

"Maybe it's too late to get my car in, it's probably encrusted by now. But I'd like to at least go check."

She finished with Jack and had to stand to attend to Martha, who had already taken care of the worst of things with her big feet. Emma rubbed her head, neck, and legs down with a dry towel. "Suit yourself," she said to Trevor, completely unconcerned. Completely unconcerned that they were going to be stuck in this house—together—for possibly longer than one night.

Right.

Just as soon as she stopped thinking about him naked in the shower, she'd be unconcerned.

"Here," he said, reaching out to take the towel from her hands. "I can finish drying her off if you'll—"

"Just because I was just out there does not mean I'm heading out to check on your car. You want it in the garage, I'll be happy to—"

"Did I ask you to go out there? All I need you to do is open one of the garage doors." He tugged the towel out of her grudging grip.

"Fine," she said, knowing she sounded like a shrew, but he did things to her equilibrium she really didn't appreciate. Too bad if he didn't understand that. She wasn't about to explain it to him. She left him with the dogs and headed down the passageway to the garage, then realized she'd forgotten the Hamilton bible with the garage code and turned around to head back. A second later two things happened almost simultaneously. The lights flickered out, casting her in immediate full darkness . . . and she ran chest first into Trevor Hamilton.

"Hold on there," he said, finding her arms easily despite the complete lack of light.

"The lights," she said. "What happened?"

"The storm, I'm guessing. Ice is heavy. It probably coated the power lines and took some of them down."

"Generator?" Surely a house as massive as this one had a backup system, but she didn't recall reading anything about one in the book.

"I don't know," he said. "I've never been up here when the power went out."

She suddenly realized she was still standing deep inside his personal space, and that he still held her arms. "I—I need to get back to the kitchen, make sure the dogs and Cicero aren't freaked out."

"Yeah, I guess my car isn't going to come inside out of the cold after all."

"Do you need anything from it?"

There was a pause and she could have sworn it wasn't a comfortable one, but given that she couldn't see even a glimmer of his face, she couldn't really tell.

"Nothing that can't wait until morning."

Whatever awkward pause Emma thought she'd detected was lost in the sudden intimacy of having a man talking about being there in the morning, his voice all deep and sexy, when they were—once again—all caught up inside each other's personal space. Yeah. She really needed to stop that.

Clearing her throat, she stepped back, bumped into the passageway wall, stepped forward again, bumped into Trevor, who was reaching out to steady her. "Sorry," she said, frustrated and, when he just chuckled, a little embarrassed. So much for getting outside the fog that seemed to envelop her every time he was near.

"Not to worry," he said. He held on to one of her arms, then turned and pulled her hand to his waist. "Here, grab hold and we'll feel our way back to the kitchen." He pushed her hand so it slid down the rock-hard side of his torso to where his belt was looped through the waistband of his jeans. "Got me?"

If he only knew. Rubbing her hands all over him . . . not exactly helping her out at the moment. That he didn't seem remotely aware of the personal nature of this kind of contact, or what it might be doing to her, didn't make her feel much better, either. Apparently she was the only one who went into some kind of hormonal stupor when the two of them were close. Not all that surprising really, but still.

"Yeah," she said, then cleared her throat when the word came out as a croak. "Go ahead. We need to check on the dogs."

Her eyes had adjusted a little to the dark, but with almost no natural light filtering into the passageway, she couldn't make out much more than his shadow in front of her.

She could feel his body heat through the fabric of his shirt, and how lean and hard his waist was as he moved in front of her. And how much she'd love to run her hands around to the front, to what was certainly to be his equally hard and flat stomach . . . then he'd pause, reach down and cover her hands, pull them more tightly around him, stop, and slide them around his waist, before tipping her chin up so he could dip his own down and—

"Watch your step," he said, quite abruptly interrupting her little fantasy. "Kitchen straight ahead."

She jerked her hand away. "I—I think I can take it from here. I have an emergency flashlight in my bag."

"Handy. Why don't you turn it on and we can root around for some candles or something, so you don't burn your batteries out."

"I'm just going to get Cicero settled, make sure the dogs are okay, then find my room."

They bumped their way into the kitchen, where they were greeted by the cold noses and the enthusiastic whining of both dogs.

"Welcome!" Cicero called, sounding a bit panicky as he rustled in his cage.

"It's okay," Emma said, as she rubbed Martha's body and crouched down to scratch Jack behind the ears. She stumbled her way to the counter and groped along, looking for her bag, but couldn't find it. "I know I left it right here."

"Left what?"

She jumped a little when she realized Trevor was right behind her. "My bag, with the flashlight."

"Oh, you meant your shoulder bag? You—uh, I think you

have it on your shoulder. At least you did when you walked out of the kitchen earlier."

Even as he said it, she realized he was right. In all the commotion, she'd sort of managed to forget that little bit of information.

"I can't find my glasses when they're on my own head," he told her, as she groped around inside her bag for the flashlight.

She appreciated him trying to make her feel better, but he didn't know everything that had been going through her mind back there in the pitch black hallway. "You wear glasses?"

"For reading. Why?"

"No reason, just . . . no reason." He struck her as this perfect, godlike specimen, so it just didn't jibe that anything about him wasn't functioning at one hundred percent. She wisely kept that part to herself. She found the flashlight and pulled it out, switched it on, casting them both in a small pool of yellow light.

"Not exactly industrial size," he said, looking at the tiny beam. "But it should do the trick."

"I—it's for reading." She started to explain that she liked to read and that she always carried a little flashlight as a sort of book light, but he already thought she was a dork. No need to give him further reason to be amused at her expense. "But it comes in handy for all sorts of things. I had a flat tire not too long ago in the middle of the night and—" She stopped. She was babbling. She never babbled. "Anyway, I'll sit it here on the counter and take care of the bird, if you want to look for candles." She propped it on its end so the beam of light cast upward, but it was so small, the glow didn't really reach very far.

"Why don't you take it and go cover Cicero for the night and get him settled, then I'll take it and root around in the cupboards.

"I'm surprised there isn't a generator," Emma said. "In a house this size, out this far from town, I'm guessing power going out isn't entirely unusual."

"Maybe there is one but it has to be turned on manually."

"I don't recall seeing it in the book or addendums, but—"

"You mean the notebook you were carrying earlier?"

"Yes. Your Uncle Lionel compiled it, or had it compiled, to help guide me through my stay here."

"And there are addendums?"

"Oh, yeah," she said, then realized she hadn't sounded entirely kind, and hurried to add, "but it can never hurt to have too much information."

Trevor chuckled. "Don't worry, you didn't offend. Lionel is nothing if not thorough with his attention to detail. At least when it suits him, anyway."

Emma looked over at him. He was rummaging through the drawers that were closest to the light. She wondered what he'd meant by that last part. There'd been a slight edge to the dry amusement. She turned back to Cicero. "Okay, big guy, let's get you your evening treat."

"Snack for Cicero! Cicero is a pretty bird."

He sounded a little less panicked, but still not settled. "Yes, yes, you are."

She grabbed the plastic container from the little cupboard next to his cage and fished out a piece of dried mango. She fed that to him and watched him hike it all the way down to his water dish, dunk it carefully a few times, then scoot down the rung to the middle of his cage and quietly enjoy his soggy feast. She changed his paper from the sliding tray beneath the cage, dumped it in the trash, then turned around and put her hands on her hips. The dogs had all but shadowed her every step since she'd come in the kitchen and were right behind her, looking at her expectantly. "I'm guessing you guys want to come with me."

Martha enthusiastically bumped her head into Emma's stomach, while Jack wriggled around her ankles, his tail slapping back and forth. "Well, we need to find out where we're bunking in first." She really wished she'd done that first upon arriving, but it was too late to worry about that now.

Cicero was done with his snack, so she said her good nights and covered him up, heard him fluff his feathers out, and relaxed a little. One down, anyway. She walked back over to the counter. "Any luck?"

"No," Trevor said, his head buried in one of the lower cupboards. "Mind sticking around here for a few minutes and letting me use the flashlight to finish looking in the cupboards and pantry? One candle and I'm good."

"Go right ahead." She handed him the flashlight and watched him as he turned his back on her and began systematically going through drawers and cupboards. This left her time to wonder how she'd ended up stuck in a house with a man who did things to her libido that should be illegal, when she was supposed to be stuck only with a couple of dogs and an unruly parrot. Why her? She scooted onto a stool, sighed, and propped her elbows on the counter.

"That was a particularly plaintive sigh. Am I keeping you from something?"

She hadn't realized she'd made a sound, but she really couldn't be faulted for it. Didn't he know how ridiculously attractive he was? Didn't he know that when he bent over like that to look through the lower cupboards, his jeans cupped a rear end so fine it was male model worthy? Didn't he know that she'd spent the last seven months building her business, leaving her no time for men of any kind? Much less the kind with magazine-cover asses? "No," she finally managed, when she realized she hadn't answered him. Because she was staring. Again.

"Not finding much," he said, and straightened. "Why don't I lead you to your room, get you settled and see if maybe there are any candles in there so you can have some lighting, then borrow this"—he waved the flashlight around—"and dig around a little more."

Oh, great. Trevor Hamilton was going to be in her bedroom after all. While she was in it. That's what she needed. Well, that was exactly what she needed, or wanted anyway, but she doubted he'd be on board with the suggestion, especially as he'd so quickly shot down her earlier assumption that he'd been looking for temporary companionship. "Sure." She slid off the stool, slapped her thigh so the dogs fell in beside her, hefted her nylon bag and reached for her other duffel.

"I'll get these."

She didn't bother arguing. With her luck she'd swing around a corner and take out some eighth-century figurine or something. Better if he was the one who took that risk. At least he was family.

"Where are we headed?" he asked, hovering at the entrance to the front hallway.

"I haven't a clue. I looked at the map earlier, but—" She stopped short of telling him she'd gone off exploring in the opposite direction. She didn't need him reporting to Lionel that his sitter had been snooping. "I think I got turned around."

He slid one bag to the floor. "Here, let me look at the map." He held out his hand for her notebook.

She hesitated.

He smiled. "Trust me, I'm not interested in Lionel's dog-sitting mandates and endless house rules."

What are you interested in? She shoved the book in his hand, thankful she'd managed not to say that out loud. In her head it had sounded sexily suggestive. Best she'd left it right there.

"Good God," Trevor murmured, juggling the book and the flashlight.

"You're skimming."

"Is there an index to this thing? How long are you staying, anyway?"

"Twelve days. And the section on my accommodations is in the front."

"Ah. Says here you can choose any room in the upper east wing." He looked up. "You were in the west wing when I found you."

She shrugged casually. Or so she hoped. "I'm better with left and right than east and west."

He eyed her for a moment longer, then flipped the book shut and handed it to her. "Follow me."

As they left the kitchen for the front hall, the air got noticeably cooler.

"Uh-oh."

"What, uh-oh?" Emma said.

"No heat." He started trudging up the main staircase. The dogs wove their way between them, with Martha quickly out in front, and Jack trying his best to kill them both by sending them falling backward as he nudged through their feet.

When Trevor got to the main landing of the second floor, he said, "Change of plans. Follow me."

"What change of plans? Wait a minute." But she had to hurry to keep up with his long-legged stride.

"We can look for the generator switch and whatever else we need in the morning when we have daylight. And, hopefully, some sun to go with it. But for tonight, we can huddle in here." He paused in front of a pair of double doors and swung them open. "Follow me."

Emma stuck her head inside the door. As Trevor moved inside, the small beam of yellow light illuminated enough furniture to show that it was a sitting room or parlor of some kind. A rather large one.

"Aha," he said, flashing his beam across the room to highlight the detailed filigree in the masonry surrounding a huge fireplace. Another flick of his wrist showed the wood stacked next to it. "That'll do. For the night anyway."

"Wait a minute. You're proposing we both stay . . . in here? Together?"

He looked back over his shoulder. "Conserve heat. There are a few bedrooms with fireplaces, but not in your designated wing. Of course, we could break Lionel's rule book and go find one with—"

Just the brief visual of her and Trevor stumbling together

through the dark house, looking for a bedroom with a fireplace—where they would both, presumably, stay for the night—was enough to make up her mind. "Here is fine."

She walked in with Jack on her heels. Martha obviously knew the room as she trotted right over to the long curtains covering one of the windows and nosed it aside. Not even a glimmer of moonlight trickled in. Once Emma's racing heartbeat subsided a little, she realized she could hear the steady tapping of ice hitting the windowpanes. Great.

She heard the scrape of a match on flint, and minutes later the room was filled with a warm yellow glow as Trevor nursed a fire to life in the fireplace.

Emma slid her satchels to the floor and watched him as he alternately blew on the embers and added more wood. Was there anything sexier than a man building a fire?

He turned and looked at her right then, and smiled. The firelight captured his features in stark relief, making his smile brighter and his eyes glow with life. "Don't worry. I'll have you warmed up in no time."

Oh, have no fear, she thought as she purposely turned her attention to the dogs. *You've got me plenty warmed up.*

4

Trevor could feel her gaze on him like a tracking beam. Oddly, it didn't bother him overly much. He'd had more than his fill of being stared at in his thirty-one years, but he'd long since made peace with the DNA gods, and no longer denied the reality that being a relatively good-looking guy came with its fair share of perks. But that didn't mean it didn't occasionally bother him anyway.

In business, it was an admitted advantage. Unfair as it was, people were more willing to open doors, and their checkbooks, for attractive people. That fact that his last name was Hamilton hadn't hurt, either. And yes, he'd taken advantage of both. For a cause.

But there were other times when it would have been a lot easier if he were a bit more invisible. Doors might open to him, but he hadn't missed the other comments made. The thinly veiled compliments that were intended to make it clear that those less fortunate didn't appreciate the "free ride" given to the "beautiful people." Especially beautiful people named Hamilton.

If they only knew.

Which was precisely why he had stolen into his great uncle's home in the middle of an ice storm. Because *he* had to know.

Had to know, once and for all, if he was really a Hamilton.

At the moment, however, he was only aware that Emma was watching him. And, for some unknown reason, that fact intrigued the hell out of him. Which made no sense. Because, while he'd come to terms with the reality that his smile and his name opened business doors on occasion, he was thoroughly done with either of those commodities getting him attention in any personal way. Sure, he'd met his fair share of women whose heads weren't completely turned by a pretty face, but once they found out he was a Hamilton . . . well, things invariably changed. Even if they claimed otherwise.

He could have told them that he lived off whatever he made, not what he'd been born into, and, in the beginning, he'd tried to do just that. But he quickly learned it made little difference. The fact that he had a healthy seven figure trust fund out there, untouched or not, was far too intoxicating not to send even the most sensible and levelheaded woman off on at least a short-term trip to "what if" land. And once he saw that particular gleam in their eye, short-lived or not, it pretty much killed the attraction from his end.

But there was something about the way Emma was looking at him that didn't shriek gold digger or player. She was clearly not the latter, having given her affections far more easily—totally, actually—to the two- and four-legged beasts in the house. She hadn't even pretended to flirt with him. As for the first part, though, well, he couldn't be sure. She was a pet sitter, and, though he had no clue about her personal circumstances, one would assume she wasn't exactly rolling in it. She might be looking at him as a potential ride. Despite the fact that he hadn't seen so much as a glimmer of that avaricious spark in her eyes when she'd found out he was a Hamilton.

Still, whenever he looked up and caught her staring at him,

her expression wasn't so much calculating as . . . hungry. Like she'd been deprived of her favorite dessert for a very long time and had just been handed the keys to Willy Wonka's place. Only, for whatever reason, she was going to force herself to be content with keeping her nose pressed to the glass, staying outside and just looking in.

And, something about the idea of being her taboo dessert turned him on. A little. He looked back toward the banked fire and poked at the glowing embers. Okay, maybe more than a little. But that was strictly the atmosphere talking. Storm raging outside, power out, a roaring fire. He found himself glancing at her again. A woman who wouldn't have likely caught his eye in a crowd, but was presently making his fingers itch to take all that long, curly hair and spread it out to see what it looked like by firelight.

He held her gaze a moment too long, that moment where she realized they were staring, at each other, and saying nothing. His body reacted, and he wondered what the state of her body was at that moment, and spent another too-long moment wondering if he should push it. Just to see. Because . . . why not?

Which had him jerking his gaze immediately back to the fire, and, after arranging another log on top of the now piping flames, pushing himself to a stand. He was here on what was, hopefully, going to be the most important night of his life. Why in the hell he was letting her distract him like that, or at all, really, he had no idea.

He scooped up the flashlight. "You'll be okay here for a while?"

She seemed to have snapped out of that momentary reverie as well, as she was presently making quite the production out of rummaging through her satchel. "Yes, of course." She glanced up, and it appeared ever-so-casual, except he was far too aware of her every move at this point. Therefore, he didn't miss the quick, hungry once-over she gave him, standing there in front of the fire, before going back to searching for whatever the hell was so important in her bag. "What are you going to do?"

"Hunt for candles," he said. Amongst other things. He willed his body to subside, and prayed it wasn't obvious in the shadows cast by the fire. But honestly, did she have any idea what that kind of swallow-you-whole look did to a man?

A quick glance showed the dogs had already collapsed on the rugs lining the floor, quite content to doze by the fire. He walked over to the door, stepping over a prostrate Jack on his way. The basset thumped his tail a few times, but didn't bother to pull himself out of his hearth-induced stupor. Trevor smiled as he paused in the doorway and looked back at Emma. It was quite the picturesque winter scene. Fire roaring, dogs sprawled, windowpanes frosted over. Emma curled up on the couch, still rummaging. But he could just as easily picture her with a throw over her lap and a book spread across her knees. He wondered if she wore glasses to read. She'd look all studious, he thought, and sexy as all hell. He shifted in the doorway to hide the reaction that little visual had caused. Really, he had to get out of here, for his own good. And hers.

If things went as he suspected, there would be quite the up-roar when word got out. Lionel wouldn't be pleased. And he didn't want Emma getting caught up in fallout not of her own making. No, he'd have to find a way to make sure she took no blame in what he was about to do. Which meant he couldn't even think about entangling himself with her. Even for one, stormswept winter night. "Do you—" He had to pause to clear his throat and the thickness from his voice. She really knew how to . . . impact a guy. "Do you need anything else at the moment?"

"No, I'm good." She pushed her hair back from her face with one hand as she kept digging with the other. "How long will you be gone?"

It rather stunned him, the strength of will it took to keep his hands to himself in that moment and not go straight to her and drag her down on the couch. Nose pressed to the window, indeed. If only she knew how badly he wanted her to come into his candy shop. That hair of hers was like a living, breathing thing. And he wanted his hands all tangled up in it. He shoved one hand in his pocket, out of apparently irreversible necessity. The other merely gripped the flashlight a little more tightly. "I'm not sure," he said.

"We have the fire, and plenty of wood. I don't mind keeping it stoked so it lasts till morning. You don't have to hunt for candles." She had no idea how easily she was keeping things stoked already.

He really needed to get the hell out of this room. "I'd just feel better if we had more alternate light sources. If we need to move around during the night. Restroom calls, refrigerator raids . . ."

"Okay."

So dismissive. The epitome of casual disinterest. Very "I'm not even paying attention to you."

Yeah. Right.

Clearly, not true. Well, not clearly, but certainly he wasn't the only one with the whole heightened awareness thing going on. Just moments ago, she'd looked at him like a woman craving a sugar rush, and he'd been a giant Everlasting Gobstopper.

He really needed to refocus. "Okay, then," he said, because apparently his ability to be a witty conversationalist had vanished. Right along with his common sense. "I'll check back in with progress reports."

"Fine."

He stared at her bent head for another too-long moment, frustrated that she didn't seem to be having as much difficulty fighting this . . . whatever it was, as he was. That, and he was wondering what her smooth, bare skin would look like by firelight. Which, when he realized what he'd been thinking, had him swearing under his breath and ducking abruptly out of the room. Considering she could have presented a major obstacle to him getting what he'd come here for, she was making his premeditated plan perfectly easy for him to execute. Even with the added problem of the power loss, he couldn't have asked for a better resulting scenario. Candle hunting. It was a brilliant off-the-cuff plan, if he did say so himself. So, why in the hell was he not racing to take full advantage of it?

"Because," he muttered, as he wound his way back to the main stairs, "the only thing I want to take advantage of is Lionel's hot little pet sitter." Except there was nothing little about her. And, on any traditional scale, she wasn't exactly pretty, much less hot.

So why was he smiling as he went down the stairs and made his way to Lionel's personal study? He wasn't sure, not entirely. But maybe it was because, although she looked at him like forbidden fruit, she talked to him like he was an annoying fly in her pet-sitting ointment.

God, he'd never thought himself perverse when it came to women, but apparently, there was a first time for everything.

Well, he'd simply use that as motivation to find the proof he'd come for as quickly as possible, and get the hell out. Complications he didn't need. And he didn't want to complicate things for her. She didn't know what she was possibly getting into by just being here at the same time as his little visit. And he was sure as hell not going to tell her. Find the Bible, get out of the house. Simple plan.

He let himself into Lionel's study and flashed the thin beam of light around the room. He groaned. Simple, huh? He'd been in this room many times, but he didn't remember there being quite so many books. Possibly because he'd never faced searching through them before.

The room was octagonal and formed part of the corner tower built into the mountain retreat. Four panels of the room contained floor-to-cathedral-ceiling bookcases, each crammed full of books. This library section of the room came complete with rolling ladder to climb to the upper echelons of each stack. He supposed he should be grateful for that much. Another panel contained the nine-foot-high door he presently stood in, and the remaining three contained windows that started around two feet from the baseboards, and, in multiple panes, covered the entire length of each section of windowed wall. Heavy curtains were drawn over them, but they barely muffled the sound of the ice pinging against the many panes of glass. In fact, the sound was far more prominent in here, possibly because the room itself protruded away from the rest of the structure of the house, making it more vulnerable to the elements. The rapid-fire tattoo of ice pellets brought with it the disturbing reminder that, even if he did find what he sought, he might not be able to get out in the morning.

In fact, given that the rural roads weren't high on the county's list of what to plow or treat in inclement weather, he could be stuck here for a few days.

A few long days. With Emma. By the fire.

He groaned and quickly made his way over to Lionel's cherrywood desk. It was a massive thing with heavy, carved legs, squatting ominously and gleaming in the center of the octagonal room. He felt a momentary pang for what he was about to do, but pushed that aside and ducked around behind the mini-fortress before he had a change of heart. This was his one chance. Once Lionel heard he'd been here, he would contact his great-nephew and demand to know why. And Trevor would tell him. And that would be the end of Trevor's visits to the mountain retreat. So, he had to make good with the one shot he was ever likely to have. Because he certainly wouldn't ask Emma to lie and say he hadn't been here, especially when she was already in potentially enough trouble just by associating with him at all.

He skimmed the light over the drawers, then knelt before the first set of books stacked on one side. The chances that Lionel kept the ancient family Bible, or any other family documentation, right in his desk drawer was slim, but he'd feel better when he'd eliminated it from the possibilities. He had to at least check it out.

Another possibility that hadn't escaped him was that Lionel might have locked the thing up in the family vault. Only Lionel had access to that code, but possibly, if the Bible wasn't in the desk, the code would be. Somewhere. Possibly jotted in a journal. Something personal, perhaps, that would trigger awareness of it's purpose in a family member, but not with a common thief.

At the moment, he felt like both as he slid each drawer open and carefully rifled through the contents. He didn't bother with worrying about things like fingerprints. If he found the proof he sought, Lionel would know soon enough, as Trevor had every intention of confronting him with it. If he didn't find it, then Lionel would never suspect him, a family member, of snooping around anyway.

Unless someone mentioned it to him. Someone like Emma.

He rocked back on his heels and ran his plan through his head. Again. Nope, he concluded, he couldn't involve her. Besides, who was to say she'd be trustworthy anyway? Her loyalty, if she had any, would be to Lionel as he was the one ultimately responsible for handing over her paycheck. And a very healthy one he imagined it would be. Lionel could be a real stick in the mud about, well, pretty much everything. But he paid people enough to put up with his bullshit. Trevor was certain he was taking good care of Emma as well.

Good enough not to risk getting herself involved in a lie. He was a virtual stranger and she owed him nothing. *Of course,* a little voice said, *there are other ways to sway her into wanting to protect you. . . .*

No, he resolutely answered. *Absolutely not.* He was not

that type. Hadn't he spent most of his life loathing the users and hangers-on? And, given that, he was the last person on earth who would ever use another person for personal gain.

He scooted over and started on the next set of drawers. And put any thoughts of seducing Emma right out of his mind.

5

Where the hell was he anyway? Emma shooed a curious
Martha back into the parlor and shut the door, closing
the dogs in. She knew they were allowed to wander freely, but,
given the circumstances, and not being fully—okay, even par-
tially—familiar with the layout of the place, she would feel
better if she knew where they were at all times until they got
the power restored. "I'll be back," she called through the door,
when Jack whined and snuffled his nose along the crack at the
bottom. "Just go lie down." The fire was banked and more glowing than burning, there was a full screen in front of it, so they
should be fine, she told herself. Mostly because she really didn't
need anything else going wrong. She hadn't even been there
twenty-four hours and already everything that could go wrong
had.

At the moment, she wanted to know where Trevor was.
He'd said he was going to check back in with her, but that had
been almost an hour ago. Just how badly did they really need
candles, anyway? Wouldn't it make more sense just to wait
until morning and search with some natural lighting to help
them along the way, instead of burning up the only batteries
she had? Surely they could make it that long.

At least, that was her excuse for heading out to look for him. And she was sticking with it.

She felt her way along the wainscoting on the hallway walls, pretty sure she was heading back toward the stairs. A minute later her sense of direction was, for once, proven to be correct when her hands hit the banister railing. She gingerly moved down the risers, wishing that even a sliver of moonlight was easing through the stained glass windows bordering the huge front door, down in the foyer below. No such luck. Her night vision, which had adjusted well with the firelight, was once again reduced to nothing. She paused at the foot of the stairs, keeping one hand on the newel post as she tried to figure out which way to launch herself with the least chance she'd crash into something extremely expensive, and extremely breakable.

Just then an actual crash resounded from somewhere to her right, followed by a thump, a grunt, and a rather long string of curse words.

"Trevor?" she called out, but got no response. Dear God, what if he'd gotten hurt? At least the curse words proved he'd survived whatever it was that had happened. "Where are you?"

All she got back was a groan. Oh, no, he was in too much pain to shout and direct her to his whereabouts. The best she could do was to strike out blindly in the direction of the crash, and hope she didn't end up in similar circumstances.

"Did the batteries wear out already?" she called, more just to hear her own voice and help to stay steady, than because she really expected him to answer. Plus, if he could hear her, he'd know she was actively trying to find him. "You've been gone a long time. I was worried, so I came looking for you." Her outstretched fingertips jabbed into a wall. A very hard wall. Now she was the one swallowing a string of swear words as she shook the life back into her fingers, then curled them into a protective ball for a moment, before reaching out more slowly, finding the wall, and spreading her palms wide on the smooth surface. She took one careful step at a time, not familiar with the hallway, or the objects that were probably lining it. If the rest of the house was any indication, Lionel liked to collect things, or hold on to things others in his family tree had collected. Either way, there was a better than average chance she was going to crash into something, and the last thing they needed was for both of them to be hurt.

"I'm coming," she called out. "I'm just not familiar with the floor plan, so I'm using the Braille method out here and it's taking some time."

There was another thud, then the sound of something tumbling over, followed by another groan, a few more choice swear words, and, finally, Trevor's voice. "I'm in Lionel's personal study," he said, sounding none too happy about the fact.

"Excellent," she called back. "And just where might that be?"

"Third door—it's a double door—on your right."

"Are you okay?" She kept skimming one hand lightly along the wall, trying to keep the rest of her body as close to the center of the hall as she could.

"Considering I was very recently wearing a good portion of Lionel's personal library, I suppose I could be worse."

"Oh, my God, what happened?" He sounded relatively close, like she was almost there, but there was no glow emanating into the hall. "You're okay, though? I mean, nothing broken?"

"Well, your flashlight didn't fare too well. Sorry."

Her fingertips hit the molding around the doorframe and she paused in the open doorway, not that it did any good, because she couldn't see a damn thing inside the room. "Trevor?"

"Present and mostly accounted for," came his disembodied voice, from somewhere in the far corner of the room.

"What happened? Where are you? I mean, I know you're in here, but can you direct me?"

"Just stay in the doorway. There are books everywhere and the damn ladder landed somewhere."

"Ladder? What—never mind. Do you need help? Should I call 911?"

"I'll be okay, just as soon as I get"—he paused, and there was a loud grunting noise, then an odd grinding noise. "Well . . . I'll be damned. That explains a lot."

"What explains a lot?" Emma asked, growing more frustrated by the moment. "Did you find any candles? Because it would help tremendously if I could see what's what right now."

"You're telling me. Yes, on the candles. No, however, on matches or a lighter. I don't suppose you smoke?"

"Ew."

"Ditto, but the match holder by the mantel in here was empty."

"We had matches upstairs in the parlor, remember? You could have just brought them up there. And how did you end up with Lionel's library crashing down on your head, anyway? Do you need help getting unpinned? Assuming you're pinned, but—"

"You're babbling."

"Stress. I'm an imperfect human. It happens."

She was surprised to hear him chuckle.

"That was amusing?"

"I'm an imperfect human, too. Quite, at the moment. I just— I like your style, Curls."

"Curls—" She stopped, not wanting to know why he felt compelled to give her a nickname, but mostly because she kind of liked it, and more mostly because, whereas to her it would be cute and a little romantic, to him it was probably something he called his kid sister. So why ruin the fantasy now? "Thanks. Now, direct me over there and—"

"I really don't need help, I just—"

"Well, you're going to get it, regardless, so stop whining and tell me where you are. And what was that 'I'll be damned' comment about?"

There was a pause. A longer pause than she felt the question warranted.

"Trevor?"

"I—why don't you go back up with the dogs, they're probably getting worried. I'll be up shortly."

"Would that be kind of like 'I'll check back in with you'? Because you'll have to pardon me if I don't rush to buy into that."

"You get a little surly when you're stressed."

And he sounded way too damn amused by that, too. "Which apparently brings out all that patronizing condescension in you."

He grunted, then there was a another sound of something tumbling, which she assumed was a pile of books. "Sorry," he managed, his voice a bit tighter. "It wasn't meant to come off that way. Like I said, I like your style."

"You mean surly and babbling? Silly me, why didn't I think of trying that angle out more often with guys?"

"You coming on to me, then, Curls?" he asked, not sounding remotely serious about the assumption, so she carefully made sure she didn't take it as the flirtatious banter she found herself wishing it was.

"Other guys," she clarified, then hurried to add as he grunted and shoved at something—"Be careful! Why don't you let me come help you?"

"Because I'm not sure everything is done falling yet. Better you steer clear. I'm . . . digging myself out. It'll just take me a few minutes, okay? I'm not hurt, the ladder sort of broke the fall of most of the books. I just don't want to inadvertently trigger another avalanche and I'm as hampered by the lack of light as you are."

"Okay. I don't guess you know where the candles you found ended up? Maybe I should go find one myself, and grab some parlor matches upstairs. Can you hold out that long? Then I could help unbury you."

"No, that's—" He broke off, then sighed, and said, "Yeah, that might not be a bad idea. Start with the east rooms down the hall to the right at the top of the stairs, then travel back to the parlor we were in, which is on the west side—left—at the top of the stairs."

"I may not be a born mapmaker, but I do usually know that if east is to the right, then west is to the left. But thank you, because, knowing me I'd probably get lost anyway."

"Anytime," he said, his voice sounding more tight than amused now.

"You sure you're okay?"

"Fine, I'm fine."

"If I don't find anything in the next ten or so minutes, I'll come back and tell you."

There was another pause, then, "Just find one. I'm okay."

She paused, too, knowing there was something more going on here, but decided it was unlikely he'd tell her even if she asked. "I'll try to hurry."

"Just be careful. And leave the dogs in the parlor. We don't need to worry about tripping over them."

"No problem. Just . . . stay where you are."

There was a light chuckle, then, "Sure thing, Curls. I'll do that."

Rather than respond, and mostly to block out the little warm fuzzy his nickname made her feel, she turned and moved slowly and carefully back down the hallway.

It wasn't until she was at the top of the stairs again, and starting down the wing to the right, that it occurred to her that he'd never told her what his "I'll be damned" moment had been about.

6

Trevor tried not to feel bad about sending Emma off on a wild goose chase. Lionel wasn't one for perfumed-scented anything and, other than some long tapers that the house-keeper had probably stored away somewhere for the dinner parties Lionel never gave, Trevor was pretty certain there weren't going to be any candles anywhere in the house. The one he'd found in here had been encrusted in some kind of antique brass family heirloom that was God knew how old.

It had just been a convenient cover for his need to snoop around. He'd been a little surprised that there hadn't been an industrial flashlight of some kind to be found in his cursory look in the kitchen earlier, but, if there was, he hadn't found it. Possibly there was one in the garage, though there weren't really any tools stored there. Or in Lionel's specially designed, but never used, workshop. He'd had that built more for appearances than anything. He could build entire conglomerates, but Trevor was pretty sure he'd never seen his great-uncle with an actual tool in his hand, much less building something with them.

However, the workshop was in a detached building, located down the hill from the house and, at the moment, out of reach while the ice storm continued to rage. And beyond that, he wasn't really sure where else to look. So, instead, he'd used what there was of Emma's flashlight, and searched for something else entirely.

He shoved more books out of the way, trying to be careful not to crash the ladder the rest of the way down on his head. He'd been skimming the spines of all the books starting at the top of the tall cases, balanced on the attached rolling ladder while he searched. And he'd been doing just fine until he'd made it halfway down the ladder, halfway down the stacks, when the whole damn contraption derailed and sent him and the ladder sailing sideways. He'd tried to grab at the shelves, which were built into the wall, only they seemed to give, which had made no sense to him at the time but he'd been too busy protecting himself as he and an avalanche of books went cascading down to the floor to think much beyond it.

Emma's flashlight, which had been on it's last dregs of power anyway, was presently buried in book rubble, leaving him to sift through things by touch, praying he wasn't going to somehow bring the entire bookcase down on his head.

Which, as it turned out, given the creaking sound of moments ago, was a rather valid concern.

He carefully continued to shovel books to one side and the other as he made his way to the newly created opening in what had been a wall of bookcases. The opening had been revealed when the bookcase he'd been dangling from swung loose from the wall it was supposedly built into.

Lionel wasn't really a gadget kind of guy. Despite keeping his business sense on the cutting edge, privately he was more the old school type when it came to gizmos and new technology. However, his wife, Trevor's favorite great-aunt, Trudy, had loved technology, and puzzles, and figuring out how things worked. Unsurprisingly, she was also a fan of mystery novels and could usually solve the riddle of the plot long before any of her contemporaries.

Since this mountain retreat had been her sanctuary, especially during the latter years of her life when she'd been ill, and long hours spent reading her favorite novels had been the mainstay of her entertainment, Trevor could only suppose that Lionel had had the secret room built as some kind of treat for his wife to enjoy.

Or, it could be where Lionel hid things he didn't want anyone to find.

Trevor usually thought of Lionel as an empire builder and stern patriarch. It was rare to think of him as a devoted, loving husband, though, from all accounts, he had been. Still, Trevor wasn't entirely inclined to believe the secret room was simply a loving gesture, no matter how much Lionel had doted on his late wife.

Wishing he had the flashlight, Trevor crawled into the opening, leaving the mass of fallen books in a wake behind him. He stopped just inside the gap, as the black void in front of him made the total lack of light in the study seem bright by comparison. He sighed in regret. He'd have to wait until morning, when at least some daylight would penetrate the big windows of the main room.

And find some excuse to keep Emma away from this room, which meant keeping her out of the study altogether, since he had no idea how to put the wall and case back together. Which, with all the books on the floor, would take some time, even if he did. He scooted back out, shoving at books again, when a bright beam of light flashed into the room and skimmed over its contents, before pinning him to the spot as he shielded his eyes.

"How very . . . Humpty Dumpty of you," Emma said from her stance in the doorway.

Great. Just great.

"Hey," he said, with feigned enthusiasm, "you found a flashlight."

She stepped just inside the door. "Bedside drawer in one of the guest rooms." She patted the pocket of her fleece vest. "Extra batteries, too."

"Could you lower the beam a little?"

"Oh, sorry."

Unfortunately, she both lowered it and shifted it slightly to the side. The side with the gaping doorway to the secret room.

"Whoa. So that's what that 'I'll be damned' was all about." She moved in closer, careful to pick her way over and around clumps of books. She stopped about ten feet away, when the tumble of books completely blocked her path. And his exit. "Did you know about the hidden room? Is the door what triggered the avalanche?"

"No, and, sort of." Sighing internally, he accepted his fate as gracefully as possible, and pushed himself to a stand. Fortunately, everything seemed to work and he didn't feel any noticeable injury.

She kept the beam of light on the open doorway, but the high-powered flashlight illuminated a fair amount of the room, making it easy for Trevor to pick his way through the books to her side, while also neatly blocking her view of the newly found hidey-hole. He had no idea what was in there, but no way was she going to search it before he did.

"Why don't we head back upstairs? I'll tackle all this in the morning."

"You don't want to see what's in the room?"

"Whatever it is, it's been there for some time and certainly won't be going anywhere before morning."

"But—"

"I wouldn't mind tracking down a bathroom with a medicine chest, preferably one stocked with some kind of pain reliever." Which wasn't entirely true, he felt fine, but it certainly sounded plausible enough. He paused behind her and shifted his body in a way that indicated she was supposed to turn in front of him and lead the way out. One thing he hadn't counted on was all that curly hair, and that fresh scent that seemed to linger on her, combining to weaken his already vulnerable state.

She held her ground, and he found himself unwilling to do anything more aggressive to move her. Well, he was having aggressive thoughts, but they had nothing to do with bodily re-moving her from the room. More like removing things from her body . . . Maybe he was wrong about needing something for his discomfort. He needed something much stronger than an aspirin, however. Preferably something shaken, not stirred. He was stirred up plenty already.

"Emma, please, can we just—"

"Why were you looking for candles in a bookshelf?" she interrupted.

A quick look at her face told him she wasn't just making casual conversation. Her expression was more like Jack with a tasty piece of rawhide; determined and single-mindedly fix-ated. She wasn't going to be easily misdirected.

His respect for her grew, even as his brain worked quickly to find some way out of this latest round. She cut him off be-fore he had a chance to figure out a solution.

"What is it you don't want me to see?" She quickly flashed the light past him toward the room.

He had to curl his fingers in to keep from reflexively grab-bing for the flashlight and thwarting her attempt at discovery.

Then she was lowering the beam, and looking directly back at him. Any other time, he'd have been drawn in by the way her eyes got darker when she was serious, the way her lips pursed, making the bottom one look almost bee-stung. So at odds with her strong cheekbones and jawline. Which shouldn't surprise him. Everything about her was at odds with him.

"What are you really looking for?" she asked.

He opened his mouth, but she cut him off, again.

"And don't try to talk me in circles, okay? You're here looking for something. And it's not an alternate light source. You wanted me out of the way when you left me upstairs ear-lier, you wanted me out of the way when you sent me candle hunting, and you want me out of the way right now. You've done a really good job. If the ladder hadn't fallen earlier—"

"I wouldn't be wanting a pain reliever and a stiff shot of something strong," he said. "But it did, so I'd really like—"

"I'd really like some answers."

Why was it he was fighting a smile, when he should be frustrated as all hell? "You seem to have forgotten which one of us is the Hamilton here."

"I haven't forgotten anything. You're interfering with the job I was hired to do. And, inadvertently or not, you're trashing the joint. A joint I'm responsible for maintaining. It's bad enough the power is out and God knows what is spoiling or . . . or going bad because of it. Not to mention the heat going off, and things freezing outside, like pipes, or—or, whatever."

He couldn't help it, he did smile. She was babbling again. Imperfect human that she was. One he was finding himself unavoidably and increasingly attracted to. But his grin was certainly not the reaction she'd been aiming for, which she proved by thumping him on the upper arm.

"Hey!" he said, rubbing at the spot, more to make a point than because she'd hurt him in any way. "No hitting."

"Fine. If you call no hitting, then I call no being obtuse. You said you were here to surprise Lionel with a visit. I'm thinking the surprise part was that he wasn't supposed to know about your visit at all."

"So, are you saying you're going to contact him and tell him I'm here?"

"I'm saying now would be a good time to tell me what's going on so I can make an educated decision, instead of being backed into a corner and forced to make a knee-jerk one."

His lips quirked. "Why do I get the feeling you're thinking the key word in that little dissertation was *jerk*?"

She sighed and dipped her chin briefly, before looking back at him. Though she had no problem standing up to him, he guessed confrontation wasn't typically her style. If either of them was frustrated as hell, at the moment, it was her. But then there was also the way she jiggled the flashlight in her hand. Like someone who was nervous. Only she was staring him right in the eye. Which begged the question . . . exactly what was fueling those nerves?

Which was something he had no business even thinking about. He had to scramble and scramble fast here. Everything was on the line, and she was standing right in the way of him getting what he came here for. Now was definitely not the time to be wondering what she'd do if he leaned in a bit closer. Then closer still. He was lifting a hand before he realized he'd put thought to deed. He managed to check the action before he touched her face, and instead toyed with a few of the curls framing her face.

"Don't—don't think you can distract me," she said. Quite unsteadily, he noticed.

His body really noticed.

"You're not answering my questions," she added, but she didn't jerk her head away, or back up so his hands would no longer be in her hair.

"I'm not trying to be frustrating," he said, thinking hair as curly as hers shouldn't feel so soft and glossy. He let another coil wrap naturally around his finger. "In fact, you have no idea how badly I'd like to reduce the frustration for both of us. At least for a few hours."

The jiggling stopped. But her gaze stayed locked on his, and he could see her throat work. Which brought his attention to that slender column, and made him wonder how the tender skin beneath her ear would taste.

"I read you wrong earlier, when we initially met, about your intent. I—I'm not reading you wrong now, am I?"

He just shook his head.

She drew in a shaky breath, and let it out again. "Right. Well, I know you're probably used to this," she said, her voice a bit tighter, and a bit lower.

"This?" he queried, letting his gaze drift from her neck to her mouth. It really was quite sinful looking. His own watered at the thought of sampling it.

"Using seduction, getting your way," she said. "You're . . . a very attractive man. I'm sure you're aware of that."

He immediately looked into her eyes, and noticed how carefully still she was holding herself. "Meaning what, exactly?"

"I don't play these kinds of games," she said, her voice more than a bit shaky now. "I'm a pretty direct person."

"Games?"

"I'm not naïve. You want to distract me from whatever it is you're up to, and sending me on wild goose chases wasn't working, so . . ."

He realized what she meant, and realized he shouldn't be insulted. She couldn't be blamed for thinking exactly that. Besides, she didn't know him. Still, it stung that she didn't think his interest in her was sincere. But, just to clarify things, he said, "So, you think I'm trying to seduce you. As a means of distraction. Or as some kind of persuasion, so you won't call my uncle."

"Yes. Maybe you don't even realize you're doing it, maybe it's second nature to you, but it's not to me. It's—"

Now he cut her off. With a kiss. His hand was fisted in her curls, finally, and he drew her mouth to his. There was nothing aggressive about the kiss, or threatening, or even demanding. But she was right about one thing, it was intentionally seductive. Because he definitely wanted to taste her, and he wanted her to like it. Beyond that, he didn't much seem to care where it got him, or what it got him. It wasn't about that. He just wasn't quite sure he'd ever get her to believe that. Not when he couldn't quite believe any of this himself.

But not because she wasn't worthy. He didn't think in those terms. He didn't believe this was happening, but that was because he'd come there looking for one thing. One very specific thing. And, it appeared, had found something else entirely.

She froze at the contact of his mouth on hers, and her lips—those lips—didn't open beneath his. "Trevor," she said, against his mouth, the soft friction making him groan a little.

"This isn't a game," he said, meaning it, though he knew she had no reason to believe him. "I just—I've been dying to do this since we met in that hallway."

She pulled back enough to look at him. "I may not run in your circles, but don't insult my intelligence."

His hand was still in her hair, her lips were still tilted up to his, and his gaze searched out hers. His body raged at him to take that mouth again, until it was pliant and open beneath his. "What circles do you think I run in?"

"Hamilton ones. Privileged ones. Ones that think nothing of toying with people to get what they want."

"That's not remotely who I am." He lowered his mouth again. "I know you can't know that, but that cliché couldn't be further from the truth of me. I don't assume anything with you, or anything else. I just know you fascinate me, and I want to kiss you, taste you, know more of you."

"Because I'm standing in the way of you getting what you want. That's the only reason you even noticed me. If we'd met anywhere else—"

"I'd have noticed this." He wrapped his hands more deeply in her never-ending mass of curls. "And these." He dipped in and dropped a hard, fast kiss on those lips. Then he looked into her eyes. "I'd have noticed you, even if you'd never spoken to me. I don't know what I'd have done about it, but I'd have noticed."

She stared into his eyes, and he hoped she saw the truth there.

"Then you did speak to me. And you didn't pull any punches, even after you found out who I was. Maybe even more so. I'm not used to that, and you can't possibly know how refreshing that was." He edged closer to her. "How much more attractive that made you to me."

"Because I didn't suck up to you?"

"Or come on to me." A grin edged his lips upward. "Though I did notice you looking at me. A lot."

Even in the dim light, he could see her cheeks actually pinked, which, considering how direct a person she was, intrigued the hell out of him.

"Normally the staring is a signal for me to run and run fast."

Now she frowned. "Because . . . ?"

"Women who stare are usually formulating strategies. Strategies that have a lot more to do with my last name and supposed bank account than about me personally."

"I wasn't—wouldn't—"

"I know," he said, his smile widening. "You just looked. Honestly, openly, and pretty frankly."

"I didn't think you saw. I'm sorry if you felt . . . I don't know, demeaned? You're right, I don't know you. I am shallow enough to say I liked what I saw, so I looked." Now her lips quirked. "Maybe a lot. You're also right that there was no game plan. I had no intention of following through on . . ." She trailed off, apparently realizing she was giving more away than she'd intended.

"On your attraction to me?"

"I didn't think it was mutual."

He traced the finger with her hair coiled around it down over her cheek and across her lips, his gaze following the motion. "You couldn't be more wrong."

Her skin warmed under his touch, and her pupils expanded. "You're either incredibly good at playing women—and I'm still not entirely sure I trust you . . . or you—"

"Really mean what I say? I always do."

She moved back, just a fraction, enough so that his fingertips were no longer brushing her chin. "Okay. If you want my trust, and you want more than the one kiss you stole, then let's put a foundation to this attraction."

He was already in it now, but that comment should have sent him scrambling for the door. Instead, it also intrigued the hell out of him. And, it was rather shocking to realize that he was perfectly okay with doing whatever it took to prove he meant what he said, to gain her trust. Mostly because, at that moment, it had absolutely nothing to do with distraction or the reason he'd come here, and everything to do with her. "I've never met anyone like you," he said, as sincere as he could be.

"Then you need to get out more. I'm quite ordinary."

"There is nothing ordinary about you."

"Trevor—"

"What did you mean, about putting a foundation to this attraction? What can I do or say to prove I'm not just using you for my own personal gain?"

"I was just pointing out that, although we're both consenting adults, in a dark house in the middle of an ice storm, and, yes, it's true, I am attracted to you—I'd have to be dead not to be—that despite the ridiculous and surprising temptation you're presenting me with, I don't just—"

"Fling yourself with great abandon into a wildly satisfying sexual affair with a man who is finding himself completely smitten with you?"

Now she laughed. "Uh, well . . . yes. More or less."

He sunk his hands under her hair and cupped the back of her head, tilting her mouth up to his once again, her gaze to his, as his body crowded into hers. "So, then, what foundation does this attraction need in order for it to move forward?"

"Your trust. Tell me why you're really here. What are you looking for?"

7

Emma watched his face closely, and though he didn't answer right away, he didn't look away, didn't flinch. Both good signs.

Good, if she was going to believe that any of this was actually happening to her. Because it was a far more plausible scenario that she'd just fallen asleep in front of the fire upstairs and was dreaming this entire sequence. Although, even in her dreams she was generally a pretty pragmatic sort. And in Emma Lafferty's basic, straightforward world, men like Trevor Hamilton simply did not fall all over themselves to seduce her. Hell, she'd have passed out in a dead faint if he'd even smiled at her. Under normal circumstances anyway. These circumstances were far from normal.

And she'd dealt with him in a way she likely wouldn't have in any real-world scenario. Or maybe she would have. Hard to say. What she wouldn't have done was flirted with him. Or played up to him. Either for personal or professional gain. That's not who she was.

And here he was, essentially trying to get her to believe the same of him. She had no reason not to believe him. Except he was hot. Rich. And was here for reasons he hadn't been quite honest about. Not that it was necessarily her business. But, for the next eleven days, this house and everything in it was her business. Which made what he was doing here her business.

"If you're the up-front person you say you are, who just happens to be finding himself completely swept away by my stunning beauty and incredible wit, then tell me why you're here. I won't go running to Lionel. It's really none of my concern. I know I'm being nosy just asking. But I'm guessing you don't want Lionel to know. So . . . you trust me with your secret. And I'll trust that you're not distracting me with all this seductive smoke and mirrors, so I won't notice or care if you rob your uncle blind."

He smiled then. "You really need to stop underselling yourself. You are stunning and incredible."

"I was not fishing for compliments."

"I know. Which is part of what compels me about you. I don't think I've ever had the pleasure of meeting a stunning, witty beauty who doesn't give a rat's ass what I think about her."

He tugged her closer again, and she had to admit she was quite liking being in his personal space. It was disarming and disconcerting, all at the same time. Which might also be part of his plan. Keep her in a pheromone-induced fog, sweet talk her into doing exactly what he wanted, believing whatever he told her.

Only he didn't seem to be spinning any tales, even if he was making her head spin.

"So, it's my complete lack of tact that attracts you? Along with the babbling and other imperfections? I really have apparently been going about the whole attracting guys thing entirely the wrong way."

"So . . . does that mean there isn't a guy? At the moment?"

"I realize we haven't exactly made any commitments here, with our bodies or our brains . . . but I wouldn't be standing here—right here—if there was someone in my world. I don't do that. I couldn't do that." She cocked her head. "And you?"

"Will you believe anything I say?"

"Answer my initial question . . . and I'll let you know."

"First, no, there is no one special. I've spent the last five years concentrating on building my own business and that hasn't left a lot of time for socializing. I'm not a monk, either, but let's just say I've found the dating world to be immensely frustrating and even more unfulfilling."

"I find that almost impossible to be true. Not for me, mind you. I personally completely agree. But it can't be that hard for you."

"I didn't say it was hard for me to find a date. I'm not trying to be disingenuous here. But finding someone I want to keep dating? Yeah, that's been a bit trickier."

"Poor, hot-looking rich guy syndrome, huh?"

He laughed. "It's more pathetic than even you realize."

"We all have our crosses to bear."

He kept grinning. "You really are . . . unlike anyone I've ever met."

"Just because I don't pull punches and I'm not staring at you because I'm trying to figure out how to part you from some portion of your trust fund—"

"Just because you're being yourself around me," he said. "And it's a self I am growing to like more every second." He tipped her chin up, and brushed a soft, incredibly hot kiss across her lips. "And it's a good thing you're attracted to me, and not my money. Because I'm not entirely sure I have any."

"Must be some empire you've been building these past five years."

He kissed the tip of her nose, then the corner of her mouth. "No, I did that completely on my own. I haven't touched any of my Hamilton money. The whole wad of it is still sitting in that trust fund."

She sighed, a part of her—most of her—wanting to rescind that entire part about not being a one-night-stand kind of girl. He kept on touching her, and talking in that low smooth voice, and looking like . . . well, how he looked, and she honestly didn't know how much longer she was going to remain the up-standing, morally centered woman she liked to believe she was. In fact, she'd far rather be down-lying, and centered beneath him right about now.

She struggled to keep track of what he was saying. "What, your uncle won't let you spend your trust fund? Is that why you're here?" She really couldn't care less about his money, but she paused and leaned back a fraction when all of what he'd said sunk past the hormone haze. "Do you think Lionel Hamilton is stealing from you? His own great-nephew? Is that why you're here?"

Trevor smiled then, and the way he looked at her . . . it was amazing she wasn't simply a puddle at his probably perfect feet. "No, no one is stealing from me. I'm here because I'm not sure I am, in fact, Lionel's great-nephew. And, if my suspicions are correct, then I'm not entitled to that trust fund."

"What? How could you not know if you're his nephew? Do you think you were adopted? And you'd still be a Hamilton, unless you're saying you have some hang-up about being a blood relative. Or you're saying Lionel does."

"I'm not adopted."

"A bastard then? No insult," she added quickly. "To you or your parentage. I just meant, if you think you're not a real Hamilton, and you're not adopted—"

"I know who my parents are, and they were legal when they had me. It's not me, personally. Well, it is me, personally, but it all started a few generations back, with my great-great-grandmother."

"Wait a minute. You mean to say you've left a—let's just say very healthy—trust fund and incredibly huge amounts of interest sit around and gather dust because somewhere up in your ancestral tree, someone parked their boots under the wrong bed?"

Trevor laughed. "I've never quite thought about it that way, but . . . kind of."

"No one is that selfless. Blindly so, I might add."

"It matters to me. Who I am, where I came from."

"And Lionel doesn't suspect this? Does anyone in your family know or believe what you suspect? Do they treat you poorly or something?"

"No, they treat me fine. Or would, if I hadn't nosed around my family tree when I was younger and started asking questions no one wanted to answer."

Now Emma frowned. "Why? It's not the Dark Ages anymore. Surely they accept that every family, even ridiculously wealthy ones, have skeletons. Why wouldn't they tell you the truth? I mean, it's still your money. If they know there were affairs and the lineage isn't perfect, but still dole out the trust funds, then . . . why does it matter? You're a Hamilton in every way that really counts, right?"

"Not right. Not to me, anyway."

She sighed. "You're really a very contrary man."

"Just an honest one. Who wants to know who he is."

"I understand that, on an emotional level. But even if you find out your lineage branches off to an entirely different tree somewhere back, will that make you feel any differently about who you are? I mean, you were raised by your parents, as part of this family, which you are. How would you feel different if you found that your great-great-whoever slept with someone other than the Hamilton she was married to?"

"That's just it. I've always felt different. For as long as I can remember."

She smiled a little. "Poor, hot-looking, rich . . . misfit?"

He grinned. "Like I said, you had no idea how pathetic. But, uh . . . essentially, yeah."

She shook her head. "I . . . really don't understand."

He slid his arm around the back of her waist, and tugged her, finally, fully into his arms. "And, you see . . . that's what so intrigues me, because, I already happen to think you're going to be the first person who really does."

"You do, do you?" she asked, unable to keep from smiling up into his beautiful blue eyes. If this really turned out to be just a dream, then the hell with it. She was going to milk it for all it was worth. "Why is that?"

"Because you see clearly. And you think clearly."

"Not when you're holding me like this, I don't."

His grin widened. "I understand the condition, trust me."

"So you're not just fogging my brain so I'll help you look for . . . whatever it was you came here to find? Proof, I presume."

"If I was thinking clearly, I wouldn't be anywhere near you, and you'd never suspect why I was here. I've waited what feels like a lifetime to finally have the chance to get to the truth. I'm a fool for risking this chance by spending my time here with you, much less confiding in you."

"You say all the right things," she said, wanting to distrust him, knowing she needed to maintain a healthy dose of skepticism around him, because, the truth was, she wasn't going to be around him for any real length of time.

Which rendered all of this as much a foolish venture on her part, as it apparently was for him. Only for vastly different reasons. She knew she was a confident person, and came off as such. But, in this arena, she was as vulnerable as anyone. Maybe more so, because she wasn't the sort that people—male people—thought needed much tending to. Emotionally anyway. And, in addition to being wildly attracted to him, she was really starting to like Trevor Hamilton. It was a killer combination.

And she didn't need the one-two sucker punch that was surely coming her way. Stuff like this only happened in movies. In real life, the pet-sitting Emma Laffertys of the world simply didn't get the trust-fund Trevor Hamiltons. Not for more than a night, anyway.

"I mean what I say," he said. "I want you to know me. Because I think you actually would. Know me. For me. You might even like me."

"I know I'm going to probably regret saying this, but I do like you. Or I'm starting to."

"Then I'm going to be completely honest with you about something else."

"See, I knew it. You're going to tell me you're dying, or that—"

"I'm going to tell you that we're going to be trapped in this house for a day or two at least. Maybe more. I'm thinking hopefully more, and you have no idea how big a surprise that is to me, considering my plans when I came here."

"So, what's the confession?"

"That I want you. Now. In front of the fire, or, for that matter, right here on the pile of books. And I know how important all that foundation stuff is. It's important to me, too. Which is why I want days with you, and maybe, if I'm insanely lucky, a lot more than that. But, right now, the secret room, the proof I need, and all the talking we need to do, all the important getting-to-know-you stuff, can wait. Has to wait. Because I'm not sure this can."

"This?"

"Yeah," he said, taking her face in his hands and pulling her mouth to his. "This."

8

"Trevor," she said, her voice catching along with her breath. "We're—"

"I know," he said. "You're not a one-night-stand kind of woman. Which is good. I don't believe in them either."

"I'm glad to hear it, but any future night potential isn't great. You're from North Carolina, I live here."

"That's just geography," he said, kissing the corners of her mouth, and along her jaw. Like a man starved, he suddenly couldn't get enough of her.

"Says the rich boy," she said, but she was tilting her head back, giving him access to that tender spot on her neck, clutching at his shoulders, nails digging in, like a woman drowning.

He understood the feeling. It all felt so overwhelming, and yet remarkably simple. He didn't have a moment's hesitation in going after what felt incredibly right, even though, having just met her, it made no rational sense. And he was nothing if not a rational man.

Just not around Emma. And damn but it felt good.

Wildly, insanely, ridiculously good. Maybe because he felt . . . safe with her. Which was kind of crazy, but as soon as the notion came to him, he realized it was exactly right. And true.

Because she would be true. Good, bad, one night or a hundred nights, she'd be true. And honest. With herself. And with him. Whatever happened, she'd be the kind of woman who would never duck, never hide, and never lie. How he knew this with such clarity, and such faith, he had no idea.

But he did. And, for now, it was enough to go on. Enough to not stop at the edge, but jump off. If he crash-landed . . . well, he'd deal with that, then. But, oh, how he wanted to fly.

"Not rich, remember," he clarified, working his way along the underline of her jaw.

"Not yet," she managed, nails still digging, breath still catching. It was damn sexy, hearing those little gasps, knowing he was the cause. "Not that it matters. I don't want your money, but you might have to come to terms with having some, at some point."

"Wouldn't matter, either way," he said. "About the distance, I mean. It's still just geography." At the moment, he was pretty sure he'd crawl through hell if that was what it took to get to her.

"Dreamer," she breathed, gasping as he nipped at the lobe of her ear.

"Realist," he countered. "Stubbornly so."

"How do you explain this then?" She moaned a little as he nibbled on her ear. "It sure as hell feels like a fantasy to me."

"Yeah, I know," he said, grinning against the side of her neck. "Pretty fucking fantastic, isn't it?"

She laughed. "I should be offended, except that's exactly what I was thinking."

He lifted his head. "See? Fated."

"We're either both going to be really sorry in the morning, or—"

"Let's go with 'or' . . . okay?" He kissed her again, but this time it was slow, and there was nothing behind it other than the need—the absolute need—to know her. And this seemed like a perfect place to start. "I never leap first," he said, against her mouth. "Not ever."

"Neither do I," she murmured back. "Crash landings suck."
He grinned at their parallel thinking, again.

"But life offers no guarantees, either," she said, taking his face in her hands and taking an active role in this fantasy they were sharing. She tilted his mouth to fit hers. "And I'm having a hard time staying safely on the ledge."

He groaned as she kissed him—really kissed him—for the first time. Damn, this was something. Really something. Everything else ceased to matter in that moment. All the other moments would come along anyway. Right now he could think of nothing more important, perhaps ever in his life, than making damn sure this particular moment, and the ones that immediately followed, were as perfect as he could make them. Because there was this feeling, this instinct, this . . . whatever the hell it was in his gut, that was telling him that they had to be perfect . . . because he was going to be remembering this exact moment for the rest of his life.

"Jump with me, Emma," he whispered against her lips. "Just . . . jump."

So she did.
She was flying. She felt weightless, her pulse soaring as she coasted along on the currents that were sweeping through her and around her, pushing her along almost effortlessly toward some great and glorious destination. Which was such a ridiculously over-the-top thing to even think, silently in her head, that she should either be laughing hysterically at herself or running, screaming, from the room, and maybe even the house.

Trevor Hamilton had cast a spell over her. And there was no way that it should be working. She was in for the mother of all crash landings. Any idiot could see that. All rational logic dictated that he had to be using her.

But then there was the fact that he had told her why he was there, giving her leverage. One call to Lionel, or Lionel's people anyway, could certainly make his life difficult. If he was telling the truth about the whole trust fund, family tree thing, that is. But . . . why make something like that up? If he was going to lie, he could have made up any one of a number of more plausible reasons for snooping about. And it hadn't sounded like a lie. He didn't look like a liar when he'd said it.

And, fool or no, this kiss sure as hell didn't seem like a lie.

So, she kissed him back.

And that made it even better.

Yeah . . . there might be a crash landing in her immediate future, but this one just might be worth the ride down.

9

Trevor felt her sink into him, and he pulled her, finally, tightly against him. She fit him, which was both stunning and the most natural thing in the world. She was shifting her mouth to fit his even before his hands slid to cup her face.

Those lips of hers, so soft, so . . . plush. Heaven. And then she parted them, and it was so sinfully sweet, sliding his tongue between them, tasting her so intimately. She wasn't tentative in tasting back, which should have surprised him, with all her talk of him being out of her league, but didn't, because it was her frank approach to life that had drawn him in in the first place. He doubted she'd be any less direct with him in this. And given the rock hard state of, oh, pretty much every inch of his body, he was very happy he was right about that.

He turned slightly to pull her more tightly against him, fit her more perfectly between his hips, causing them both to trip over a few scattered books. He'd completely forgotten his surroundings, he'd been so focused on her.

"This isn't exactly . . . can we—"

"Find a nicer room," he finished. "I think there might be one or two that we could choose from."

"The animals . . ." She was kissing the corners of his mouth, and now running her teeth lightly along his jaw, which made it almost impossible for him to comprehend any words being spoken, but they eventually sunk in.

"Sleeping. By the fire. Very content."

"The fire. Should we go . . . stoke it? Or something?"

"Oh, we're doing just fine stoking the fire. Come on." He kissed her again, hard and fast this time, and they were both gasping a little when he broke it off and took her hand. "I'll lead the way, you provide the light."

"Oh, right. I—I think I dropped it . . . at some point." She crouched down and fished around, finding the flashlight quickly and flicking it back on. "I don't even remember turning it off."

He had the immense pleasure of looking into her face now, seeing her eyes, all dark and sparkling when she looked at him. Her hair was a wild halo of curls, which only accentuated the sultry way her lips parted when he tugged her back against him and took her mouth again. "It's kind of insane, how badly I want you," he said.

"I'd be insulted, except—"

"Not what I meant."

She tugged his mouth back to hers and smiled against his lips. "I know. I'm not that lacking in self-esteem." She crowded her hips against his. "Besides, you're being pretty convincing about wanting me."

He laughed. Why was it so easy with her? "Promise you'll always be this open and direct," he said, as he led her from the room.

"Not everyone appreciates my . . . directness."

"You have no idea how refreshing it is."

Now she laughed. "Let's hope you still feel that way . . . later."

He caught the hesitation, and knew that, despite leaping along with him tonight, she was still unconvinced on how they could do anything beyond share this night together, or maybe the next ice-bound few. . . . Well, he wasn't exactly sure himself. But no way was he walking away from this, from her. So, he'd just have to do whatever it took to make sure she didn't want to walk away, either.

He led her down the dark hallway, and back upstairs, only he ducked down the right wing this time, not toward the left where the parlor and the dogs were. He felt her hand shudder a little in his. "I know, it's getting chilly up here. But I know where—" He broke off as he stopped in front of a set of double doors. "This was my aunt's favorite guest room, and I was lucky that I was her favorite great-nephew, so it was always mine when I stayed here." He opened the doors, and Emma flashed the beam of light around the interior, stopping first on the beautiful, ornately carved fireplace, then a bit longer on the equally beautifully hand-carved sleigh bed.

"I can see why you both loved it," Emma said, as he pulled her inside and closed the door to the hall.

There was wood stacked by the fireplace, which, given Lionel's attentiveness to detail, he'd expected to find. "It will only take me a few minutes to get the fire going."

She let go of his hand, and helped illuminate the area in front of the hearth so he could get things set up. "How long has it been since you've been here? You said things sort of broke down between you and your family . . ." She trailed off, then said, "I'm sorry. We don't have to talk about that now. I was just—this is a lovely room and the way you spoke about your great-aunt . . . it sounded like you loved her very much."

"I did. She was the best. And if she were still around, I think she'd have been my ally in finding out the truth. She was the only one who could stand up to Lionel without pissing him off. If anyone was going to make him understand why it was so important to me to know, it would have been her."

He stacked the wood, stuffed in the tinder and kindling, then sparked one of the long fireplace matches he'd drawn from their special brass container beside the mantel.

"How long has it been? I mean, since she's been gone?"

"I was seventeen. And just starting to make noise about things."

"Why did you even suspect?"

"I know it sounds hokey, but I never felt like I fit in. I didn't have the same killer instinct my family did, or the same mindset about conquering all for the sake of the victory. Amassing wealth—or more of it, I should say—wasn't how I wanted to judge my success in the world. And no one seemed to get that in this family."

"Not even your parents?"

"My father was a true Hamilton, through and through, and my mother lived to serve my father . . . and her own societal needs. I know that sounds rather harsh, but . . . we knew who we were, and who we weren't. We got along fine, mostly because we just pretended not to notice our differences. They just wanted me to be a fine, upstanding young Hamilton, and I wanted to keep the peace."

"You said 'was.' Are they—"

"Gone? Yes, right after I graduated from college. Drunk driver."

"I'm so sorry—"

"That's when I decided to forge my own path. I graduated, decided to stay in North Carolina—"

"And start your own empire."

He laughed. "Hardly. My degree is in environmental geology. I started a company that works with builders to make sure the land they build on is safe. I also work with already established communities, older communities, to pin down problem areas and help them work with the local authorities to clean things up."

"That's—"

"Not very Hamilton-esque. I know." He shrugged. "I really enjoy it. I have good people working for me. And, unless being a Hamilton will open doors to helping the people I'm trying to help, I don't have to pretend to be something I'm not. Or never felt like, anyway."

"So . . . because you felt different, you assumed your family tree was—"

"A bit twisted? Well, not specifically. But you know how some kids feel like they were adopted, or should have been? Like they're aliens in their own family? That's what it was like for me. When I was in school, I had a class on psychology and one of the projects we did was working on our own family tree. That got me started, and I kept digging. Not because I intended to prove that there was a bastard line somewhere up the tree, but, I guess in hopes that I'd find at least one ancestor I identified with personally. Just to feel connected in some way, to know more about who I was and where I came from."

"I can understand that. But that trust fund would help a lot of people, and it's yours, regardless of how you feel, so why not—"

"I tried to talk to Lionel about my feelings, which was pretty foolish, looking back. I went to Aunt Trudy first, though, and she encouraged me to talk to him. I should have known better. And that's when I realized that there really was something to my concerns. It was clear I'd struck a nerve, and he all but shoved me out of the conversation. As I said earlier, I can be stubborn. And, unless he was going to confide the truth in me, about my heritage—all our heritage—then I wasn't going to touch anything that came from it. I know it sounds high and mighty, and it's really not. It's more—"

"You being a stubborn idiot?"

He laughed, which surprised him. But she made it easy to see things with a bit more perspective. "I'm sure it looks that way. And, I probably am, a little. But it was a choice I made. To live on my own terms. Not Hamilton terms, and that meant not living on Hamilton money."

"And you've still never found out the whole truth."

"No. And it's not like something that colors my every waking moment. I have moved on with my life. But, yes, it is something I want to know, need to know, at some point. I hope to have a family some day, and I want to know what legacy it is I'm passing down, skeletons and all. I don't want any child of mine to question where he or she came from, or why they might not feel the same as I do about things."

"Why do you think the proof you need is here? Wouldn't Lionel keep important family documentation like that at the family estate in town?"

"Trudy was the matriarch of the Hamilton family, and, in that arena, she took great pride in the caring and maintaining of the history we've accumulated, both in physical artifacts and written history. She had all the certificates—birth, death—from generations back, along with journals and Bibles."

"And you think that's the missing link for you?"

"Yes."

"Did you get to see any of it while she was alive?"

"I was just starting to dig when she first got sick. She was sick a very long time, and spent most of her time here. She loved this place, and Lionel had most of her things and anything dear to her, moved here. He's never changed that since her death."

"How long was she sick?"

"A little over two years. And when I had the chance to see her, I didn't want to bother her with everything I was thinking or feeling. We all knew she wasn't going to get better, she knew it, too. So we enjoyed our time together."

"Any regrets about that?"

He stopped poking at the fire and looked over his shoulder at her. She'd perched herself on the edge of the bed, with the flashlight dangling in her hands, which were pressed between her knees. "No," he said, never more sincere. "None." He replaced the poker in the wrought iron stand, and pushed to his feet, turning to face her. "Lionel and I don't see things the same way, and though I haven't exactly been banished or anything, we don't exactly enjoy each other's company. So he politely invites me to family functions, and I politely decline, and we coexist with little adversity."

"Like you did with your folks."

"Sort of runs in the family, it seems, yes."

"Until now."

He stepped closer. "Until I heard he was going overseas for two weeks and giving his staff some seasonal time off. Usually he rattles around up here alone, just him and the dogs and that damn parrot, as he calls him. Cicero was one of Trudy's . . . eccentricities. She loved that bird. And Lionel loved Trudy, so he put up with him. I'm somewhat surprised he's kept him all these years, since he really can be obnoxious. And Lionel doesn't put up with obnoxious from anyone."

"People do interesting things to keep the memories of loved ones close. My dad actually keeps my granddad's—his dad's—ashes in this huge, cheap trophy he had them sealed into. It was a thing he won when he was, like, twelve years old. But his dad had coached his team that year and it had been the thing that had brought them close after my grandmother died. So that's where my grandfather is spending eternity." She smiled, and looked a little embarrassed about sharing something so personal and, perhaps, unusual.

He moved closer, bumping her knees apart and stepping between her thighs. He took the flashlight from her, flicked it off, and tossed it to the carpeted floor beside the bed. "You know," he said, "there is another reason I have no regrets about not pursuing things when Aunt Tru was alive." He took her hands in his, and lifted them up.

"Why is that?" Emma asked, her voice trembling just the slightest bit. But the look in her eyes wasn't one of trepidation. It was one of anticipation.

Which made Trevor smile. "Because then I wouldn't be here. On this stormy night." He kissed the back of her hands, then pressed them to the bed beside her legs, and started scooting her backwards, climbing right up with her, and over her. "Finding you." They reached the pillows and he pinned her hands beside her head, lowering his body to hers, until they both groaned in satisfaction at the perfect fit of his hips between hers. "And discovering that, maybe, I've been right in pursuing my own life. Because what's really important isn't where you came from . . . but what you do with who you are." He nipped the point of her chin, then at her bottom lip. "But I'm thinking now that I stopped short of the real goal."

"What goal?"

"Of figuring out the rest, which is that it's all fine and well to find yourself, create and pursue your own path, and stick with what works for you and let go of what doesn't." He grinned then, and looked into those sparkling, direct, honest eyes. "But, it's not entirely complete until you find someone to share yourself with, and maybe leave something behind when you go, that makes other people smile." He kissed her then, tenderly. "Like you did, talking about your dad and grand-dad."

"And like you do, talking about Aunt Trudy."

"Yeah . . . like that."

She leaned up this time, and tugged her fingers free so she could hold onto his face and kiss him, taking his mouth, staking her claim, making her stand. Her kisses were passionate and strong, like her body presently moving beneath him.

He drove his fingers into her hair, taking in return, tangling his tongue with hers, his groans mixing with her gasps. He moved his hips against hers as she lifted them off the bed, moving beneath him, with him.

"This is a little insane, you know," she panted when he reared back suddenly and tugged off his shirt. She worked just as feverishly to divest herself of her clothes, too. "I just met you."

It should have been comical, their frantic disrobing. It certainly wasn't the slow, tantalizing unveiling of her for the first time he'd have liked for them both to indulge in. "I know," he said. "But I feel like I've already waited a lifetime for you." He kicked free of his shoes, shucked his pants, helped her tug off her own. "You are so beautiful, and there will be many times in the future where I will pay rapt attention to every inch of your lovely body—some, perhaps, with more detailed focus than others—but right now—"

"I know," she said, and all but yanked him on top of her.

He grinned. "Did I tell you how much I like that you're not a fragile flower?"

She rolled him to his back, and he sat up and pulled her legs around his hips. The flickering fire behind her made the tips of her curls appear as if they were glowing embers. "My very own Vesta."

She twined her arms around his neck and started to tease him with kisses along the side of his neck.

"You," he said, as he pushed her backward, making her squeal in delight, while keeping her legs twined over his hips as he lowered himself slowly between her legs, "are going to drive me delightfully insane." He stopped just short of pushing inside her. "I hope you'll let me do the same.

In response, she tightened her legs around him, bringing him into her body. "Start now."

10

Trevor drove into her, long, deep, and fully, staying there even as she arched up on a long groan of satisfaction. She felt tight around him, so tight, and he began moving before she could acclimate to having him inside her, filling her so completely. But where she expected discomfort, there was only this intense, pervasive heat, like a hot glow spreading inside her as he moved his body within hers, and she responded to it like they'd established this rhythm years before. Perhaps lifetimes before. His own Vesta, indeed.

She didn't question it, didn't question the ridiculous things they were saying to one another. Two strangers, caught up in the moment, in the center of a raging storm, trapped during a time of year when sentiments ran high and emotions weren't always steady. Later. She'd worry about all of that later. Because, this . . . this was worth every foolish thing she might say, and whatever mortification could possibly follow.

Besides, they'd both said things. Made claims. Staked claims. If she was going to be made a fool, she wasn't going to suffer alone.

Which, having mentally settled that, should have allowed

her to push everything else aside and just go on this glorious, intense pleasure trip he was taking her on.

Except it didn't. Because every time he drove into her, she felt something . . . more. And it had nothing to do with friction and the lovely places he was reaching inside her body. When he moved his head so he could tease her nipples, lick at the tips, make her squirm, make her scream, and ultimately make her come, writhing beneath him . . . it didn't feel like simple, sweaty sex.

It . . . mattered. More than slaking lust and exhausting pent-up sexual tension.

He slowed in his thrusts, letting her climax ripple through her until every last shudder was spent. Like he knew her, he was partnering her, being in it with her, not just along for the ride. When she opened her eyes, she found herself looking into his, and there was so much there to see, naked on his face. This mattered to him, too.

And because it did, her heart ached. Physically squeezed, as she felt him gather inside her, his strokes moving deeper, more rhythmically, and finally picking up speed and intensity . . . and his gaze never once left hers. He wasn't just taking her, he was joining with her. It might have been just another foolish sentiment, except there were tears gathering at the corners of her eyes as he built higher, and came ever closer.

And she never cried. Not ever.

But when she moved, tightened her muscles just enough, tugging him over the edge into that long, sweet, groaning release, she didn't just feel slaked and pleasantly fulfilled. She didn't just feel him, the weight of him, lying spent on top of her. She felt like a part of him was hers now. A part no one else had. A part worthy of being tended to, of being held dear. She felt that he was hers now.

And all she had to do was find a way to keep him.

11

He pressed his lips to her temple, then buried his face in her hair. "That was . . ." He had no words for it. None that would do justice to what had just happened between them. It should have been sex. First sex. Awkward, getting-to-know-your-body sex. Even with someone who held all the promise in the world of being special to him, it was still, at first, just sex.

Only, not this. Not with her.

"I know," she said.

He slid to his side, pulling her to him even as she was naturally turning into his body, her leg draped across his, her head finding its natural spot between the crook of his arm, and the space over his heart.

He slipped his hand into her hair, keeping her cheek gently pressed over his slowly recovering heartbeat, and pulled her tightly against his hip with his other arm. "You do know, don't you?" he said, somewhat in awe.

"What do I know?"

"Just that . . . you're right, we're strangers. And yet, not. I don't know you, but I know of you, if that makes any sense. And, it would be insane, and ridiculous, to think I know what you are and what you can be to me, except you look at me, and I see that same understanding on your face." He tilted her face up to his, and looked down into those stunning, knowing eyes of hers. "It's not crazy if we're both thinking it, feeling it . . . saying it. Right?"

She smiled, and he actually felt his heart tip inside his chest. That was a smile he wanted to be blessed with, graced with, every chance he got.

"I say yes," she said. "Because the alternative is we've gone to some parallel universe, or this really is a dream. Except even I don't dream this big, or this good."

He smiled, too, then, and stroked a curl-entwined finger down along her cheek. "So, by default then, it has to be real."

She turned her face, kissed his palm. "I sure as hell hope so."

He rolled them both slightly, reaching down for the coverlet and sheets they'd already tangled up, finally tugging and pulling the covers over their bodies, before settling them both back deeply into the down mattress and soft pile of pillows. "Stay with me."

"Try to make me leave," she said, making him laugh.

"You . . ." He shook his head, then kissed the top of hers before tightening his arms around her. ". . . better still be here when I wake up in the morning. Because if this is a dream, I'm going to be really pissed."

She laughed, and traced her fingers through the hair on his chest, as their breathing evened out. He felt an almost liquid warmth seep through him, relaxing him in a way he'd never felt before, like it went past muscle, past mind, somewhere beyond, somewhere deeper, as if soothing his very soul. He'd wanted to talk more, find out more, if for no other reason than to ground the fantasy of this connection they'd forged in as much reality as possible, as quickly as possible, before something in the real world shattered their dream one.

But then her hand was drifting downward, and despite how sated he'd felt a moment earlier, his body began to stir to life all over again. This time there was no frantic coupling.

This time they relished in every breath, every moan. She tasted him . . . and he tasted her. He spent the most glorious hour of his life exploring her body . . . then lay back in stunned shock as she, very delightfully and deliberately did the same with him.

And when she could take no more teasing with his tongue, and he could take no more of her little nips down along his spine, he pulled her beneath him, and slowly pushed into her. Their gazes, as he was coming to know would always be the case, found each other unerringly, and remained locked, as he drove . . . and she took, then more, when she rose to meet him, holding him so tightly inside her he thought he'd die from the pleasure of it. And this time, when she climbed that last peak, so did he.

"Emma," he said, groaning as she arched beneath him and fell sweetly, perfectly apart around him. He took her mouth then, and took her. Claimed that last piece of her, and thought to himself that this time, there would be no being complacent and keeping the peace. This time, he would fight, and cause a scene, and do whatever it took, because this time, finally, he had something worth fighting for.

He wanted to tell her, make her understand, only the sandman had other ideas, and they both drifted even as his heartbeat was still finding its balance. The last thing he remembered was the soft kiss she pressed directly over his heart.

12

The first thing Emma heard was howling. She blinked her eyes open and instinctively stretched, only to realize—and immediately recall every last detail of the fact—that she was in bed with Trevor. Naked, in bed. With a naked Trevor. A naked Trevor who had made love to her last night like she was the last woman on earth, or maybe the only woman for him.

She closed her eyes, wanting to hold onto the fantasy that surely must be. But Jack was howling, the fire had gone out, and the thin gray light coming in through the tall, floor-to-ceiling windows announced that bad weather was still continuing. And the warm, hard body next to her, along with the wide, firm palm cupping her backside, were all far too real for her to pretend that any of this was a dream.

"Jack needs to be put out of his misery," Trevor said, his body still heavy against hers, his eyes still closed, and his voice deliciously gravelly.

"He just needs to go out," Emma said, hearing the roughness in her own voice as well.

"Not if he was dead he wouldn't."

She smiled even as she gently pinched his waist. "Not funny."

"Neither is a howling dog at o'dark-thirty."

"I think it's later than that, but outside isn't looking so good."

"All the more reason we shouldn't have dogs."

"We don't have dogs. Lionel has dogs. And I need to go take them outside."

Trevor clamped his arm down more firmly around her waist and pulled her more snugly into the very warm and wonderful body heat he was also wrapping around her. "You need to stay here and keep the real world from intruding."

That sounded like a great idea. Jack howled even more mournfully, which made her groan. "Keep that thought. I'll be right back."

What she was, however, was on her back. For a sleepy, drowsy guy, he moved remarkably fast when he wanted to. Something to make note of, she thought, then smiled at the idea that keeping track of his habits might be something she needed to be doing at all. It was the morning after . . . and there had been no crash landing yet.

In fact, this felt pretty remarkably . . . normal. And nice. And . . . something she'd like to keep doing. With him. For a very long time.

Jack's howl took on a particularly plaintive tone, and Emma found herself thinking that Trevor had a point about owning dogs. But then, the only thing keeping her warm at night, up until the last one anyway, was her grandmother's frayed quilt. So she could be excused for not being overly enthusiastic about her stubby-legged charge since it meant leaving Trevor's delectable warmth, and what felt like a . . . growing interest in keeping her tucked away for at least a little while longer this morning.

"I love dogs, I love dogs, I love dogs," she repeated under her breath as she very reluctantly disengaged herself from Trevor's arms.

"Then I love big backyards with well-built fences and self-serve doggy doors," Trevor said, rolling over to cover the spot she'd just vacated with his amazingly stunning body and burying his face in her pillow.

She had to curl her fingers into her palms until the bite of her nails proved that yes, in fact, she really was awake. And that remarkably fine ass she was staring at, had, just recently, been cupped into the curve of her body. Really. She didn't get this lucky. Except she just had. And, if she played her cards right, was about to get lucky again. And maybe again.

Merry Christmas, indeed.

He turned just enough to cock one eye open to look at her. "You're staring."

"Sue me," she said. "You have a world-class backside, and I get to have my hands all over it again. So, I'm going to stare. You'll have to get used to it from me. Promise me you won't move and I'll be the fastest little dog-walker in Virginia."

"As long as those hands are warm when you get back, you have a deal."

But a moment later, before she could scramble around and find her clothes, shivering in the morning cold—still no electricity apparently—Trevor was dragging himself into an upright sitting position and raking his hand through his hair. He did rumpled, morning-after beard stubble really well, too. "Wait a second, and I'll go with you."

"You don't have to do that. Enjoy the warm bed. It's freezing out here. We should probably rebuild the fire. I think the dogs will be okay in the house while it's light outside, but if we keep the fire going in the parlor, too, I'm betting they'll just stay up here where it's warmer. I can put Cicero in his smaller, portable cage and move him in there, too. He shouldn't be anywhere drafty."

"Which is why I'm going to go with you and help."

"Trevor—"

"Emma," he said, only it was quite adorable and she had to admit, she rather liked hearing him say her name, in any tone.

"Would it help if I said my willingness to help you was entirely selfish in motivation?"

"A great deal. I guilt very easily."

He grinned at that. "I am not a greedy man when it comes to money or possessions, however, it's becoming apparent I am going to be a very greedy man when it comes to you."

She smiled. "I'm listening."

"So, if I help with critter control and fire patrol, then that means I get you back here sooner rather than later."

"What about your search?" She put the question out there quite deliberately. The real world was going to come back, and she didn't think she could bear keeping this wonderful cocoon of cozy perfection going any longer without poking a little bit to see how sturdy a cocoon it was going to be.

"It'll be waiting for us—if you want to join me, that is—."

She hurried to button her jeans. "I'll walk the dogs and move Cicero if you rebuild the fires and dig up something to eat."

"A deal which I'd be a fool not to take, but I guilt easily, too. And I can't have you turning into popsicles with the pup-sicles, while I'm all warm inside. Doesn't seem right."

"Except I'm getting paid to take them out. It's not like I'm being the altruistic one."

"Meaning if they were our dogs, you'd just say screw it and jump back into bed with me?"

"Well, no, because then I'd be obligated as their owner to take care of them. If we had dogs, which we don't."

"Do you? Have dogs, I mean?"

"No. I can't where I live. Which I hate, but I'll get my own place eventually. So, I have everybody else's dogs. And cats. The occasional guinea pig. I'm an all-service pet provider, you see."

He looked over her as she tugged on her sweater. "I happen to like what I see."

"I'm sure I look rather frightening at the moment, but you lie really well. You must really be feeling . . . greedy."

"I never lie." He scooted his legs off the edge of the bed, still quite beautifully naked, and snaked out a hand, snagging her wrist, and tugging her into his lap. "Not about you. Not about this."

"This?" she asked, this time knowing exactly what he meant, but delighting in letting him express it.

He smiled, and he was such a beautiful man, in ways that went far past his surface beauty, it made her heart catch a little.

"Yeah," he said, softly. "This." And he tipped her chin up and claimed her mouth with a kiss that was unlike any they'd shared yet, and they'd shared many during their night together. It was morning, and there had been no bathroom-toothbrush run, so she should have been cringing, but the fairy tale continued and it was simply warm, sweet, and magically wonderful. She really, really didn't want the real world reality check that was likely in store.

She sighed as he lifted his mouth from hers, and kissed the tip of her nose, then the corner of her eye, then her temple, before pulling her more deeply into his arms. Tended to, indeed. She'd always been the caregiver—strong, healthy, and never thinking about needing it herself. And she was still all those things . . . but this touched her on a level, soothed her on a level she hadn't realized needed soothing. Maybe everybody needed tending to, in some way. Maybe he'd been right, about finding your path in life, then sharing it with the person who would enhance the joy already found in it.

Jack's howl reached new heights of discomfort, making them both laugh. She got up from Trevor's lap, and liked that he reluctantly let her go, but did, indeed, let her go. He might be greedy—which she heartily endorsed—but he wasn't selfish. Another trait to admire and respect.

"I'm on dog patrol, you're fire captain. We'll meet back here in, say, twenty minutes?"

"You drive a hard bargain."

She grinned. "No, I believe you're the one who will have to do that."

"Cute."

She leaned in and kissed the tip of his nose, surprising him, and maybe delighting him a little with the unexpected move. "Yes, you are. And after the hard bargain, we can arm wrestle over who has to figure out what to have for breakfast."

"I'll help."

"I'll let you. I'll feed the dogs. Then we'll hunt. And if we can get the power back on, I believe there is a game on later today that has stakes attached to it. If you're very lucky, you'll win, and I won't have to cook."

"How is it lucky for me to end up cooking?"

She walked to the door. "Did I mention I make really good dessert?"

"Maybe, but I'm thinking you'd make a really a good dessert, so we'll arm wrestle for that later, too."

She was smiling when she left the room. And despite the fact that the air in the house was downright frigid, she all but danced down the hallway, let two very anxious dogs out of the parlor, then floated down the stairs and got all three of them into their outdoor winter gear, and out into the frigid, gray morning . . . still smiling all the while.

And the smile was still on her face right up until the moment she stepped back into the Florida room, and faced a no-longer-smiling Trevor.

Apparently the reality check had begun.

13

"Lionel called," Trevor said.

"Okay," Emma said, cautiously, not entirely sure yet exactly what he was frowning about. But given the phone still in his hand, Emma could hazard a guess it wasn't going to be good. "Wishing us a happy holiday, was he?" Her attempt to lighten the mood fell flat, but his expression did smooth a little.

"I debated on answering it, but I know I've put you in an awkward and potentially costly situation with him, so I thought a good offense would be your best defense."

She appreciated that he'd thought of her. It hadn't occurred to her what her liaison with Trevor might cost her, in terms of her new career, but she realized she didn't much care. Some things were more important, and what Lionel Hamilton thought of her was quickly becoming unimportant. "Not so much, huh?"

"Not so much."

Emma grabbed two towels and handed him one. Better to keep going through the motions of things being normal. Which was sort of ridiculous since nothing about being here was part of her own personal normal. She started rubbing Jack down. "What did he say about you being here?"

"I told him why I was here."

"Which went over marvelously, apparently."

"Actually, he was surprised I was still thinking about it. It's been a number of years since the subject has come up."

"But he still wouldn't tell you. He does know the truth, right?"

"I assume so, but I'm not sure. I know he knows there are things in our family history he's not particularly proud of, and he's an intensely proud man. Which is mostly why he'd just as soon I forget my little hunt and pretend I'm fine with who I am and what I was born into. It flabbergasts him that I'd want to believe any different."

"Do you?" She rocked back on her haunches when he frowned at her. "I mean, what are you hoping to find? That you really are a Hamilton, or that you're from some other genetic pool?"

"I—I don't know, really. I mean, I've asked myself that. A thousand times. But I've grown up a lot in the past six or seven years, and I'm looking more to my future than to my past. It's more just an old doubt that I need to lay to rest, I guess."

"What did Lionel say about it?"

"He told me that while he didn't appreciate my subterfuge, he wanted me to just be done with it, once and for all, then never speak of it again."

Emma smiled. "Not a surprise, given what you've said about him. So . . . did you tell him you'd found the hidden room in his study?"

"I didn't mention the avalanche, but yes."

"And?"

"And he's rightfully pissed off that I was snooping in what wasn't mine, but he didn't bluster too much when I reminded him that I wouldn't have needed to snoop if he had just treated this like the adult conversation it should have been, years ago, and told me what he knew."

Emma patted Jack on the head and scratched at his ears, then pushed to a stand. "Why do you think he won't? I mean,

I know he's a proud man, but . . . do you think that whatever you unwittingly prodded him to uncover would rock the family in some other way? And, by extension, the foundation of Hamilton Industries?"

Trevor stopped rubbing Martha and looked at her. "You know . . . I never really thought about that. I mean, it's a couple generations past, so far as I know, so I wouldn't think so, but—"

"So, legally, it could still matter. If the liaison was something that might jeopardize true ownership of the company, or something earthshaking like that. Maybe it's not just a matter of him being embarrassed by family skeletons, but there's something serious and specific he doesn't want to get out. Any idea who the adulterous liaison in question might have been with? A rival of some sort, perhaps?"

Trevor tossed the damp towel on the laundry pile with the others and shoved his hands in the pockets of his jeans.

Emma was momentarily distracted by the realization when his pants rode down to reveal . . . more skin, that he wasn't wearing anything under his jeans.

"Like I said, it was generations ago. I'm not sure how it would still be that critical."

"Hamilton Industries is more than a few generations old."

"True, but aren't there limits on certain things?"

"Legally, maybe. But this is a small county, with close ties. It might not matter what the law says. People's opinion does hold a lot of sway and everybody loves a scandal."

Trevor sighed, then swore under his breath. "Everything you're saying . . . thinking back over my conversations with Lionel . . . I think you might be right. I can't believe I never went in that direction."

"Why would you have? All you wanted to know was who was in your direct lineage. Did he tell you where the answers were?"

"He said everything I needed to know was in the hidden room."

Emma's gaze jerked up to his. "Then why are we standing here?"

"Because," he said, a hint of a smile coming out now. "Perversely, now that I've been handed the key to unlock my own personal kingdom, given what you've just said, I'm not sure I want to know what I've inherited."

Emma smiled. "It's perfectly normal to be nervous, but . . . you have to know. I mean, you do know that, right? You can't let anything I've said change your mind. I know you're looking to the future, and that's right and good and healthy, but . . . this is a part of who you are."

"More foundation talk?" he said, smiling, even though he was clearly distracted, his mind probably on new ideas, possible other answers.

"Yeah, of a sort. Do you want me to go with you? Or would you rather go through things alone?" Then another thought occurred to her. "Or . . . were you coming to tell me you wanted me to leave altogether? Did Lionel fire me for letting you in?"

Trevor reached for her then, and pulled her into his arms. It felt like forever since she'd been there, and she was very happy to be back.

"I did tell him you had nothing to do with letting me in. And no, he hasn't fired you. In fact, he didn't even ask after you. He's not exactly known for treating his hired help like human beings, but then I gather you've noticed that."

"So . . . he doesn't know about—"

"Us?"

She smiled, she couldn't help it. She liked that word. A lot. "Yeah. Us. Is that going to cause other problems for you?" She tried to move out of his arms, her smile fading. "Because this is a much bigger thing than you and I—"

"You and I are a very big thing. And, when Lionel finds out, he'll feel about it however he feels. I'm not particularly concerned about that."

"Okay," she said, trusting him on that. Besides, she wasn't

going to fall apart if every last thing wasn't perfect. It was pretty damn perfect enough.

"I will be honest and say that I'm not sure how it might impact your future business opportunities in Randolph County. Lionel can be . . . punitive. And since I don't know what I'm going to find—"

She stopped him. "Why don't you do that, then we'll worry about my business opportunities or sudden lack thereof."

He kissed her then, surprising her with the intensity of it.

"What was that for?"

"Your business opportunities or lack thereof are a real problem. What I find in that room is an ancient one. It'll wait."

"Trevor—"

"Let me ask you something, and I know it's a bit over-reaching, all things considered, but . . . Does your family live here? In Virginia, I mean?"

She shook her head. "Connecticut. Much like you, I went to college here, stayed. I work with my college roommate, or did, for your uncle's company. Chelsea still does, in HR, but I quit seven months ago after I inherited some money from my grandma on my mom's side. I was good at my job, but I hated it. I love animals, and always wanted to work with them. I can't stand to see them suffering though, so being a vet was out. I came up with the pet-sitting service idea and . . ." She smiled. "I'm babbling again."

"You're human. And I like mine imperfect."

She laughed. "Well, you're getting that with me in spades."

"So . . . seven-month-old business." He pulled her more tightly against him. "Did you know that there are pets in need of sitting in North Carolina? At least, I'm assuming there must be."

"Huh," she thought aloud, trying to be calm and casual, when her insides were erupting into a party of hope and expectation. Was he really saying what she thought he was saying? "Is that so?"

"I think it is quite probably so. Maybe you'd consider relocating. Just saying to think about it. We can figure things out long distance if you want, or I could even think about—"

She cut him off with a kiss. "Did I mention I love an adventure?"

"No. No, I don't believe you did. But I'm immensely happy that you do. So, you'll consider it? After we've had time to make sure that—"

"How much time would that be?"

He grinned. "Want to celebrate the new year in Chapel Hill? Test things out?"

"If we can celebrate after I'm done house-sitting."

"That can be arranged."

She wrapped her arms around his neck. "You know, Santa is being very, very good to me this year."

He scooped her up against him. "That Santa is a hell of a guy, I hear."

"Well," she said, kissing him, "he's got some competition."

The kiss started out gentle and sweet, but quickly turned into something fiery and passionate. He started to back walk her out of the kitchen, and toward the staircase leading upstairs.

"Trevor," she said, sighing as he started his way along her neck with those kisses she already knew would drive her wild. "The hidden room. Your legacy."

"Is in my arms."

She melted a little, but moved away from his tempting lips all the same. "You want to know. It's there for you."

"I don't think it's going to change anything. Being a Hamilton or not. I mean, it is who I am, like it or not. It's helped me, whether I've wanted it to or not. But I like who I've become, on my own, and whether or not there's another surname out there I don't know about that should rightfully be mine, what's come to me through the family is mine. But that doesn't matter now. Because I know what I am, and what I'm not."

"What do you mean?"

"Whether I'm a Hamilton, or a Smith, or a Jones won't change anything. My world is still in North Carolina, my life is my own, and that trust fund will stay where it is, because that's the decision I'd make whether it's rightfully mine by ancestry or not. I guess I've always known that. I just hadn't come to terms with it."

"What changed? Not what I said about Lionel hiding something, because—"

"It just put it in a different perspective for me, one I've been too narrow-minded and locked into past thinking to consider."

"So, even if that other surname isn't attached to you? But, maybe to some other branch of the family?"

He nodded. "It's immaterial to who I am. It might be important to Lionel, and if that's the case, I'll respect that. I know it's not how I want to define myself, it's not how I have defined myself."

"So . . . what will you do with it? Your Hamilton legacy, I mean."

"The money?"

"And whatever other responsibilities or inheritances might be in your future, yes."

"Keep them for our offspring?"

She laughed. "You really are forward-thinking."

"Okay, let's just say I'll make sure it stays somewhere safe, on the off chance my progeny feels differently about his or her legacy than I do." He tipped her face up to his. "Are you okay with that?"

"It's not your money or your name I'm after, Mr. Smith."

"Good." His grin was quite suggestive. "So . . . what are you after, then?"

"Starting the new year in Chapel Hill. And the best chicken Marsala a girl can get."

"Feeling lucky, are you?"

"Oh, there's no feeling about it. Lottery winners the world over should envy me right now."

"I rather like that notion."

"So . . . upstairs? Or hidden room?"

"You know, whatever secrets Lionel might be protecting will be his cross to bear. That's been his choice."

"So, you're not going to look."

He shook his head. "No. I'm not going to look."

She glanced over her shoulder, toward the hall leading to the study. "The whole secret room . . ."

He laughed. "It's killing you, isn't it?"

"I can't believe it isn't killing you. Just for curiosity's sake."

"How about this—come upstairs with me, and we'll talk about the future."

"Talk?"

"Amongst other things."

He really did have the most wicked twinkle in his eyes.

"And then?"

"And then if you want to go treasure hunting, you can go while I cook."

Her eyes widened. "You'd really let me go find out?"

"Just because I've decided not to doesn't mean you shouldn't know everything you might need to know about the family you're entangling yourself with."

"And if I find something . . . interesting?"

"Your call."

"I'm warning you, no way will I be able to not tell you. I'm a terrible secret-keeper."

"Okay."

"You really are the most perverse man."

"I know it seems that way, but honestly, my perspective has shifted into an entirely new orbit." He tugged her up the stairs. "One that involves you, me, and whatever we might discover as we head down our path. It's going to come with Hamilton stuff. And I hope it comes with a lot of Lafferty stuff, too. There will be good, and bad, and frustrating, and wonderful. But, at the core, it's just us. That's what I want to focus on."

"Then you'd rather me not look?"

"I'm telling you that what matters is that we both do what we need to do, and the other of us will respect that. Want me to hunt with you?"

"I know it's presumptuous of me to say this, but yes, I think you should know."

"Okay." He tucked her hand in his and they went back down the stairs.

"Right now?"

"Seems like as good a time as any. I don't want you distracted when I take you back upstairs and have my way with you."

"But—this could be a very momentous occasion."

He swung around and brought her flush up against him. "The momentous occasion happened when I met you. And the momentum has been building ever since."

"You really mean that, don't you? I mean, you really don't care what's in that room."

"I think what's in that room is a burden Lionel chose to adopt. And he's requested it be left that way. And you're right . . . as to the rest, I truly, honestly don't care. It's so odd, after all this time, but I've really come to peace with it. I know my path." He backed her into the corner between the foyer and the hallway leading to the study. "And I want you on it with me."

"Okay."

"Okay?"

She smiled. "Okay. So . . . who do we get to clean up the mess?"

"You're okay with me sealing the room back up?"

"I'm okay with you taking me upstairs and talking about our path and having your way with me and clouding my mind with all kinds of wonderful future things. I'm okay with respecting your uncle's wishes, and I'm thinking he will be more than happy to take care of his study, especially when you tell him you decided to leave the Hamilton skeletons be."

"You know, I never thought I'd say this, but I actually feel sorry for him," Trevor said. "And I feel a little bad, pushing him like I have. The whole time I was angry because he wouldn't put my needs first, because he wouldn't trust me with the truth. I thought he was being overly conservative, and keeping up appearances above all, like my family has always been. I never thought I was being selfish. Or that I was truly asking him to jeopardize something that might really matter to him."

"You had a right to know."

"I think he is protecting something, or someone. And it might not mean anything to anyone but him, but I should have respected that, or even at least considered it."

"You didn't know." She kissed him. "You do now, and you're respecting his wishes to handle it his own way."

"If he lets whatever secrets he's harboring die with him—"

"Then maybe that's where they should lie."

"Maybe you're right."

She grinned. "I'm always right."

"I thought you were imperfect."

"Usually right, then."

"Well, for me, you're just right."

She melted. "The things you say."

"The way you look at me."

She smiled. He grinned.

"Come on, Curls. We have a date with destiny."

"Well, never let it be said I'd keep destiny waiting. Or you."

He pulled her right down on the center of the grand staircase and, grinning, began unbuttoning her shirt. "The things you say."

Epilogue

Trevor and Emma did forge their own path. Chapel Hill became home to Emma's pet-sitting service as well as their new home together, which housed several mutts, two stray cats, and a recalcitrant pygmy goat. With a lot of hard work, Trevor's business continued to grow, and did even better when Emma lured Chelsea away from Hamilton Industries to come work for her new husband.

Lionel continued to rattle around in his mountaintop retreat, never alone, always a staff around him, but intensely lonely, nonetheless. Thinking about the love he'd lost, as he often did, with the passing of his dear Tru. And the secrets he'd kept, both selfishly and selflessly, realizing now just how great the cost had been to him. And he wondered if he'd made the right decisions. . . . And yet, what choice did he have? He'd been protecting Trudy's legacy as well.

And at that very same time, in a neighboring county, another young man was about to make a discovery that would change his life. Sending him on a quest that would shake the very foundations of everything Lionel, and those who had come before him, had believed to be true. Secrets would finally be exposed, and nothing would be safe and secure again.

FINDING
MR. RIGHT

1

For two months, Maggie Bell walked past him every day on her way out of the office, and every day she took in that tall, leanly muscled body, those incredibly well-fitted Levi's hanging low on his hips thanks to his tool belt, and forgot everything else just to take it all in.

Take *him* in.

As the guy in charge of earthquake retrofitting her office building, he usually carried a roll of architectural plans in one hand and a radio in his other as he dealt with his men, looking confident—not to mention smoking-hot—and every day she thought the same thing.

Yum.

She actually knew him, at least vaguely. Not that he'd remember, but twelve years ago they'd gone to high school together for one semester. Back then, she'd been a bookworm and a true science geek, and little had changed. Jacob Wahler had been the basketball star, a tough kid, though kind enough to be the only guy on his team to ever bother to smile at her. Twice she'd helped him with his chemistry homework, and then there'd been that one time he'd asked her to shut the door—when she'd walked in on him in a dark classroom with his hands down the jeans of a cheerleader.

God, she'd hated high school.

Twelve years, and she'd not ever looked back, but she was looking now. Jacob had gotten a little taller, and had filled out that long rangy body, which now appeared to be rock hard and clearly honed from the physicality of his job. And then there was everything from the neck up, which packed just as much sexual heat as the rest of him. Dark hair curling just past his collar, even darker eyes, olive skin, and a quick smile capable of melting Greenland faster than global warming.

But no matter how gorgeous, she reminded herself that guys like him weren't her fantasy, and never had been. She was a cerebral woman, and she went for cerebral men.

It was her thing.

Unfortunately her thing wasn't working so well. Somehow her Mr. Right always turned into Mr. Wrong, but she had other issues to worry about, such as her job.

She was lead chemist at Data Tech, a company run by two brothers, scientists who together employed other scientists on the cutting edge of technology. Tim and Scott West funded individual projects and innovative inventions that they deemed impressive and viable.

She planned on being both impressive *and* viable. In light of that goal, she'd been working on a skin care technology that acted as a drug delivery for cancer prevention treatments and gene repair agents. The idea wasn't new, it was actually in the preliminary experimental stages at many labs across the world, but no one had been consistently successful, not yet. She was close to it though, possibly within the next year or so—if Data Tech continued to fund her.

Tim and Scott had a lot to gain in her success, as they would claim the fame and fortune from it. Maggie didn't care about that, what she cared about was revolutionizing the delivery of drugs to the bloodstream. Every time she thought about it and the possibilities—treating skin cancer, for example, a method which could have saved her own mother—she felt so hopeful about the future, about saving lives, that she could hardly stand it.

What this meant, what it had meant for two long years, was work, work, and more work, and little-to-no social life— hence drooling after Jacob Wahler, aka Sexy Contractor Guy. Today alone she'd been in her lab since eight A.M., and as it was six P.M. now, her eyes were a little blurry. She knew she needed to call it a day and go home to the empty condo she'd bought last year.

Unbelievably, here it was again, a week before Christmas and she'd scarcely noticed the festive decorations all around her, much less even pulled out her own boxed tree and Christmas stocking for Santa. And really, what could Santa possibly bring her anyway?

A man . . .

That thought came out of nowhere but it was true. She wanted a man for Christmas. She realized it was sexist and anti-feminist, and set women back decades but she didn't care. She was a chemist, a woman with a brain who knew how to use it, and she was using it now to wish for a man.

Tonight she'd settle for a man-made orgasm . . .

Wow, she was more tired than she'd thought, and she slipped out of her lab coat, flipped off the lights in the lab, and headed into her connecting office. There she shut her laptop and slid it into her briefcase. She was going to go home, find her Christmas decorations, and get festive. Maybe sip some eggnog and try to figure out how to get un-alone. She walked out of her office and into the construction zone as she headed toward the elevators and told herself in the grand scheme of things, she was fine. Fine.

Fine.

Okay, that was a few too many fines, but she really was.

"Hey, Mags." Scott West, boss number one, poked his head out of his office, having to peer around a ladder. He was very cute, which usually made her dizzy if she looked at him too long. He wore a white lab coat over his expensive Hugo Boss shirt and pants, looking like a very expensive Doogie Howser. He was a nice catch, and they'd gone out once several weeks back, and that had been really nice, too. But then he'd gone traveling, and she'd been buried in her lab testing and reporting on the results, and . . . and they'd not gotten together again.

"Did you get a look at the showroom today?" he asked.

The showroom was on the lobby floor, filled with all the inventions Data Tech had funded, like the rainmaker that harvested water from the air, a motorized pool lounger, a human exoskeleton that could carry heavy loads over long distances, snorkel radio gear, lightbulb sheets, and any of a hundred other wild and crazy things.

"There's a new exhibit," he told her. "Floating furniture made with matching sets of repelling magnets. The couch can support up to two thousand pounds, can you believe it? How cool is that, a floating couch?"

"Very," she said, wondering who would want a floating couch.

He smiled. "I'm putting one in my office. They're carrying it up now. Want to stick around and see?"

Was he gearing up to finally ask her out again? Unlike Jacob, Scott *was* her type. She knew this. He was cerebral, brilliant really, and extremely into science, which made him perfect.

"Hey." This from boss number two, who poked his head out of *his* office, right next to his brother's.

They were identical twins. Crazily competitive twins, with Tim into robotics and Scott into molecular bionics. They ran Data Tech as a legacy to their father, while each doing their damnedest to one up the other, at work, at play, in any way they could.

Tim tossed a glass vial to Maggie. Her latest formula, which she'd given him a few days ago. "It's beautiful," he told her. "But we've added a secret ingredient. Let us know what you think."

She held the vial up to the light but didn't see any change. "What is it?"

"Tim," Scott said, suddenly looking unhappy. "I—"

"Just something to smooth the formula," Tim said over Scott. "It's a secret until you let us know if you like it."

"I'll try it out tonight." She'd been running test groups on the drug delivery formula using Vitamin B3 and other essential oils as the drug of choice. So far, she'd been inconsistently successful, but she *would* get there.

"*Tim.*" Scott sent his brother a long look. "I thought we— you know I wanted to . . ."

"Spit it out, bro."

But Scott appeared to have lost his words, and just glanced at his brother.

"Lethologica," Maggie said. "The state of not being able to find the word you want." She patted Scott's arm. "Don't worry, it happens to me all the time, it'll pass."

Scott blinked and she smiled, but he didn't return it. "I'll test it for you," he said instead, reaching for the vial. "No need for you to have to."

"Oh, no, that's okay. I don't mind at all."

"She doesn't mind," Tim said to Scott. "Let it go. 'Night, Maggie."

Maggie looked at Scott, who clearly wasn't going to ask her out now. " 'Night."

"Maggie." Scott eyed the vial. "I really think—"

" *'Night,*" Tim repeated, putting a hand over his twin's face and pushing him back into his office. "Don't have too much fun tonight, Maggie."

Okay, they were acting strange. But who was she to judge? As for having fun, ha. After a lifetime of being the nerd, of going to Stanford three years ahead of her peers, of completing college before anyone her age had even begun, she'd gotten damn good at *not* having fun.

And wasn't that just the problem.

Turning, she walked to the elevator. She could see Jacob

and his crew at work, just down the hall. He stood on a ladder, pulling a hammer out of his tool belt, reaching far above him to a ceiling tile, that long, hard body all stretched taut . . .

The elevator dinged and she stepped into it, craning her neck, not to see all the pretty decorations, but to catch the last view of Jacob's tush as the doors slid shut. Was Scott's butt that cute? Since he always wore a white lab coat, she couldn't say.

Outside, she drew in a breath of the cool L.A. evening air and headed to her car as her cell phone rang. It was her sister Janie, a UCLA professor who did *not* have the geek gene. Nope, Janie had somehow snagged a normal life for herself. She'd married and brought two beautiful kids into the world, and was determined to make sure Maggie did the same.

"Hey, Mags." Janie's mouth was clearly full. "Sorry, chocolate stuck in my teeth."

"Don't tell me you're still eating leftover Halloween candy."

"A Baby Ruth bar. Sinful, I'm telling you. Why do you think they call it a Baby Ruth? Why not a Baby Jane or something?"

"It was supposedly named for Grover Cleveland's baby daughter."

"Your brain works in the oddest ways."

"I know."

"Uh-huh. And do you also know if you're coming for Christmas Eve?"

"Bringing the pumpkin pie."

"Spending the night?"

"Wouldn't want to miss Santa."

A lie, and they both knew it. Maggie just didn't want to be alone in her condo on Christmas morning. "What am I supposed to get you for Christmas, by the way? You already have everything you could want."

"You could bring a date."

When Maggie laughed, Janie sighed. "Well, you could *try*. Your Mr. Right is just right around the corner, I know it."

"Yes, but which corner?" Maggie stopped beside her sensible Toyota and searched for her keys, blowing out an irritated breath when she realized she was completely blocked in by Tim's *not* sensible Porsche. "Dammit." She whirled back to the building. "I have to go kill my boss."

"Invite someone from work," Janie said. "Not the boss you're going to kill, but the other one."

"I want *him* to ask *me* out. But my Mr. Rights all seem gun shy."

"Then invite a Mr. Wrong."

"You mean *purposely* go out with someone who isn't right for me?"

"Honey, you've gone two years without sex. What do you have to lose by changing tactics? I mean, honest to God, your good parts are going to wither from nonuse."

"Well, what am I supposed to do, just take off my clothes and have wild sex with the first guy I come across?"

"Yes," Janie said. "The first *wrong* guy, the one you wouldn't normally go out with."

"You want me to have sex with Mr. Wrong."

"Use a condom."

Maggie laughed. "You can't be serious."

"Seriously serious. You need to go for the first Mr. Wrong to cross your path—as long as he's not an ax murderer or rapist," she qualified. "And probably he should have a job and love his mother. *That* can be my Christmas present—you having sex with Mr. Wrong. Promise me."

Since that was as unlikely to happen as having sex with a Mr. Right, Maggie laughed as she walked back into the building. Back on the sixth floor, she dodged through the obstacle course of construction equipment. The construction crew was desperately trying to finish before Christmas, and apparently they were working late tonight. Still on the phone with her sister, she ducked under a ladder, over a cord, and then around a huge stack of unused drywall, catching her shoulder on the sharp edge. She heard the rip of her coat and sighed as she dropped her briefcase to look. *"Dammit."*

"What?" Janie asked. "Mr. Wrong?"

"No! Jeez. Hold on." She bent for her briefcase, just as someone beat her to it, scooping up the loose change that had spilled out.

"Thanks—" Maggie lifted her head and froze at the wide chest in her vision.

A chest that once upon a time she'd dreamed about in chemistry. She took the coins from Jacob's big, work-roughened palm, her nerves suddenly crackling as well as all the good spots Janie had mentioned, which meant that they hadn't withered up, at least not yet. "Three quarters, four dimes, and four pennies," she said. "$1.19."

"That's fast math."

Yes, her brain always sped up when she was anxious. Plus, there was the other thing. She was also a little revved up. Sexually speaking. Which was Janie's fault, she decided, for putting the idea of hot sex in her head in the first place. "A dollar and nineteen cents is the largest amount of money in coins you can have and still not be able to make change for a dollar."

He blinked, then nodded. "That's . . . interesting."

"It's fact." Oh, God. *Shut up.*

"Who's that?" Janie whispered in her ear. "Who are you talking to? A man? It's got to be a man because you're spouting off useless trivia like you do when you're nervous. Oh! He's your Mr. Wrong, isn't he? *Ask him to have hot sex with you!*"

"Hush," Maggie said, and Jacob blinked again. Oh, God. "Not you." She stood, and he did the same, giving her a quick peek of him close up and personal. His scuffed work boots, the mile-long legs and lean hips, covered in Levi's, all faded and stressed white in all the right places, of which there appeared to be a tantalizing many. God bless denim . . . "Thanks, Jacob."

At his surprise, she nodded. "Yeah, we know each other, or used to. Chem 101, your junior year at South Pasadena High. Before you moved to New Orleans."

"Maggie Bell?" His eyes warmed. "I remember now. You

came up directly from eighth grade, right? You saved my ass that year."

"Jacob . . ." Janie whispered in her ear. "I don't remember a Jacob. Is he cute?"

Yeah, he was cute. Cute like a wild cheetah. As in look but don't touch. And while she stood there, still enjoying his jeans—what was with her?—her mouth ran loose. "Until you and your crew started retrofitting the building, the dress code around here was pretty much limited to white lab coats."

His mouth quirked. "I can't climb ladders in a white lab coat."

"No, no it's okay." *So okay.* "I get tired of looking at all that white anyway. So it's good that you're not." *Oh, just shut up already!* "Wearing one," she added weakly.

"You should probably not talk anymore," Janie said, ever so helpfully over the phone.

Maggie bit her lip to keep it shut. He was so close, so big. And she felt a little like a doe caught in the headlights.

"You tore your coat," he said, and fingered the hole.

At his touch, her body tightened, and her mouth opened again. "It's okay. I tend to do things like this a lot."

"Run into drywall?"

"Run into stuff, period." Someone had opened a window, and the evening breeze came in, as well as the sounds from the street six floors below. Traffic, an airplane, a sudden blare of a horn so loud she jumped.

"Just a car," he said.

"In the tone of an F."

"Excuse me?"

"All car horns are in the chord of F."

He did that eyebrow arch thing again.

"Jesus, Mags. *Stop talking!*" Janie demanded in her ear.

"Okay, I've really got to go."

"Wait!" Janie yelled. "Ask him out first, you promised! You have to do him, and get him to do you—"

Maggie slapped her phone shut before Jacob could hear her

crazy sister. Yes, he was Mr. Wrong. Wrong, wrong, wrong. But what was she supposed to do, say *Hey, how do you feel about me jumping your bones?* Probably she should start with a dinner invite and work her way up to the jumping bones part. Yeah, that was it, that was how *normal* women did these things. Okay. She took both a big breath and a small step backwards for distance, but Jacob curled his fingers into the front of her jacket and caught her up against him.

Not that she was complaining, but . . . "Um—"

He gestured to the bucket of nails she'd nearly stepped in, and she winced. His body, plastered to hers, was as hard as it appeared. And warm. Very, very warm. "Thanks."

"Maybe you should just stand real still," he suggested, and let go of her.

"Yes, except I don't stand still very well. I only do still when I'm lying down."

He arched a brow, those deep chocolate brown eyes lighting up with amusement to go with the heat still there, making her realize the double entendre she'd just said. "You know what I mean."

He just smiled, and turned his head toward a crew member who came up to him with a McDonald's bag.

"Burgers on the run." Jacob took the food. "Thanks."

Maggie's mouth once again ran away from her brain. "There're one hundred seventy-eight sesame seeds on each of those hamburger buns."

He leaned back against the wall, all casual like, in direct contrast to her uptightness. "One hundred seventy-eight, huh?" He was clearly biting back a smile. "Exactly?"

"Or thereabouts," she muttered, wondering how it was she could be so smart and yet not be able to keep her mouth shut.

"So you graduated early to become a sesame seed counter?"

"No." She laughed. "No. I'm sort of a chemist."

"How does one become a *sort of* chemist?"

Yeah, still amusing him. Terrific. Just what she wanted to do, amuse the gorgeous man, at her own expense. "Okay, it's not sort of. It's really. I'm really a chemist." Wow, so much better. Now all she had to do to complete her humiliation was ask him out. No sweat. "So—"

But he pushed away from the wall, calling out to one of his workers. "Dave, not there, over a foot! Check the specs!" He glanced back at Maggie. "Do me a favor and watch where you walk in here tonight."

Yes, she'd just watch where she was going, she thought with a sigh as he walked away. That was her. Always watching. Never doing. She opened Tim's office door. "Your car's in my way."

He looked up with concern. "You didn't bump it?"

"No, of course not."

He rushed off to check on his precious baby, and Maggie followed at a slower pace, calling back her sister as she went. "He walked away from me."

"Who, your Mr. Wrong? Did you ask him out?"

"No, I ran out of words."

"You tell him that car horns are in the chord of F and you can't find the words to ask him out? God, you need help."

"I know!"

2

When the alarm went off well before dawn, Jacob groaned, squelched the urge to toss the thing out his window, and rolled out of bed. He strode naked to the shower, which he cranked up to scalding.

This eighty-hour workweek shit had to stop.

After pulling on his last set of clean clothes—damn, he really needed a night at home to catch up—he headed to work, already on his cell phone with his crew, who wanted to get this job finished as badly as he did. He wanted to fly to New Orleans as scheduled in two days, hang out with his family, and possibly do the stacked blonde his brother had set him up with for New Year's Eve.

Simple needs, really. Except there was a glitch. Christ, he hated glitches, and he had the mother of all glitches staring him in the face. He had to finish this job before anyone could leave. He'd signed a contract with Data Tech and he had two days left on that contract. Two days or he'd lose his ten percent bonus—only thanks to delay after delay, they had at least a week's worth of work still to be done in that two days.

Not good odds, but then again, he'd faced worse. Much worse.

He left his house, skirted the jammed L.A. freeways like a pro, and was on the job before the sun had even thought about coming up. And since he had a kick-ass crew, they'd joined him without complaint.

Okay, there was complaining, but they all wanted that ten percent bonus as badly as he did, so they bitched and worked at the same time. After they finished this building, they were jumping right into another job on Fourth Street. Business was good. Actually, business was great.

So why he felt so damn restless, he really had no idea. Maybe the trip would help. He could see his mom and sister, and make sure they were doing okay in their new place. He could see his brother and catch up.

And get laid.

Yeah. All systems go on that one. After moving to New Orleans in his senior year of high school, he'd come back out to Los Angeles five years ago with his best friend and partner, Sam. They'd started out in the hole, practically having to beg, borrow, and steal jobs, but they'd managed. And then they'd gotten their first big contract, and that had led to two more, and they'd been on their way.

Then Sam had gone home for his brother's birthday and had gotten killed in Katrina, and things hadn't been the same for Jacob since. He'd been left with five large contracts already signed, when all he'd wanted to do was go home and wallow. In hindsight, those jobs had probably saved his sorry ass. Even if this one just might kill him. But he wanted that damn bonus. It'd help both his mother and sister pay off the mortgages on homes that no longer even existed, and it would ease their tight financial situation.

He was busy laying out some electrical lines when he heard the *click click clicking* of heels and knew it was 8:03 exactly, because at 8:03 every single morning, she appeared. Maggie Bell, his new favorite "sort of" chemist with the encyclopedia brain filled with odd facts.

She'd grown up. Filled out. And looked damn good. She wore black pumps today, her long legs covered in sheer silk, a business skirt and blouse, and since it was December and chilly, an overcoat, open and flapping behind her as she rushed along, working her cell phone, sipping her caffeine, and balancing a briefcase. She looked a little bit harried, a little bit late, and in spite of the fact that she screamed class, also just a little bit messy.

God, he loved that part. He had a feeling if the right guy came along and took that pen out from behind her ear, then slid his fingers into her hair and kissed her long and hard and wet, she'd melt. That fantasy alone had gotten him through the past two months.

As he did every single morning, he stopped whatever he was doing to watch. She didn't disappoint. Today her honey-colored hair was piled on top of her head in what looked to be a precarious hold. She didn't wear much makeup that he could tell, but her lips were glossed. Her eyes were covered by reflective sunglasses but he knew them to be a jade green, and that in five seconds they'd focus in on him and she'd stumble just a little. Then her mouth would tremble open in a perfect little O, and time would stop, just literally stop.

And then she'd blink. Her eyes would cool, as if she'd just remembered that they were virtual strangers. She'd pretend to be occupied by something in her hands and rush into her lab, not to be seen again until at least six—

Ah, there it was. She glanced up, saw him only a few yards away with the electrical wiring in his hands. She came to an abrupt halt, prompting two of his guys behind her to nearly plow into her.

Her mouth opened and apologies tumbled out from everyone, and then his guys made their way around her and she gripped her things, once again turning her head in his direction, this time with a hint of pink in her cheeks.

He lifted his hand and waggled his fingers.

Her mouth curved in a self-deprecatory smile. "Whoops." Her voice was soft and musical, and if he'd let it, it would have gone straight to his head. And other places.

In high school, she'd been the quietest little thing. He remembered sitting near her, watching her absorb school in a way he'd never quite managed. He'd actually wished he could be more like her. She'd helped him out, and he'd been grateful, but she'd been too shy to get to know, not to mention far too young. And then he'd moved and had never seen her again.

He was seeing her now—warm eyes, sweet smile, and a body made for sin. Not too young now, was she . . . ?

Scott West came out of the elevator, dressed like a man who didn't have to worry about any ten-percent potential profit loss. "Hey, Maggie," he said. "Jacob."

Scott had been a tough-ass at the negotiating table, but was looking much softer now that he was taking in Maggie's sweet morning appearance. "So what's today's fact?" he asked her, flashing a set of perfect teeth.

"Odontophobia," she said, staring at his extremely white teeth. "The fear of teeth. Point one percent of the population suffers from it."

Scott laughed and shook his head. "Good one. So . . . about that vial Tim gave you—"

"Oh! I tried it last night. The secret ingredient . . . it's sweet almond oil, right? For that extra vitamin E? It's a little too thick now but I'll—"

"No, no, don't worry about it. I'll have Tim rework it." He held out his hand, presumably for said vial, but she shook her head.

"It's at my condo, sorry."

"Gotcha. Well . . ." He opened his office door with a smile not quite the same wattage as before. "See you at the staff meeting."

Maggie turned back to Jacob, but stopped short when her cell phone rang. With a look of apology, she opened her bag and pulled it out to answer it. Immediately a frown crossed her brow, and she forgot about him, he could tell. She was on the move again, talking, gesturing with her full hands, not watching where she was going as she headed beneath his scaffolding to enter her lab, just barely ducking as two men from his crew moved a heavy piece of equipment in front of her.

The woman was a walking/talking accident just waiting to happen. The cutest, sexiest, walking/talking accident he'd ever seen.

Maggie spent the entire morning hunched over her laptop, going over lab results, ignoring a flood of pesky texts from a nosy-body Janie.

Alice showed up at noon with lunch. "Men suck," she said, handing a wrapped sandwich to Maggie. "And I think the bottle for your cream should be blue."

Alice was twenty-two, an intern on loan from UCLA to do Data Tech's filing, but she'd latched onto Maggie because she wanted to be a scientist, too. Dressed like a Goth superhero, all in black and lace, with some interesting deep purple lipstick, she sighed glumly as she sat and opened her sandwich. "I think my boyfriend is cheating on me with his lab partner."

"Oh, Alice. I'm sorry."

"Yeah." Alice usually wore an expression of general angry-at-the-world emo-ism. But today there was something new, hurt. "Me, too. But definitely blue glass. For your cream. My grandmother loves blue glass."

Talking with Alice made her dizzy. "I'm aiming for a younger crowd here."

"Hey, my grandmother is a tough chick. She rides with the Hells Angels, and is armed to the teeth at all times. And isn't it a wrinkle cream?"

Maggie looked into Alice's face, which was gorgeous, smooth, and covered in pale, pale foundation. "Yes, I've made several wrinkle creams. But I'm also working on a drug delivery system. And trust me, you're only a few years away from your first wrinkle."

"I am not. I don't allow my skin to touch the sun. Haven't you heard? Goth is the new tan." She took a big bite of her PB&J. "The drug delivery system thing is cool. I should start reading the reports I'm filing for you guys."

Scott poked his head in the lab, his gaze passing over Alice to meet Maggie's. "Lunch?"

Maggie had been waiting so long to have him ask her out again it almost seemed surreal. She was crazy not to jump up and say "yes!" but the fact was, Scott was a Mr. Right and she'd given up Mr. Rights. Thanks to Janie, she was going to go for her Mr. Wrong.

Soon as she figured out exactly how to do that. She held up her half-eaten sandwich. "Sorry, I'm almost done."

He nodded, nonchalantly looking around her lab, as if not sure what to do with himself. "Well, okay then. See you later."

When he was gone, Alice looked at Maggie. "He wants into your pants."

"Because he offered me lunch?"

"Yeah, I think you should go for it. He's rich and he's hot. And *rich*. Which always trumps hot. My boyfriend's rich. Or his family is." Some of her perpetual anger made room for that hurt again. "Unfortunately he's also a dick."

Maggie squeezed her hand in sympathy. "Neither hot nor rich are important criteria for me."

Alice seemed baffled by this. "What's more important than rich?"

Maggie sighed. "Scott's my type."

"The bastard."

"No, I mean . . . I'm trying a new thing. I'm going for the *opposite* of my type. I'm going for Mr. Wrong."

Alice put down her sandwich. "Okay, this is interesting. Go on."

"It's my sister's idea. She made me promise that my Christmas present to her would be me ignoring all the Mr. Rights and going for Mr. Wrong."

"So have you found him yet?"

Maggie hesitated, and Alice pounced with glee. "You have, haven't you?" She grinned. "Who is he, that geek in accounting—what's his name, the one who actually carries pencils and pens and a calculator in his shirt pocket?"

"Alan, and he's a great guy, but no. He's not a Mr. Wrong, he's . . ." Her own type. The overeducated thinker, nice but distracted, and to be honest, a little aloof. She wanted passion, she wanted aggression, she wanted . . . *wild sex*.

Oh, God, it was true. She wanted wild sex from her Mr. Wrong. "I'm not really ready to share."

Alice sighed and packed up the trash from lunch. "Fine. It's none of my business and it's going to end badly anyway, these things always do."

"Alice—"

"I have to go. It's time to get filing. Hey, maybe I'll learn something."

Maggie got back to work. At the end of the day, she closed up and left her lab. The place was completely void of Data Tech employees, which was typical of Christmas week. Everyone wanted to rush home to their families.

Their significant others.

She sighed again and kept walking, trying not to notice the boughs of holly, the lights . . . the noise of the construction workers. Two of them were mumbling about the long night ahead and their looming deadline, and she wondered if their boss was still in the building. Maybe like *her* boss, Jacob had deserted his workers. Maybe he was home drinking eggnog with his friends, enjoying the holiday; maybe he was on a date, which for some reason tightened a knot in her gut and made her head hurt. She rubbed her forehead and—

And tripped over an open tool box, hitting the floor on all fours. Her briefcase went flying, and the pen she'd forgotten she had behind her ear skittered across the floor. "Dammit."

"So much for watching where you're going."

Accompanying this most annoying statement, two big, warm hands gripped her waist and hoisted her up. When she tilted her head back, her gaze collided with a set of dark brown eyes. Terrific. *Now* he showed up. She bent to look at her burning knees, which were both skinned good and already starting to bleed. *"Dammit."*

"You said that." Jacob crouched down, seeming big and bad and just a little irritated. He had drywall dust and sawdust all over him, and was hot and sweaty, and clearly not exactly thrilled at the interruption. He picked up all her things, easily tucking them beneath one arm. "Shit, you're bleeding," he said, looking at the trickle running down her calf. "Tommy, bring me a clean rag!"

"It's okay." She sucked in a painful breath. Liar, liar . . .

But she smiled into his solemn eyes as her heart kicked hard. "The human heart can create enough pressure to squirt blood thirty feet, so this is nothing, relatively speaking." Even if her knees were on fire . . . "I'm fine," she said, and stood up.

He straightened, too, and she suddenly became aware of exactly how close they were. Inches apart, which was waaaay closer than they'd ever been. Someone, presumably Tommy, tossed him a rag, which he caught over her head and handed to her.

"Thanks." She hadn't skinned her knees in years and she didn't remember it hurting this bad. She dabbed at her knees and hissed out a breath. "You don't by any chance have a Band-Aid? Or two?"

"Sure do." He led her down the hall, past the elevators. The building was in a U-shape, curved around a courtyard six stories below. Out of the corner of her eye, she watched him walk, his broad shoulders stretching the seams of his shirt, his Levi's lovingly cupping a most drool-worthy butt.

Odd to be so attracted to a Mr. Wrong, but her body was humming again in spite of her knees. He hadn't gotten himself a haircut, and the dark strands of his hair looked soft and silky. He hadn't shaved that morning, and maybe not yesterday morning either, and that growth didn't look soft and silky at all. It would be rough against her skin, which for some reason, gave her a little shiver. "I was wondering . . ." *If I could ask you to do me.*

Still walking, he glanced over at her. His jaw was square, his mouth generous, but it was his eyes that held her. They were fathomless, and in those swirling depths was a mix of emotions with a barely restrained impatience leading the pack. He was busy, needing to get back to work, and at the knowledge, her nerve packed up and went on vacation. "Never mind."

Two years without sex, her good parts whined. . . .

They turned a corner, tight with stacks of boxes. "Watch where you're going," Jacob reminded her.

Right. Watch where she was going instead of watching him and daydreaming. Time to stop daydreaming! "Yes, well, in my defense, I rarely do watch where I'm going."

"And we've got a mess all around you, I know. But your boss promised he'd give you all this week off so we'd have the empty building to ourselves. Then he didn't."

"Tim's a good guy, but he's tight with his money, so tight he squeaks when he walks." She smiled when he laughed. He had a good laugh. "He's never given us a week off."

"We're attempting to not miss our deadline. Some of us have flights to catch out of here tomorrow, if we finish."

"You'll finish."

He looked a little surprised, and a little amused. "How do you know?"

She was doing her best not to limp. No limping in front of the cute guy from high school—but she wanted to. "In high school, you finished everything you started, even when it was hard. Basketball, chemistry . . ." *The 36-D blonde in that empty classroom . . .* God, she'd been so jealous of that girl. "You just seem like a guy who still finishes what he starts."

His eyes heated, and oh, Lord, so did her body, but had she really just said he looked like a guy who finished what he started? Why didn't she just strip down right here and ask him to finish her? "Where are you flying out to?" she asked instead, desperate for a subject change. "New Orleans?"

"You remember."

She remembered everything about him, but gave a slight shrug. Playing it cool.

"My mom lost her house in Katrina," he said. "She's in a new place now and we're all meeting there for Christmas."

"Sounds lovely." She was happy for him, but wistful for herself. Yes, she had Janie, but she missed having her mom, too.

Jacob stopped at an empty lab on the far side of the building, which he and his crew used as an office and for tool storage. Knees on fire, Maggie sat on a chair while he dug into a large toolbox and came up with a first-aid kit.

"Here's some antiseptic spray," he said. "It'll take out the sting. Pull up your skirt."

No can do. Not when she'd just remembered she hadn't shaved her legs. "I'll do it." She held out her hand for the spray, which she shoved beneath her skirt, gave a cursory spritz and gritted her teeth. "All better."

"Maggie, I can see the blood dripping down your calves. This is my fault, so let me see."

"I'm good."

With a sigh, he reached for the hem of her skirt himself.

3

Jacob's fingers brushed Maggie's skirt, and suddenly he wasn't thinking about her knees but other things altogether, until Maggie put her hands over his, flashing a quick and definitely fake smile. "I just remembered. I have my own Band-Aids."

He pushed a smile of his own, one that usually got him a lot more than a peek at an injured knee. "Maggie, it's just your knees."

"It's not my knees I'm worried about."

She was blushing. Was she for real? He had a million other things to do, and yet he was crouched before her watching her most mesmerizing face. She was the ultimate science geek fantasy, if one was into that sort of thing. And apparently, given his pheromone level whenever she got within sight, he was. Her hair was still piled on top of her head, her lips fully glossed, and that smoking body covered up with her coat. Her killer eyes were magnified behind her lab glasses, which she'd clearly forgotten to take off. She'd put the pen behind her ear again.

She flashed another fake smile and rose, then winced and sat back down. "Honestly, it's not hurting at all."

"God, you are such a liar." He shuffled through the kit.

"Damn, I don't have Band-Aids. I can't believe it. Joe must have used them all last week when he staple-gunned his finger to the ceiling. The spray should help, though. Did you get a lot of it? Come on, let me see."

"Can't."

"Why not? You have ugly knees?"

She rolled her eyes. "If you must know, I didn't shave my legs."

"Jesus, really? I'll call the fashion police, stat."

She wasn't amused at his grin. "It's not funny. I haven't been as diligent lately since I'm not dating."

He sat back on his heels, fascinated by this, by her. "So you only shave your legs for a date?"

"Well, it's a time sink otherwise, and— Never mind." She lifted her chin. "My point is, I can't show you my legs if I haven't shaved them."

"Maggie, I don't care."

With a look that said she was prepared for his disgust, she finally pulled her skirt up past her knees.

His smile caught in his throat. Disgust was the last thing he felt. She was definitely wearing silk, which had torn and snagged at both knees, but that wasn't what caught his interest and held it. Nope, that honor went to the fact that her silk stopped at mid-thigh, or one did; the other had sagged down just above her bloody knee, held there by what appeared to be an inch-wide strip of stretchy lace.

If she'd been this sexy in high school, he'd been blind. He tried to control himself, but suddenly all he could think about was what she'd look like in that silk and her white lab coat and nothing else.

As if she could see his wicked, dirty little thoughts, she let out a sound that managed to convey what she thought of him, and snatched the antiseptic herself. "I got this."

"Okay." He straightened and jammed his hands in his pockets, waiting for her to deal with it, letting out a slow, long breath, practicing some multiplication problems in his head . . . anything to make sure his brain didn't focus in on those sexy as hell thigh-highs. But she slowly rolled the stocking down, past the scraped knee, and—

"*Don't look!*"

"I'm not."

"You are so."

Yeah, he was.

"What, you've never seen a clumsy woman tear her stockings before?"

"I've never seen a beautiful woman so unaware of herself before."

Her gaze snapped up to his, and he let her look her fill, which she did with a wary hunger that quite frankly turned him on more than the stockings, more than any woman had in a long time.

"So I have a little thing for lingerie," she said defensively, and sprayed her knees again. "And dammit, *ouch*."

He put a hand on her thigh, bent, and blew on the scrapes. She gasped.

Nope, he wasn't alone in this odd and inexplicable attraction. "Maggie?"

"Yeah?"

"You're crazy if you think I have a problem with your lingerie."

"It's not that I'm crazy. Although in general, women are thirty-seven percent more likely to need a psychiatrist."

That made him smile. "You know some interesting things."

"I know, it's odd. I'm . . . odd. I dress in lab coats every day and I wear glasses, and my hair— Well, just never mind about my hair. I know what I look like. Wearing sexy underwear gives me the illusion of *being* sexy, at least in my own mind."

He took in her slightly disheveled, sexy-as-hell appearance and shook his head. "Hate to argue with someone thirty-seven percent more likely to need professional help, but there's no illusion here. You *are* sexy as hell."

She blushed beet red. "And not that it's any of your business, but the thigh-highs are far better for the female body

138 / *Jill Shalvis*

anyway, and—" She broke off when he slipped his hand around the back of one calf and lifted her leg enough to get a good look at her trashed knees.

"And . . . ?" he prompted, when she didn't finish.

"And . . ." She slid her eyes to his hand on her. "I lost my train of thought."

"You were talking about your lingerie fetish."

She pushed him back a step. "It's not a fetish!"

"Okay."

"It's not!" She shook her head and let out a breath. "Oh, forget it." She thrust the antiseptic spray at him and got up. As she straightened her legs, she sucked in another breath.

"Still hurt?"

"It's just scraped knees." She shoved her nose up into nose-bleed heights. "I'll be fine." She put a hand to his chest to push him out of her way, then frowned down at her hand.

"Yeah," he said, feeling the pull at the touch. "Quite a punch, huh?"

"What's quite a punch?"

"The chemistry. Our chemistry. Fitting, I think, since chemistry is where we first met."

She paused. "You think we have chemistry?"

"I guess it could be static electricity."

She choked out a laugh, looking down at her fingers, still spread over his chest. "Do you remember me catching you in that empty classroom with that girl?"

He went blank a moment, then grimaced. "Oh, shit. Yeah. Look, in my defense, I was an idiot back then."

She limped to the window, which looked over the courtyard, and farther, back to her own lab. "Hey, my light's on," she said with surprise. "I didn't leave my light on."

"Maybe you forgot."

"No. I shut down my laptop, locked my files, filled my briefcase with everything I need to work at home tonight, and then shut off my light. Like I do every single night."

"It happens."

"Not to me." She took a hobbling step toward the door, and he sighed. "Give me your keys. I'll run back and flip it off for you."

She hugged her keys to her chest. "That would be against the rules."

"And you always follow the rules. Even if your gut tells you otherwise."

"Well, yes."

"Doing my homework for me was against the rules."

"I didn't look at it like that." She sagged a little. "I was trying to help you, and . . ."

"And?"

"And I had a crush on you. Which you had to know."

He paused, then let out a breath. "Yeah, but like I said, I was an idiot back then."

"No, I think you're onto something. Not about breaking the rules, but about following your gut. I need to do that for this situation." She looked very determined. "Follow my gut."

"Which situation?"

She hesitated.

"Tell me."

"You're very different," she said. "Direct."

"Saves a lot of time. Save time, Maggie."

"Okay, if you must know, I'm determined to need to shave my legs more often. How's that for direct? But not for my usual Mr. Right, because my usual Mr. Right always turns out to be Mr. Wrong. Using reverse psychology, when I shave my legs, it's going to be for a Mr. Wrong, and a night I won't easily forget. One night, and then we both just walk away. Do you understand?"

He blinked. "You need a razor."

With a frustrated sound, she walked out of the lab. He followed her limping form back down the hallway. "At least let me give you a lift."

"No, I'm good."

He watched her hobble another moment, then grabbed her,

and turning his back to her, bent at the knees and hoisted her up.

"Hey—"

"Just a piggyback, relax." Which he realized was going to be next to impossible for the woman who probably never relaxed, just as she never broke the rules.

"Don't touch my legs."

How did a woman like this even have sex? "Hold on," he commanded, locking her hands together across his chest.

"Oh, God."

Yeah. If their *accidental* touch had set off sparks, there was a fire blazing now that she had her breasts smashed to his back and her legs around his waist. He lowered his hands to her thighs to hold her up. Her skirt was long and gauzy, and stretchy enough that she wasn't flashing anyone behind him. Her modesty was perfectly intact, except for the fact that her crotch was pressed against his lower back, but he decided not to mention that.

But he felt it, felt the heat of her, and suddenly he needed to do some relaxing of his own, especially when he spread his fingers to touch as much of her as he could and she shivered, pressing her forehead to his shoulder.

He understood. But it was one thing to fantasize about the pretty scientist geek, and another entirely to think about doing more than just fantasizing.

As he strode with her down the hallway, a few of his men gave him a second look, some even taking a third and fourth look. No one said a word, though, as he carried her, trying not to enjoy the feel of her legs hugging his hips, her breasts up against his back, and utterly failing as he took her past the offending tool box and to her closed lab.

Which was locked up tighter than a drum.

"Key's in my pocket," she said in his ear.

He slid a hand to her hip, and she sucked in a breath. "I'll get it!"

"Okay, okay. Just trying to help you out."

"Letting me down would be helping me out."

"Sure." He loosened his hold on her legs, allowing her to slide down his back, making sure it was a slooowwwww slide, because there was something about having her legs wrapped around him, about the heat between those legs—

"You have a dirty mind," she said.

"Hey, I didn't say a word."

"You were thinking it. You were thinking about us . . ."

"Yes?"

"Having sex," she whispered.

"We'd both have to be facing the other way for that."

"Argh," she responded, or something close to that, and dug into her own pockets for her key. She unlocked the door, flipped on the lights, and nearly shut the door in his face when he didn't step inside fast enough. "I've got it from here, thanks."

"Just wanted to see your world." He stepped into the room, which was as neat and tidy as he imagined it would be. There was a long table against one wall, lined with microscopes and other various equipment, another worktable along a second wall, with sinks and burners and lights, and a center workstation, behind which sat a neat black chair and a white lab coat over the back of it.

"Home sweet home," she said, and strode toward the center workstation. "Thanks for the TLC, good night."

"What's your hurry, you have your Mr. Wrong waiting for you at home?"

The tips of her ears went pink. "I shouldn't have told you. In any case, I changed my mind."

"Look at that, you're lying again."

"I . . ." She flipped on another light. "Okay, yes, I'm lying."

"Why? Am I your Mr. Wrong?"

"What?" She whipped back to face him, dropping her keys.

One look at her face had him letting out a surprised laugh. "Me? Really?"

"You were only guessing." She let out a breath and shook her head at herself. "Of course you were only guessing."

Fascinated, he moved in close. "So what exactly was it that you wanted from your Mr. Wrong?"

"Nothing. Because trust me, I'm so over it." And with that, she walked out of the lab, into a connecting bathroom, which she shut and locked.

4

Maggie stared at herself in the small mirror over the bathroom vanity. "You are an idiot." She opened a drawer, searched around, and *yes,* found her own damn Band-Aids. Then she pulled out her cell and called Janie. "You're *not* getting a Christmas present."

"Oh, no. You promised. You're going to do Mr. Wrong."

"I am not going to have hot sex with that man. He's . . ." *Gorgeous. Hot.* "Insufferable."

Jacob's voice came through the door. "I'm not insufferable during hot sex, I promise."

Dammit! "I've got to go," she hissed to Janie. Red as a beet, she opened the door and found Jacob sitting on one of the worktables, a big mixing bowl on one side, toying with her electric mixer on his other. He held up a thistle tube and dropper. "I feel like we're back in chem lab."

She just looked at him, tall, big, and rough-and-tumble, a bull in her china shop. She couldn't help but picture them back in chem lab, where she'd once dreamed of him clearing the workstation with one swooping hand, then lying her down and—

He hopped off the table and patted the spot he'd just vacated. "Come here."

When she didn't, he merely scooped her up himself and put her on the counter himself.

"Hey—"

Taking the Band-Aids from her fingers, he tore one open and smiled at her as he took ahold of the hem of her skirt. "It's like we're playing doctor."

She slapped at his hand, which didn't deter him. "We are *not* playing doctor."

"Spoilsport." He pushed her skirt up above her knees and put on the Band-Aids, during which time she became hyperaware of the feel of his fingers on her skin, of the fact that when he was bent over her that way, she could smell his soap and absorb the heat of his body. But mostly she became aware of her own breathing and how it'd quickened, but once he'd finished and yet left his hands on her, the opposite happened and she stopped breathing entirely. "You listened to my conversation with my sister."

"Yes."

"This is a little awkward."

"Not for me."

Dammit. "Okay, so you were my Mr. Wrong of choice."

"Because . . ."

She grimaced, hating to admit this. "Because historically speaking, I tend to go for a certain type of guy."

"Uh-huh. Someone like yourself probably. A little anal, a little uptight—"

"Yes," she agreed, trying not to be insulted. How was it that he could be both so gorgeous and so irritating? "But it's no longer working for me. Hence the juvenile behavior of my sister and I, and me going for my Mr. Wrong in the first place. I just wanted to . . . feel. I wanted . . ."

"Hot sex."

He was smiling again, and she gritted her teeth. "Nothing permanent."

"How long has it been for you?"

"That's not really any of your business."

"How long?"

"Not quite two years." One year, eleven months, two weeks and three days, not that she was counting or anything.

"So you wanted me to be your Mr. Wrong," he said. "To break your not-quite-two-year dry spell with some hot sex." He arched his brow. "Were there any particulars? Special requests? Kinks?"

She sighed. "Do you have to be crude?"

"Oh, baby, if you think that's crude, then we're going to be in trouble when we get down to the doing."

"I'm not doing! Not with you!" She covered her face. "I'm over it."

He put a hand on either side of her hips. "But you wanted to. With me."

"Could you shut up now?" she begged. "Please?"

"I've got a better idea." His mouth nuzzled at her jaw and she attempted not to melt. "How about I keep my mouth busy with other things? God, something smells delicious."

"It's not me, it's the stuff in that mixing bowl."

He lifted the bowl. "What is it?"

"Organic honey cream. Sort of." It was a skin repair formula, and also a cell rejuvenation. Magic lotion, really.

"Organic?" There was a light in his eyes that made her nipples tingle. "As in edible?"

"I s-suppose."

"I like honey." He smiled, and it was so wicked she quivered. He dipped a finger into the bowl.

"Jacob—"

"I leave for New Orleans tomorrow, so that is your last chance at the whole Mr. Wrong experiment."

"Oh. Well. I don't think—"

Which was the last thing she got out before his mouth claimed hers. And while he distracted her with his very tal-

ented tongue, he gently urged her legs open and stepped between them, putting their bodies up flush together.

Oh, God. "This is such a bad idea," she managed as he
took his lips on a tour over her jaw.

"This kind of bad is good." He took his finger, the one he'd
dipped in the lotion, and touched it to her throat, then leaned
in and licked it off. "Yum."

Dizzy, she clutched at him, holding him so tight to her that
he couldn't have gotten away if he'd wanted to. "I really think
we should take a moment and discuss this."

"Okay," he said agreeably, against her flesh. "You go ahead
and discuss."

"You sh-should know, I might just be using you for the fantasy I've had since high school. The one where *I* was the girl in
the empty classroom with you."

"Use me," he murmured, his tongue taking a hot lick at the
dip in the hollow of her throat. "You locked the door, right?"

"No."

"I got it." He slipped the lock and kissed her again.

God, he was a great kisser. The king of great kissers.
Greedy yet generous, soft yet firm, hot and wet but not too
wet, and while he was going about rendering her incapable of
remembering her own name, he undid the buttons on her
blouse, letting out a low, appreciative throaty groan at the sight
of her white lace demi bra, which was doing its job of holding
up and displaying—until he unhooked it, that is. Dipping his
head, he pressed his mouth to the full curves plumping out of
the top of the lace as he dipped his fingers into the lotion
again.

"Jacob—" The word choked off as he painted the honey lotion over her bared breasts, following up with his mouth as his
very busy hands skimmed down her legs and then back up
again, taking the material of her skirt up with them.

Her pulse skittered. "I don't know about—"

"You taste better than the honey."

"Thanks, but—"

"You never answered my question. Just hot sex? Or . . ." With a naughty bad boy grin, he flipped on the vibrating mixer at her hip and wriggled his eyebrows. "Extra stuff?"

She took a big gulp as he nudged her blouse off one shoulder. The soft material of his shirt was stretched taut over his leanly muscled chest, loose over his belly, which she could feel beneath her fingers, fingers that somehow slipped beneath the tee to touch warm, hard abs.

"Tell me," he said.

She played with the waistband of his jeans. "Um . . ."

"Oh, don't lose your nerve now." His mouth was at her ear. "Tell me, Maggie. Slow and sweet?" He skimmed his thumb over a nipple, making her arch into him. "Or fast and hard?" His other hand was up her skirt, playing with the edging of her panties. "Or somewhere in between?"

"Fast and hard," she decided as she shoved up his shirt, revealing his stomach, which made her mouth water. "Really fast," she choked out, as his finger slipped just beneath her panties.

"I can do fast." He glided the pad of his finger over her, his own breathing uneven, his body tight against hers.

She was breathing just as erratically, and her body was every bit as tight, and also trembling.

And wet.

She dropped her forehead to his chest. She could tell he was holding back, being careful with her, and she'd have expected that from Mr. Right but not Mr. Wrong.

She didn't want careful.

She wanted wild, unmitigated, unadulterated passion, from him, for her, and she wanted that now, along with her fast. So she kissed him, gliding her tongue to his. He made a low, rough, intimately thrilling sound from deep in his throat and his arms came up, banding tightly around her, pulling her flush to him.

Careful restraint gone. Mission accomplished.

"Tell me it's like getting back on a bike," she gasped. "That I'm going to remember what to do next."

"Trust me, you're going to remember."

"Okay." Desire was getting the best of her, and her fingers outlined the bulge of him straining the front of his jeans.

"See?" He breathed shakily. "You're remembering already."

She could hear the loud beat of his heart in her ear, could feel him shudder in pleasure when she stroked him. He wanted her. Her Mr. Wrong wanted her. Unlike her last encounter, the man she was with wasn't worrying about the time, or his next meeting, or how he looked. He was thinking of her, touching her, kissing her, completely lost in her, and she let herself get a little lost in that, lost in the heat, the passion, the need, all the things she'd deprived herself of for so long.

He tugged off her blouse, let out an extremely satisfying growl at the sight of her, and lapped up some of the honey concoction he'd left on her breasts, his thumbs rasping over her nipples until she thunked her head back against the wall. "Definitely remembering."

"Good." He laved one nipple with special, tender care, then gave the other the same attention, until her hips were rocking restlessly, needing, desperately needing. His hands danced up the back of her thighs, cupped her bottom and squeezed. "That's real good."

She tried to tug off his T-shirt, murmuring in delight when he helped, pulling it over his head. When she leaned in to kiss his chest, he let his head fall back, his hand coming up to cup the back of hers, which tightened on her as she licked his nipple. Egged on by his shaky exhale and the way he moved hungrily against her, she did it again, lapping up his magnificent body, all lean, long, hard angles, so male, so hot. It was incredible, it was freeing, knowing this was just sex, that's all, and for that moment she felt like a different woman, and she loved it. Loved how he made her feel. "I'm ready for the fast and hard portion of the program," she whispered against his skin.

"Me, too." He urged her hand lower to prove it, helping her unzip his pants to free the essentials.

"Oh," she breathed, wrapping her fingers around him. "You've definitely got the hard part covered."

"Yeah. Let's work on the fast." Pressing his mouth to her shoulder, he hooked his fingers in her panties. "Lift up, Maggie." He tugged the material off and over his shoulder. The table was cold against her butt, making her gasp, but he slid his hands beneath her.

She'd meant to do this quick, meant to get only what she needed and get out, but suddenly, getting out was the furthest thing from her mind. Awash in sensory overload, she wanted to do this for the next hour.

All night.

Straining against him, breathing like a lunatic, she murmured in surprise when he suddenly dropped to his knees and yanked her forward.

Right against his mouth.

He kissed her then, using his tongue, his teeth, and she lost herself.

Completely.

Lost.

Herself.

When she'd stopped shuddering, he surged back to his feet, produced a condom—God bless the condom—then in the next breath filled her so full she nearly came again on impact.

And then he began to move, and she did come.

Instantaneous orgasm.

It boggled her mind, coming like that, coming without even trying, certainly without straining for it. He brought her up again with fierce thrusts that took her so far beyond her own experiences, she wasn't sure she could even bear it. But then he whispered her name in a voice that assured her she wasn't alone in this, that he was just as lost in her as she was in him.

Right there in the very lab where she'd had endless fantasies about him for the past two months, he made them all come to life. And suddenly she wasn't lost at all, but found, one-hundred-percent found.

Jacob was still trying to find his legs and gather his senses when he heard it, a soft click, like a door closing. With Maggie plopped against him like a rag doll, he lifted his head but the lab door was closed.

In his arms, Maggie stirred, and frowned. "Was that the door?"

"I thought so but—"

"No." She peeked over his shoulder. "Couldn't be. It's locked. Oh my God, do you think someone saw us?"

"Who has the key?"

She blanched and straightened. "My bosses. And probably others. But they're all gone for the day, or so I thought." She pushed at him and he released his hold on her, stepping back as she hopped down and tried to put her bra back on. "Someone was in here."

Yeah. Very likely, which pissed him off.

"But why? No one could have known we were going to . . ."

"What do you keep in here? Anything you don't want anyone to see?"

She struggled with her blouse a moment, then whirled around, snatching her panties off a microscope with a sound of distress. "Plenty."

Her answer had him taking a second look at her as she fumbled to right her skirt, which was all twisted around her waist, a hot look he might add. He knew Data Tech specialized in the latest technology and inventions, putting new and innovative things on the market, often years ahead of their competition, but he had no idea what Maggie did exactly except make edible honey lotion. She limped away and into her office, still trying to fix her clothes. "I don't know what anyone could have been looking for . . ." Then she turned back to him. "My briefcase. I left it and my purse in your temporary office—"

"Wait here." He ran back to the other side of the building, grabbed her briefcase and purse and turned to head back to her, but she'd come up behind him, standing there pale and quiet as he handed everything over.

"There's no one on my floor," she said. "No one who might have come into my lab. Everyone's office is dark." She opened up her briefcase, searching inside for . . .

A glass vial.

Looking extremely thankful to see it, she flipped through the rest of the briefcase, checked her laptop, and then took a deep sigh of intense relief.

"Important stuff?"

"Two years' worth of work, and this sample is definitely valuable enough to steal. If you know what you're looking for."

"What is it?"

"Transdermal drug delivery."

"Trans what?"

"It's a way to get cancer prevention and gene repair medication through skin care."

"Impressive," he said, staring at her, suddenly understanding exactly what someone was doing snooping in her lab. "And definitely worth stealing."

"Yes. When the formula is right, just a little bit of this stuff could deliver a critical dose of meds, and if done correctly, virtually eliminate the side effects common with injections. I'm in testing now, the dosing is still inconsistent."

"But you're close," he guessed.

"Yes. I believe I'm nearly there."

"That's amazing."

"Not yet it's not. At the moment what I've got is some fairly fabulous face cream that works better than cosmetic surgery, suitable for acne, anti-aging, and psoriasis, as well as repairing sun-damaged skin. But I'll get there."

"Is that why your skin is so amazing?"

Her gaze flew to his, startled. "You think my skin is amazing?"

He slipped his fingers into her hair, letting his thumb trace her jaw. He'd just had her, and yet the simple touch still electrified him to the core. "I do."

"It's my lotions, not me." She clasped her hands and avoided his gaze. "So . . . thanks for tonight." She grimaced. "I mean, for taking care of me after I fell, not for . . ." Her eyes drifted shut. "You know."

"For being your Mr. Wrong?"

"Well, yes." She was still flushed, her shirt a little crooked. She covered her eyes and laughed, and the sound did something low in his belly. "Look," she said. "I know this is silly but I really do want to thank you. Can I buy you a coffee?"

"Do I have to wait for you to shave your legs?"

"Ha. No, it's a little late now."

"I'd love a coffee, *and* the thanks, but I've got to get back to work. We're working through the night and all of tomorrow so we can be done in time for the holidays."

"Oh. Right." She backed up a step. "No problem." She grabbed her briefcase and purse. "I understand."

She didn't, he could tell. She thought he was rejecting her. "Maggie—"

"No, I don't want to keep you. Don't work too hard!"

And with that, she quickly rushed toward the elevator, out of sight, but not, most definitely not, out of mind.

5

That night, Maggie was home making chocolate chip cookies and eating most of the dough before she could bake it, still unable to believe she'd had sex in her lab—her lab!—when her phone rang.

It was Scott. "Maggie?" he said, sounding caught off guard. "You're . . . home?"

"Well, yes. I am. Is there something wrong?"

"No, but . . ." He let out a laugh. "You know what? This is embarrassing. I hit the wrong number, sorry."

Click.

Maggie looked at the phone. "Okay." Good to know she wasn't the only one smart enough to calculate the mass of any object in her head but not socially talented enough to hold a conversation with the opposite sex.

And yet she'd held the attention of a man earlier, hadn't she? And even though the good-bye had been painfully awkward, everything between the Band-Aids and that awkward good-bye had been . . . perfect. She'd been wearing a stupid grin for hours. And still was. God, orgasms were good.

She should bring him some of these cookies, as that thank

you she owed him. It was the right thing to do, the polite thing to do. Thank-you-for-the-perfect-sex cookies.

Still grinning, she put a batch in the oven and ate some more dough, which made her happy, and received two prank calls, which annoyed her. She watched Letterman, which didn't annoy her, and finally went to bed, still grinning a little bit.

When she got to work the next morning, she'd managed to downgrade the grin to a smile, but as she entered the building, nerves replaced it. How was she going to look Jacob in the eye after getting naked with him? *On her work table.* She still had the imprint of a slide on her ass. . . .

But it turned out she'd worried for nothing. While the construction equipment was still blocking most of the hallway, Jacob was nowhere in sight. If he'd worked all night long, he was probably catching a quick nap, or maybe breakfast, so she brought the container of cookies she'd made him into her office, where they proceeded to call her name all morning. By lunch she'd peeked out her door so often for a sight of her Mr. Wrong that two of his workers thought she was stalking them. Annoyed at herself, she ate a few of the cookies.

Just a few.

All afternoon she could hear Jacob's voice on the Nextels of his workers as they communicated, and every time she did, she felt the urge to eat a few more cookies.

By quitting time she'd consumed a total of seven, leaving only five.

Alice stuck her head in Maggie's door to wave good-bye and Maggie absentmindedly waved back, sneaking out one more cookie. She was thinking about the last four when Alice called her cell phone.

"Didn't you just leave?" Maggie asked her.

"I did. I am. Your car has a flat."

Dammit. She needed new tires. "Okay, I'll call Triple A, thanks."

"Call now so you don't have to wait."

"I will." She hung up and looked at the cookies. Stress. Stress made her hungry. Jacob didn't need four cookies, they were huge. So she took one more while she went back to her computer, and when she looked up again another hour had passed and the construction workers were gone.

And so was their stuff.

They were done, they were gone, and Mr. Wrong hadn't even come to say good-bye. That hurt. But it also meant that the cookies were hers, so she ate one more and called Janie. "I made Jacob a dozen cookies and ate all but two by myself. Not counting the dozen I ate last night."

"This is why you're single."

"Thanks." She hung up and took her loser self to the parking lot where she found her flat tire and remembered that she'd forgotten to call Triple A. With a sigh, she sank to the curb by her car and pulled out the Tupperware.

Yep, two cookies left.

A double loser.

Jacob had his final check in hand, including the bonus that they'd earned by the skin of their teeth. It'd been a helluva tough forty-eight hours but he was done.

Free.

Leaving Scott's office, he went by Maggie's to say good-bye before heading to the airport. He hadn't had a moment to breathe all day, but he'd thought about her. Thought about her and how she'd looked sitting on her worktable with no panties . . .

Her office was dark. He'd missed her. Frustrated, exhausted, and now disappointed, he left the building. It was a typical L.A. winter evening, fifty-five degrees with a rare addition—clouds gathering, blocking out any moon or starlight—not that there was ever much of that visible in downtown Los Angeles anyway.

The streets were decorated with red garland and festive colored lights, along with a long string of red brake lights—business traffic trying to get to the freeway. He walked through the parking lot and came to a surprised stop in front of Maggie, sitting on the curb by her car, eating . . . a cookie? "Hey."

"Hey, yourself."

"What are you doing?"

"Eating a cookie."

"Okay." He waited for her to expand on that but she didn't.

"You can just ignore me," she said instead.

Uh-huh. As if he could. Nothing about her was ignorable, not from the tips of her toes poking out her high-heeled sandals all the way up those sweet, lush curves to the strands of her adorably messy hair. "Why are you sitting on the curb?"

"I was talking on my cell to my sister. Just doing my part of the statistic that says the average American spends two years on the phone."

"I'm not anywhere close to average."

"I know. You're bigger." She covered her face. "Sorry. Sugar rush. Too many cookies. Waaay too many."

She had a dab of chocolate on the corner of her mouth, and he found himself fixated on that. "What, no facts on cookies?"

"Oh, I have cookie facts. I was just trying to hold back."

"You don't have to hold back with me, Maggie."

"Okay. Did you know it was Ruth Graves Wakefield who first used candy-bar chocolate in a cookie recipe while at the Toll House Inn circa 1930?" She waved a cookie. "And *voilà*, chocolate chip cookies were born."

"Good one. So why are you sitting out here eating cookies?"

"Actually, technically, they're *your* cookies."

She was wearing another skirt today, a pencil skirt, with her legs demurely tucked beneath her, but he could see her knees, and the Band-Aids there. Her jacket was open over a blouse the same light blue as her eyes. She looked extremely buttoned up and extremely put together—if one didn't count her hair, which was once again defying gravity with what appeared to be a stir stick shoved into it.

And the chocolate at the corner of her mouth, let's not forget that, because he couldn't tear his eyes off of it, or understand the sudden insane urge to lean down and lick it off.

But he had his bag packed and in his truck, and a plane to catch.

Maggie took the last bite of the cookie and brushed her fingers off. "I should have baked three dozen."

"You bake?"

"Yes, and I'm good, too."

"I bet you are." He sat at her side, so tired he had no idea if he could get back up again. She smelled like chocolate. He had a feeling she would taste even better. Reaching out with his finger, he ran it over the corner of her mouth.

She pulled back. "What are you doing?"

"You have a little chocolate—"

"Oh, God." Her tongue darted out, collided with the pad of his finger. It was like an electric bolt straight to his groin.

"Did I get it?"

"No." He smiled. "You smeared it a little. Here." Again he glided his finger over her lips, then sucked that finger into his own mouth.

Her eyes were glued to him. "Oh," she breathed softly.

Yeah, oh. Traffic rushed all around them, and they sat there in their own little world. He had to get to the airport, and yet he didn't get back up. Instead, he leaned in so that their mouths were only a breath apart. "Let me get that last little bit—"

"Where—" Her tongue darted out, attempting to lick the chocolate off. "There?"

He smiled. "No."

She licked it again. "Now?"

"No."

"Dammit, Jacob."

"That's Mr. Wrong, to you." And still holding her face, he dropped his gaze from hers to look at her mouth, absorbing her little murmur of anticipation before he closed the gap and kissed her.

6

It was the sugar rush, Maggie told herself. That, combined with the feel of Jacob pressed up against her again, and the warmth of his mouth . . . God. This was all his fault for being such a good kisser, all his fault, she thought as she pulled him even closer.

His reaction was an immediate approving rumble from deep in his chest and a tightening of his arms. So she hugged him tighter and gave him some tongue.

Hauling her into his lap with a groan, he kissed her long and hard and wet right there in the parking lot, until her entire body shivered in delight and anticipation.

She knew what he could do for her now, to her, and that made the longing worse. Given the sound he made, and how deliciously hard he'd gotten, he felt the same. The thrill of that surged through her. This big, bad, gorgeous man had already had her and *still* wanted her.

She felt drunk on the knowledge. Or it might have been the sugar. Either way, he had one arm around her, the other on her jaw, holding her face for his kiss; but then he pulled back, let out an unsteady breath and a short laugh. "There's no door to lock this time." He rose and offered her a hand, turning to her car. "Uh-oh. What happened to your tire?"

"It got a flat."

He crouched down next to it. "Yes, because someone slashed it." He took a careful look around them before cutting his no-longer-heated eyes to hers. "How long were you sitting here alone before I came?

"Wait. *Slashed*?" She took a closer look. "Do you think it was random?"

"Slashed tire seems pretty personal. "You annoy anyone lately?"

"I annoy a lot of people. It's part of my charming nature." Spooked, she just stared at him. Her brain didn't feel like it was getting enough oxygen, so she decided to sit. Her tire had been slashed. Merry Christmas to her.

Ah, hell. Jacob looked over Maggie's head to where his truck was parked, complete with a plane ticket sitting on the front seat.

But he wasn't going anywhere.

And not just because his heart rate was still affected by that kiss, or because Maggie's lush mouth was still wet from his and he wanted to see what else was wet, but because he had a bad feeling that this smart, adorable, sexy woman who was nothing but trouble was *in* trouble. "Do you have a spare?"

"Yes." Her voice was muffled, but then she lifted her head. "And I took a class on how to change it, too."

Of course she had. He had a feeling this careful, organized, brilliant sexy mess could do anything she set her mind to.

"Is it hot?" she asked. "I feel hot. Maybe it's nerves."

"It's not hot. It's actually chilly."

"Did you know that minus forty degrees Celsius is exactly the same as minus forty degrees Fahrenheit?"

"That's a new one for me." Knowing she was about to lose it, he took her hand. "Listen, how about I change the tire for you, while you call the police and make a report."

"What if it's just one of the twenty-two percent of random, senseless acts of violence that people face in their lifetime?"

He slid her a glance. "You know, you'd really kick ass on *Jeopardy*."

"I already did. That's how I paid for my PhD."

He shook his head in admiration as he pulled out his cell phone and called the police himself, but due to a high volume of calls, they wouldn't even come out and take a report.

"It's okay." Maggie pulled out her keys. "I'll just get the spare— Uh-oh," she said when she opened the trunk.

"Uh-oh?" He peered over her shoulder and saw nothing but stacks of craft supplies. "Where's your spare?"

"My sister borrowed my car. She's been volunteering at her kids' school, and my trunk is bigger than hers. She must have taken out the spare." She sighed. "Dammit. I'll call her."

"How about I just take you home?"

She lifted her gaze to his, her eyes still soft and heated, her cheeks flushed. "I don't know."

"You're not spooked at having your tire slashed but you're spooked at me driving you home?"

"Of course not." She gnawed her cheek a moment. "It's just that if we go to my house . . ."

He liked where that sentence was going. "Yeah?"

"Nothing. A ride would be great, thank you."

She squirmed all the way to her place in the Glendale Hills above L.A., her brain working so hard he could practically hear the wheels whirling. He pulled into the gated complex of her condo unit and looked at her. "Maggie."

She jumped. "Yes?"

"You do know this was just a ride, right?"

Her face flushed. "Of course. Just because we . . ."

"Had sex."

She winced. "Yes, that. Which doesn't mean we're going to pull off all our clothes and have *more* sex."

"Do you want to?"

She stared at him. "It was just a one-time thing." She seemed to hold her breath. "Right?"

He stroked a strand of hair along her temple. "It's whatever we want it to be. What do you want it to be, Maggie?"

"That's sort of the problem," she whispered. "I didn't think this far ahead, which is really unlike me."

"You like to think ahead."

"I really do.

"Okay, you go ahead and think on it then." He walked her to her door, where she turned to face him, pressing her spine up against the wood. "Thanks so much for the ride, but you don't have to come in."

"I want to. I want to make sure you're okay."

"Why wouldn't I be?"

"Because someone slashed your tire."

"That was random."

"Okay, but if I promise not to look at you even if you do strip your clothes off, can I please come in and make sure everything's okay?"

"You wouldn't look?" She looked intrigued at this. "Really?"

"Not if you didn't want me to."

"Oh." She looked so crestfallen, he laughed, and unable to help himself, he put his hands on her hips and pulled her in. "If you begged me," he murmured in her ear. "Maybe I'd look then."

She smiled, and it obliterated a few million of her brain cells.

"Okay, truth," he said. "I'd look. I'd look for a long time, and then I'd touch."

"Oh," she breathed, sounding a little turned on. "Really?"

"And then I'd taste. I'd lick and nibble and—"

The sound of glass shattering broke the night's silence. "What was that?" he asked.

"I don't know." She pulled out her keys and unlocked her front door, looking up at him questioningly when he held her back so he could enter first.

Her condo was dark, but enough of the streetlights shined

in through the windows that he could see the living room was empty, and so was the kitchen. But the sliding glass door between the two, leading out onto a deck, was wide open to the night. "Did you leave the door like that?"

"No. No way."

Which, given her anal tendencies, he believed without question. He ran to the glass and looked out, where he could see a tipped-over ceramic bowl and plant—the source of the noise they'd heard.

Someone had just left, in a big hurry. He glanced down, saw the broken lock and moved to the edge of the deck, leaning over to see the path that lined the entire complex, which was well lit both ways for as far as he could see. There wasn't a single soul.

Her mysterious visitor had vanished.

He turned around and went back inside, where Maggie was turning on lights in the living room, revealing soft, muted beachy colors and a neat, minimalist style. He pulled out his cell phone to call the police. "Is anything missing?"

"No."

He spoke to dispatch, was assured a car would come out to investigate, and slipped his phone into his pocket. He eyed the couch and matching chair, the coffee table, all perfectly arranged and perfectly neat. Much like the woman. "Let's check upstairs."

The minimalist trend continued on the second floor, with one big exception—her bathroom. While he stood in the doorway, mouth open, enthralled by the sight, she was hastily yanking down a forest of hanging lingerie. Yellow silk, blue satin, black lace, a virtual cornucopia of exoticness that made thinking all but impossible.

"Don't look!" she demanded, shoving everything in a small drawer. She pulled at a simple white cotton thong that was maybe two square inches of material. "You're still looking!" She was all breathless and adorably sexy, and desperate to hide her things. "Close your eyes!"

"I'm sorry," he said with a laugh, when she twisted to glare at him. "I can't hear a word you're saying, you just blew all my remaining brain cells. Do you really wear all this . . . ?" He fingered a set of garters, black silk, and felt himself get hard.

"Yes." She yanked it out of his fingers and shoved it into one of her pockets. "Lots of women wear pretty things beneath their clothes, you know. It's not like I'm a freak."

"Oh, baby, I never thought you were a freak." He put his hands on her arms and halted her frenetic movements. "That's not what I was thinking at all."

"What are you thinking?" she whispered.

He looked into her beautiful face and those eyes that had a way of sneaking past all his defenses. "I'm thinking you're the smartest, funniest, most fascinating woman I've ever met. And you're so desperate to hide your sexy garters that I'm wondering what else you're hiding."

She ignored that. "Fascinating is a euphemism. You might as well say I have a good personality."

"You do."

"We both know what it means when someone says that. It means I'm a dog."

At that, he tossed back his head and laughed.

"That's funny?"

"Yes." He hugged her from behind, turning them so that she faced the bathroom mirror. She had a baby blue bra in one hand and sea green panties in her other. Her hair was its usual rioted, gorgeous mess, and her face . . . Good God, she had a face that reached out and slayed his heart. "You're beautiful," he said, meeting her eyes in the mirror. "So goddamned beautiful, you take my breath away."

She dropped the lingerie. Twisting in his arms until she faced him, she cupped his face. "You're beautiful, too. I know you're not supposed to tell a guy that, but it's true. And I don't mean just on the outside." She sighed. "I'm sorry I ate all the cookies I made you, and I'm sorry I needed a ride home. You should go, I know you have a flight."

Had a flight. "Are you sorry you chose me as your Mr. Wrong?"

"No." Her gaze dropped to his mouth. "Do you think it was a fluke? You know, how good it was between us?"

He arched a brow. "A fluke?"

"Yeah. Maybe . . . maybe we should do it again. Just to make sure, you know?"

Suddenly the blood was rushing from his head for parts south. He nodded, and in the interest of getting to the "again"— which hopefully would involve some of that hot as hell lingerie, he leaned in. He'd just touched his mouth to hers, body hot and hard and ready, when from down below, her doorbell rang.

The police had arrived.

"Maybe we can pretend we don't hear them," she whispered against his lips, all flushed and heated and sweet, sexy acquiescence in his arms.

He was all for that idea, but unfortunately the police weren't going to be ignored. The doorbell rang again, and with a sigh, she backed out of his arms and headed out of the bathroom, the black garters sticking out of her pocket.

7

The police took a report, but with nothing missing, nothing even out of place other than the broken lock, they didn't seem too hopeful on getting Maggie answers anytime soon.

When they were gone, she settled back against the front door and eyed the big, bad, sexy man standing in the middle of her living room. "Thanks for staying," she said, her hormones much more firmly in control now that he wasn't touching her. "I'll be fine."

He came close. His hands settled on the wood on either side of her face as he leaned in. He smelled like her idea of heaven, and looked good enough to eat—better than even her cookies.

"Will you?" he murmured.

"Absolutely. Maybe you can still catch your flight."

"That ship has sailed." He was so close that his body heat seeped into her bones, so close that she could feel that there wasn't an ounce of softness to him, anywhere. "Back to our other conversation. So, Maggie Bell, what other secrets are you hiding?" He tilted his head, letting the tip of his nose glide along her jawline.

Oh, God. What was she hiding? Nothing. Nothing at all. Well, except that she'd apparently renewed her huge crush . . .

He came in even closer, and opened his mouth on her ear-lobe, making her eyes cross with lust.

"D-did you know that Kansas state law requires pedestrians crossing the highways at night to wear taillights?" she stammered.

"I didn't. But what I do want to know is, how come you've denied your body pleasure for two years?"

"*Nearly* two years," she corrected, and felt him smile against her skin. "And I haven't completely denied myself. I have a shower head."

He laughed silkily and she bit her lip to keep any more ridiculous admissions from escaping, sucking in desperately needed air as he glided his mouth along her jaw to her throat. She was melting into a boneless puddle of longing when the doorbell rang again—making her nearly jump out of her skin. Pushing him aside, she ran down the stairs and opened the door to . . .

"Scott," she said, in surprise. She heard Jacob come into the entryway and stop just on the other side of the door, not visible to Scott. Behind the door, she put her hand on his chest to hold him there.

"I saw your car in the lot," Scott told her. "But you weren't in the building anywhere. I got worried. Your tire—"

"I know." Funny how just looking at him had always made her a little dizzy from all his fabulousness, but now she didn't want to look at him.

She wanted to look at Jacob. Jacob, whose warm chest was pushing back just a little against her palm.

"I called our mechanic for you. It'll be fixed by morning," Scott said. "But how did you get home?"

She leaned into the door, trapping Jacob between the wall and the door. "I thought you were already gone. I thought everyone was gone. A friend brought me here. Thank you for calling your mechanic."

"No problem." He was looking past her, as if hoping he'd

get invited in, and also trying to see the "friend." The friend who with shocking stealth filched the garters right out of her pocket, the thief.

"So who slashed your tire?" Scott asked.

"Probably just a random thing. Well . . ." She flashed a quick smile. "Thanks for coming by—" She tried to shut the door but he put a hand on it.

"Want to grab dinner?"

How long had she imagined this, him asking her out, then having her realize she was the woman of his dreams? But then, she'd been with Jacob and now . . . and now she couldn't imagine being with Scott at all. "Actually, Scott, I'm—"

"Trying to figure out who might have broken into her house."

Maggie turned her head and locked gazes with Jacob, who smiled sweetly—*sweetly?*—as he came out from the other side of the door, standing a little close as he smiled politely at Scott.

Scott blinked. "Jacob? What are you doing here? And break-in? Here? Was anything stolen?"

Jacob narrowed his eyes. "Usually the first question is, are you okay?"

"Of course, of course." Scott slapped his forehead. "I'm just flustered. A slashed tire and now a break-in. And you . . . you visiting. Maggie, are you okay?"

Well, let's see. She had Jacob—who now had her garters in his pocket—on one side, and Scott, her maybe Mr. Right—who was currently eyeing Jacob—on the other.

Who was eyeing Scott right back.

Two men. Both wanting her. "I'm fine."

"Maybe you should come back with me until we know you're safe."

"I'm staying," Jacob said casually. "She'll be safe."

The testosterone level in the air rose to dangerous heights.

"I could stay, too," Scott said. "No problem."

Oh, yes it was a problem. They were *both* a problem. And she had no experience with which to deal with this. She needed

Janie. "Okay," she said, gently pushing Scott over the threshold. "Thank you very much for coming by, but I'm going to be fine."

Jacob smirked.

So she shoved *him* over the threshold as well. "And you have a flight to catch."

"But—"

"Good night," she said, firmly. "To the both of you." She shut the door, letting out a slow, shaky breath as she leaned back against the wood, suddenly thankful she had Mr. Showerhead after all.

She ate a can of soup and a piece of toast, and didn't let herself think about the nice dinner Scott might have taken her to. Or what she might be doing with Jacob right now if Scott hadn't interrupted them. She changed into her pj's and slathered on some of her skin care from the vial.

Someone knocked at her door and she hesitated, then looked through the peephole.

A dark eye looked back at her. A dark eye that seemed to be filled with both wry humor and annoyance, complete with a dash of affection.

Jacob pulled back so that she could see all six-feet-two inches of his leanly muscled frame, the one that tended to make her brain cells simultaneously combust.

He waggled his fingers at her.

She pressed her forehead to the door while her heart went off like a jackhammer. "Go away, Jacob."

"Let me in."

Just his voice made her quiver. What was wrong with her?

"Stress," he said through the wood when she inadvertently spoke out loud. "That's what's wrong. I have the cure for that, by the way."

Oh, God. "Stressed is desserts spelled backwards." She could use a dessert right about now. . . .

Then he did something to really turn her on. He lifted a bag of chocolate cookies to the peephole. "Cookies that you don't have to make. And unlike someone I know, I didn't eat them all. Open up, Maggie."

With a sigh, she grabbed a throw blanket from her couch and threw it around her. "I'm in my pj's."

"I won't look."

A reluctant smile tugged at her mouth, and she pulled open the door. He was wearing clean clothes: a pair of dark Levi's, a dark polo shirt, and a dark smile to match, which had her pulse leaping to attention.

Bad pulse. "I don't need you to stay—"

"I know." He pushed past her and tossed a duffel bag down to her couch. "But I am."

He smelled good. Dammit, why did he always have to smell good?

She put her hands on her hips. "Jacob—"

Turning back to her, he gripped her waist, pulled her up against him and kissed her until she didn't know her name. Disarmed, she stared up at him when he pulled back. "What does that have to do with anything?"

"It has to do with the fact that I wouldn't leave you alone tonight even if I didn't want to do *that* all the damn time." He shoved his fingers through his hair and turned in a slow circle, coming back to face her, his eyes dark and full of things that took her breath. "Look, you were there for me once. Let me be here for you now. Don't ask me to leave you alone tonight."

She thought about how she'd felt earlier standing between him and Scott, how really, there hadn't been any choice to make at all. And how that scared her because she no longer understood herself or what she wanted. "We're not having sex."

"Let me guess. Because you have your showerhead."

She'd known that would come back and bite her on the ass.

"Don't worry, I understand. I doubt any guy could compete with a showerhead. How about a blanket? Can I ask for a blanket?"

She pulled one out from the small chest she used as an ottoman, then watched him kick off his shoes and lie down on her couch. He was of course too long for it, with his calves and feet sticking off the end, but he merely tossed the blanket over himself and closed his eyes. "Could you get the light?"

She just stared at him. "You missed your flight for me. Why did you miss your flight for me?"

"I realize you've been using a showerhead as a boyfriend, so you might have forgotten how the friend part works. Friends stick by each other when they're in trouble."

"We're friends?"

"Well we're not sleeping together."

He said this a little irritably, which made her want to smile. "I'm not in trouble, Jacob."

"I think you're mistaken. Go to sleep, Maggie. I'm exhausted, far too exhausted to argue with you. Maybe even too exhausted to have all that sex you don't want to have."

She turned off the light. "Is there anything else you need?"

"Probably you should be more specific."

There in the dark, she both rolled her eyes and felt . . . hungry. "Good night."

"Night."

She went to bed, and fell sleep while trying to remember why they weren't having sex. *Just a one-time thing,* she reminded herself . . . and woke up in the middle of the night dying of thirst. Or at least that was the excuse she gave herself for wanting to steal a peek at the gorgeous man sleeping over. She tiptoed into the living room and found him sprawled on her couch, both legs hanging off, one arm dangling down, face relaxed, chest rising and falling in a slow rhythm.

He wasn't a snorer. Good to know. God, she really wished she'd asked for a *two*-time thing instead of a one-time thing. If he opened his eyes right now, she'd just tell him so.

But he didn't.

She shuffled her feet. Cleared her throat.

He still didn't budge.

Dammit. Stepping closer, she touched his blanket. Faked a

sneeze. *Nothing*. Feeling like an idiot, she went to the kitchen. There were no clean glasses in the cupboard, but her dishwasher was clean so she grabbed one from there. Then she opened the refrigerator door for something to drink, and in the harsh glare of the refrigerator light, caught a glimpse of movement on her right.

Her intruder. Without thinking, she shoved the refrigerator door into him, hearing the "oomph" of air leaving a set of lungs.

Irrational fear took over, and she backed up, tripping over the open dishwasher, which she fell into, hitting her butt on the still open bottom tray, *hard*. The whole thing gave, falling out of its hinges, hitting the floor, taking her down with it.

"Maggie!" At the crashing sound, Jacob slapped his hands along the wall, looking for the light.

"Don't turn on the light!" she cried.

Okay, she was alive, but he could hear the pain in her voice. Although *he* was the one who'd been hit in the belly with a refrigerator . . .

He'd been asleep for maybe an hour before the sheer discomfort of the short sofa had gotten to him. That and the soft padded footsteps of Maggie leaving her bedroom. When she'd stood over him, he'd held his breath rather than say anything, because what would have come out of his mouth would have been "I like your pj's, now take them off." Then she'd gone into the kitchen, and he had no idea why, but he'd followed without saying a word, which turned out to be a mistake because she'd slammed the refrigerator door into his gut.

Finally, he found a light switch and hit it, and then went still as he took in the sight.

"I told you not to," Maggie said on a sigh.

She was sitting in the opened dishwater tray in a camisole and panty set, bare legs dangling over the sides, her arms bracing her up as she attempted to lever herself off the broken plates beneath her. "Jesus, Maggie." She had to be cut all to hell, and he rushed forward to lift her out.

But she held him off. "Don't touch me." She tried to lift herself out and failed. "Okay, touch me."

Yeah. He just wished she meant it.

8

"I'm fine!" Maggie shouted this for the third time in as many minutes through her bedroom door to a worried sounding Jacob.

How she'd managed to lift herself off of the broken plates and glasses—and let's not forget the utensils—she hardly knew. She'd managed only with Jacob's help, as if the whole situation hadn't been embarrassing enough, and then she'd escaped down the hall and into her bedroom.

The mirror over her dresser wasn't telling her much so she moved into her bathroom, stood on the toilet to get onto the counter, pulled down her panties, and twisted around to look into the vanity mirror.

Not good. She had a few cuts oozing a little blood, and already bruises were blooming. Nothing appearing too serious, but they weren't pretty. At the knock on her bedroom door, she nearly fell off the counter. "Don't come in!"

"Maggie, let me see."

"*No!*"

"You've got to be cut up. There's blood in the dishwasher."

Ew.

"You might have glass splinters."

Oh, no, she did not. She poked at one of the cuts, sucked in a harsh breath of pain, and admitted he might be right. But if she did have glass in there, it was staying in there.

Forever.

Jacob knocked one more time, didn't get an answer, and thought *fuck it*. He opened her bedroom door.

He had a quick view of the four-poster iron-rod bed piled high with pillows and thick bedding before he turned to the open bathroom door.

She was standing on the counter yanking up her panties, where she'd clearly been trying to get an up close and personal view of her injuries.

"Hey! The bedroom door was shut!"

"And I opened it." He strode over to her, scooped her up off the counter and put her down, accidentally knocking her toothbrush to the floor. "How bad is it?"

She slid her hands to her ass. "Not bad at all."

"Liar." He picked up her toothbrush and put it back on the counter, but she shook her head. "Wrong side."

"Huh?"

"That's the toilet side of the counter. Dentists recommend that a toothbrush be kept at least six feet away from the toilet to avoid airborne particles resulting from the flush. You just put it within four feet. I'll have to throw it away."

"I'll buy you a new one. Enough stalling. Let me see."

Resignation flashed across her face, as well as discomfort at the realization he saw right through her. "No," she said.

"This isn't the time for modesty, Maggie."

"I'm fine."

Uh-huh. And he was the damn tooth fairy. He peeked around her to catch sight of her in the mirror. The back of her camisole dipped low, revealing her shoulders and spine, lovely and smooth. And as he already knew, the panties were small, boy cut, and revealed more lovely, smooth skin. They rode low on her hips, yet slid up high enough to reveal the bottom curve of her sweet ass. She was holding said sweet ass but he could still see that one cheek was bleeding. "You're not fine."

She sagged, letting her shoulders fall as she dropped her gaze from his and pulled out a box of Band-Aids. "Okay, dammit, I'm not."

All irritation vanished. "Come on," he said gently, and grabbing the box of Band-Aids, pulled her into her bedroom. "You should really buy stock in these." He sat on the bed and patted the mattress next to him.

Miserably, she shook her head. "I can't sit."

"Lie down."

"Oh, God," she moaned, still holding her butt. "I should have just stayed sleeping. Did you know that we burn more calories sleeping than we do watching TV?"

"Fascinating. Come on, it won't be that bad."

"That's because it's not you baring *your* ass."

"True." He patted the mattress again. "How about I close one eye, will that help?"

She let out a low, glum laugh, and crawled up on the bed. "Did you know that elephants are the only animals with four knees?"

"I did not know that." He was trying not to know other things. Like she possibly had the sweetest ass he'd ever seen.

Slowly, carefully, she sprawled out on her tummy. "Did you know that every human spent about a half hour as a single cell?"

"Maggie, don't be nervous."

"Or that every year about ninety-eight percent of the atoms in your body are replaced?"

"Fascinating. Listen, it's going to be okay, I promise." One spaghetti strap of her cami had slid down over her arm. The hem had risen to mid back, revealing a strip of skin that he wanted to nibble. Her legs and feet were bare. He wanted to start at her toes and lick his way up to the world-class wedgie she had going on.

"Jacob?"

He cleared his throat. The last time a woman had lain on

her belly for him, he'd been naked and about to have a very different experience. "Yeah?"

"Just look already!"

"Okay." He very gently slid the material of her panties over one cheek, so that it further bunched in the middle. Her entire body was clenched so tight, she quivered. "Relax," he said, stroking his finger over the already blooming bruise.

She let out a sound that might have been a laugh. "You pull down your pants and we'll see if you can relax. What do you see?"

He saw two creamy cheeks that were so perfect he wanted to lean down and kiss them, divided by the bunched up silk that much to his regret managed to hide all the feminine secrets between her thighs.

"Jacob!"

Right. What did he see? Since she didn't want to hear that he saw things that made him weak in the knees, he cleared his throat. "You're already bruising and need ice."

She wriggled around. "Any glass?"

"Hold still." She had two long cuts from the broken plate. He probed them both while she hissed out a breath. "No glass," he finally said, reaching for the Band-Aids. "All you need is a little TLC. . . ." He covered the wounds and then, because he couldn't seem to help himself, he bent over her and did as he'd been dying to, and kissed the spot.

She gasped and rolled painfully to her side, her hair in her face, her eyes wide. "What was that?"

"I was kissing it all better. Did it work?"

"I . . ." She blinked and slid her hands beneath her to cup her bottom. "Yeah."

Both cami straps had slipped down now. Her breasts were full, pressing against the thin material, her nipples two hard, mouthwatering points. Her gently curved belly was rising and falling with each breath, of which she took many. Her panties were snug, the effect being that the satin did little more than outline her every dip and nuance, and if he thought he'd wanted to nibble her ass, it was nothing compared with this particular area.

"Jacob?"

With difficulty, he lifted his gaze to her face.

"You really are different," she whispered.

"From . . . ?"

"Me."

That tugged a laugh out of him. "Yeah, and trust me, I'm very grateful for those differences."

"No, it's just that you were right before. The guys I usually fall for are the male version of me."

He paused as that sank in. "Are you falling for me, Maggie?"

Now it was her turn to pause. "I didn't think it would be possible."

"Because we're so different."

"That's right."

He felt himself go very still. Shit, he'd really been an idiot. Standing, he walked out of the bedroom, away from the gorgeous creature in silk, so he could think a moment. And what he thought made him very unhappy. All the alluding to Mr. Right and Mr. Wrong, the times she'd mentioned their differences . . . While he'd been enjoying those differences, *she'd* been thinking he was a step down for her. A big step. How it'd never occurred to him, he had no idea, but—

"Jacob."

She'd followed him into the living room. He let out a breath and stared out her window into the dark night. "I realize I don't have the fancy degrees or the high-paying job, but I don't like the idea that you're just slumming with me."

"No. No, you misunderstood. We're different, yes. As in I'm anal, single-minded to the point of obsession, and frankly, socially handicapped."

He turned to face her but she held up a hand before he could speak. "You, however . . ." she continued softly, "you're tough and confident and funny and effortlessly sexy. I've never been with a guy like you, Jacob, and now I know I short-changed myself. That's what I meant before. Yes, I've been interested in you since I first saw you again on your ladder in a pair of worn Levi's, looking in charge of your world, and yeah, that's extremely shallow of me, but it's so much more than that. I love the way you think, how you always say what you mean, no guesswork. What you see is what you get with you, and that's . . ." She searched for the words. "Incredibly appealing."

"I've been interested in you since I first saw you again," he said. "Before I even knew it was *again*."

She looked surprised. "Really?"

"Yeah, really. You were wearing a black skirt and a white blouse, with a peekaboo hint of lace beneath. And fuck-me heels."

She choked out a laugh. "I was not. They were higher than my usual, but I had a meeting that day and was looking for power."

"You got lust."

"My hair was out of control."

"It was up in some complicated twist and you had a few strands of hair falling out the back, dangling against your sweet neck. You were late, you were rushing, and you looked like a hot mess. Emphasis on the hot. But even then it was your brain that attracted me most. I love watching you think, Maggie."

"Do you know what I'm thinking now?" She stepped closer and slid her hands up his chest. Wrapping her arms around his neck, she pressed all that hotness up against him.

"I could guess," he murmured.

She smiled, and it staggered him. "My life has always been MapQuested out," she whispered. "The route carefully highlighted. But with you, I don't know what to expect, I don't know what you're thinking or what you're going to do. Nothing is planned out, nothing is guaranteed, and it's . . . exciting, Jacob."

His hand swept down her body and up again. "So I turn your body on."

"You turn my head on." She caught his face in her hands and went up on tiptoe. He could feel her breasts, nipples hard, pressing into his chest. "Do you understand?" she murmured against his mouth. "This isn't a fifth date, where I've carefully reflected and decided it's time to put 'have sex' on the calendar. I haven't lit a candle or turned on the music like I usually do because that's what sets the mood and helps me relax. I haven't slathered myself in some pretty-scented lotion to make sure I'm turning you on. Hell, I didn't shave my legs—" She went still and closed her eyes, relaxing back down on the balls of her feet. "Dammit, I didn't shave my legs."

He grabbed her before she could turn away, hauling her back up against him. "I don't care. Finish. Finish what you were going to say."

"I want you because you're different from the norm for me. I want you because when I'm with you, I don't have to think. I can just feel. I know we said this was a one-time thing, but make me feel again, Jacob, just once more." She stepped back, then slowly slid first one spaghetti strap off her shoulder, and then the other, letting the cami slip. It snagged on her nipples for one heart-stopping second, then fell, revealing her mouth-watering breasts. She nudged it past her hips, where it landed in a puddle of silk at her feet. Eyes on his, she hooked her fingers in her panties, and he stopped breathing. "Love me, Jacob," she whispered, gliding them down past her injuries— which made her want to wince, he could tell—past her thighs to join the cami at her feet. Straightening, she reached for his shirt. "Love me."

He had a feeling he already did, but that wasn't what she meant, and all she wanted from him was this adventure, was what he could do to her in bed, so he tugged his shirt off over his head, lifted her up, and carried her back to her bedroom.

*   *   *

Maggie expected Jacob to put her on the bed and then follow her down, but instead he sat on the mattress with her in his lap, his spine against the headboard.

"So you don't put your weight on your cuts," he said, pulling her thighs on either side of his hips so that she straddled him, letting her feel exactly what her kisses and touches had done to him.

There was something about being entirely naked while he still wore his jeans. It made her feel exposed, and yet so aroused she could hardly stand it. "I'm a little underdressed here."

"I know." His eyes were lit with heat and desire as they took her naked body in. "I like it." Then he covered her mouth with his, going in for a long, drugging kiss that did something shocking to her brain that she'd never managed before.

It turned off.

She wasn't worried about what she looked like naked, or wondering if she'd turned off her cell phone, or if her front door was locked. She wasn't doing anything but feeling—and oh, God, what a feeling she had with his hands skimming down her bare back, cupping her bottom, gently pulling her in closer, careful of her cuts and bruises, until she was as snug against him as she could be, making her intimately aware of his jeans. The denim rubbed her inner thighs, and between.

He was hard. Big and hard and she pulled her mouth free to pop open his buttons, while his hands stroked her breasts, gliding over her nipples, leaving her to restlessly rock her hips. "Jacob—"

"I know." He took his hands on a tour down her ribs, her quivering belly, her thighs, which he urged even wider. His gaze dropped from hers, and he looked his fill, exhaling very heavily, very slowly, only to suck the air back in when she freed him from his jeans. Lifting his hips, he helped her shove them out of the way as his hands swept up her back, pulling her in close for another deep, soul-wrenching kiss, his hands making their way back down, over her bandages, between her legs. "God, you're wet. So wet. I want to taste—"

"Later—" She gasped out the word as he slid a finger into her. Needing him inside her, she lifted her hips.

"Wait," he rasped out. "Maggie, wait. I want to—"

She sank onto him, and he gripped her hips to hold her still, his eyes trapping hers. Their twin sighs comingled in the air, and she knew right then, nothing about this was a one-time fluke.

"Maggie," he said, just that. She rocked her hips to meet his, staring with wide wonder into his eyes, her hands touching as much of his hard, damp, straining body as she could. Yeah, it'd been a while, a long while since she'd been with anyone else, and yet she could say with the utmost authority that it had *never* felt like this.

And then he began to move. Her toes curled, her entire body tingled from the inside out as sheer, unadulterated pleasure hummed through her. It was perfect, it was heaven, and when he banded his arms tightly around her, pushing up, thrusting hard, his teeth scraping her throat, she felt herself start to come apart for him again.

But this time, he was right there with her, just as far gone himself, and when she came on a cry of sheer surprise at the infusion of pleasure, she heard his own low, rough groan as he shuddered and followed her over.

9

Jacob woke up to a knock, and opened his eyes. Plastered against his side was a soft, naked, sleeping woman with a smile on her face that said *I'm in an orgasmic coma*.

He'd put her there, which gave him more than a little satisfaction. With a smile, he leaned over her with the intention of waking her up and starting all over again but then he heard another knock and realized someone was at the door. Maggie didn't budge, so he slipped out of bed. At the loss of his body heat, she rolled to her belly and snuggled into her pillow—with two Band-Aids on her cute ass, and a bruise in the shape of a fork.

Someone knocked for a third time and he pulled on his jeans, padded through the condo, and opened the front door.

Scott stared at Jacob for a long beat, holding two Starbucks cups and a brown bag that smelled good. He took in Jacob's lack of a shirt and shoes and socks, and clearly added two and two. "Uh . . ."

"You're looking for Maggie."

Scott nodded, looking very unhappy. "Yes."

"She's still in bed—"

"No, I'm here." Maggie came around from behind him,

wearing a robe and a wide-eyed, sexy, rumpled, I've-just-been-laid look in spite of how tightly she held her robe closed. "Scott?"

He held out one of the coffees, and then on second thought, politely handed the other to Jacob. "I came by to check in on you, but I can see you're . . . busy."

"Scott—"

"No, it's okay. See you at work." With a smile that didn't reach his eyes, he turned and walked off.

"*Scott.*"

He didn't respond, and shutting the door, Maggie leaned back against it and sighed. "That's probably not good."

"Actually, it is." Jacob took a second sip. "For how over-priced it is, it's very good."

Maggie didn't smile. "You didn't have to act so . . . ."

"So what?"

"Territorial."

That stopped him cold. Territorial? He wasn't territorial. Territorial was for committed guys, guys who had a thing for being with the same woman, guys who wanted stability and routine—not guys just being a woman's Mr. Wrong. He was just . . . ah, hell. *He was acting territorial.* While he chewed on that shocking fact, she made a noise of disgust and brushed past him, heading into the shower. She'd just shut the curtain when he caught up with her and peeled back the shower curtain.

With a squeak, she tried to cover herself up.

"I've already seen it all." He stepped out of his jeans and into the shower with her, crowding her back against the tile.

"*Jacob.*"

"*Maggie.*" He dropped his attitude and set his forehead to hers. "Truth. I guess I am feeling . . . territorial."

She was no longer covering herself up but looking at him with a rather complimentary wide-eyed wonder. "Are we going to—"

"Oh, yeah. We're going to."

* * *

When Maggie finally got to work, thanks to a ride from Janie, she'd had two more orgasms and had completely revised her opinion of the dreaded "morning after." In fact, she grinned all the way into the building, was *still* grinning when she passed by Alice's desk.

Alice took one look at her face and swore. "Are you kidding me? *You* got laid? I can't get a freaking return phone call from my supposed boyfriend and you, of the Church of Chemistry, got laid?"

Maggie looked around to make sure no one was listening. "How can you tell?"

"I know Scott went by your place last night, and you look all loose and relaxed. Two scientist geeks doing the nasty." Alice sighed. "Some people have all the luck."

"I didn't sleep with Scott."

"No sleeping, huh? Sure. Rub it in."

"Alice," Maggie said on a laugh. "I didn't have sex with Scott."

"Hey, you don't want to dish. I get it. You don't know me all that well, and—"

"No, it's not that—" She broke off as Jacob walked down the hall. He looked . . . different. And it wasn't just because she'd seen his big, bad body in the buff now, had in fact nibbled her way up and down every inch of that six-foot-two frame.

He didn't look like the Jacob she'd seen every day for two months. He wasn't wearing his tool belt, or his jeans, but a pair of nice-fitting cargoes and a white button-down. If he put on a white lab coat, he'd look every bit as much the on-the-go professional as any of the guys in this building. In fact, suddenly he looked like . . . like her Mr. Right, which should have been thrilling, but oddly enough it didn't matter. Because sexy and gorgeous as he was, it happened to be what was on the inside that attracted her. He made her smile, he made her think, he made her feel like so much more than the sum of her chemistry degrees—he made her feel like a warm, sexy woman.

Somehow, in some way, her Mr. Wrong had become her Mr. Right.

"Ohmigod," Alice whispered, dividing a stare between Maggie and Jacob. "*Him*? You slept with him?"

Maggie gave a guilty little start. "I have no idea what you're talking about."

Alice laughed. "Oh, yes, you do." She watched Jacob walk toward them. "So was he as hot as he looks?"

Maggie bit her lip, and Alice shook her head. "You don't have to say a word, your face is saying it all for you. So you two are what, dating now?"

"No. It was . . . a one-time thing." Okay, *two* . . .

"Well, that's just a damn shame."

Jacob came to a stop in front of Maggie. As if he couldn't care less that there were people milling around, not to mention Alice staring at him with open curiosity. He leaned in and gave Maggie a kiss. "Hi."

"Hi." She was breathless. He'd given her a peck and she couldn't breathe.

Oh, and her nipples were hard.

But it was more than that. Just looking at him had her heart tipping over on its side and exposing its tender underbelly. Oh, no. She'd fallen for him and couldn't get up. . . .

"You okay?" he asked.

No. No, she wasn't. She shifted away from Alice's desk for privacy, pulling him with her. "What are you doing here?"

"I wanted to say good-bye before I got on the plane. And make sure that you stay with your sister the next few nights."

"I will, but I'll be okay."

"I know. But I didn't want to walk away without making sure."

Walk away. Damn, she'd nearly forgotten that part, which had been her own idea. "I hope you have a great holiday with your family."

He just looked at her for a long moment, saying nothing. Then finally he nodded, his eyes fathomless and unreadable. "Thanks. You, too."

"Maggie?" Alice called out, waving her back over. "Did you leave your office light on last night?"

"No, I—" She whipped around and saw the light gleaming from beneath the door. *Not again.* What the hell was going on? Pulling out her key, she let herself in and gasped. Her files, locked when she'd left yesterday, were all open and disheveled.

"So they got the chance to search this time," Jacob said, coming in behind her. "What are they looking for, your formula?"

"I'm not sure." There were only two people in this building besides herself who had keys to her office, she'd checked yesterday. Well, three. Alice, of course.

And Scott and Tim.

They'd been acting strange and just a little bit off all week now, and she'd ignored it. "Alice?"

"Yes?"

"Could you give us a minute?"

"Oh! Sure."

When she was gone, Maggie pulled the vial of her formula from her briefcase and turned to Jacob. "I think it's all connected to this." She slipped the vial into her pocket. "The slashed tire. My home intruder. The odd visits from Scott . . ."

The odd visits from Scott. *He* was behind this? *Why?* It made no sense at all. "Wait here. I'll be right back." Leaving him, she rushed down the hall and barged into Scott's office.

The room was large and plush, the desk and other furniture all inventions he'd sponsored. The desk was an alloy material that couldn't be scratched. The couch was one of the brand new magnetic designs, a flat pad sitting on the floor now but when a switch on Scott's desk was hit, the cushion bent in half, providing back support, and floated off the ground, held there by the opposing magnets buried in the cushion. It wasn't activated because of the fatal flaw of the design—when switched on, everything in the room that was metal—the phone receiver, paper clips, letter openers—went flying rather violently through the air to stick to the couch. The inventor still had the scars to prove it.

Scott sat at the desk now, with three big screen computer monitors going, one that looked like a patient monitor, revealing blood pressure, heart rate, pulse, etcetera. The second screen was a global positioning system, but before she could catch sight of the third, Scott looked up at her, jumped guiltily, and hit a button on his keyboard that shut everything down.

"What was all that?" she asked.

"Nothing. Just . . . work."

"Are you stalking me, Scott?"

"What?" He looked genuinely shocked. "Why would I stalk you?"

"I wish I knew. Someone's been in my office twice now, clearly looking for something. And then there's my tire. And someone in my condo. And you and Tim acting . . . weird."

"No. Not weird, I swear. And maybe Tim needed something—"

"My files were trashed, Scott. Maybe I should just call the police and let them sort it out."

"Okay, let's not get crazy here," he said, losing a little of the tan he'd bought himself. "I'm sure we can figure this out in-house. *I* can figure this out in-house, I'm sure of it."

She looked at his computer, wishing she could see what he'd been working on, what had made him jump so guiltily. "So you want me to . . ."

"Do nothing. I'll handle it. I'll check into it immediately and get back to you."

"I still think that the police—"

"Totally not necessary."

"*Scott.*"

"Give me until noon, okay? Just a few hours, Maggie. If I don't have answers by then, you can go to the police. *We'll* go to the police."

"Fine. Noon." She walked out of his office, knowing that somehow she needed to get a look at his computer—alone.

Jacob found Maggie walking the hallway, lost in thought. "What are you doing?"

"The average person walks the equivalent of five times around the equator in their lifetime. I'm just doing my part."

"Maggie." She was clearly tense again, as she'd been before last night. He'd had great success at unwinding her then, getting her to relax, turning her into a pile of boneless jelly.

She'd done the same for him.

And that had been great, but it'd gone deeper for him. It'd always been deeper for him. Walking away was going to hurt, big time, and yet that's what the plan had been.

She looked at him with those gorgeous, heart-and-soul eyes, and voiced his thoughts. "I know I said I wanted a one-time thing."

"Technically, it's been a three-time thing, at least for me. For you, it's been more like a six- or seven-time thing—"

"My point," she said, blushing, "is that I lied, and not just because I need your help now. I *do* need your help, but I just want you to know I lied because you scare me."

That was just convoluted enough to make sense, and he linked his fingers with hers. "Well, we're even there. You scare me too. How can I help, Maggie?"

She stared up at him, her heart in her eyes. "I need Scott preoccupied for a few minutes so I can snoop on his computer. Any ideas?"

"Yes." He pulled out his cell and called the crane operator, who happened to be in the lot still loading his equipment. "Dan? I have a favor . . ."

Two minutes later, Scott got word his Mercedes was blocked in by a crane, and he went running out of the building.

Maggie helped herself into his office, locked the door behind her, and went immediately to his desk. One touch to the mouse had all the computer windows flickering to life. It took her a moment to grasp what she was seeing, and when she did, her heart stopped, then kicked back into gear when someone knocked.

"Maggie?"

At Jacob's voice, she ran to the door to let him in, then locked it again behind him.

"No one saw me," he said, looking around at the neat office, at the pad sitting on the floor. "What is that?"

"Magnetic couch. When you flip that switch on the desk, it floats in the air, but duck because anything metal in the room goes flying through the air. Look at this." She pointed to the screen. "Scott's been busy." One window had Maggie's picture and bio up, along with the stats and ingredients on her body cream, with the surprise and critical element Scott had alluded to, and it wasn't a thickening agent. The second window revealed a heart rate and pulse monitor. The third was the GPS system, with a grid map of the city, the highlighted portion blinking in on downtown, specifically Sixth Street. More specifically, this building.

Here.

As it all sank in, the heart rate and pulse monitored on the screen picked up speed, beeping, beeping, beeping in rhythm to her own.

"It's you," Jacob guessed, his voice was low, calm, and furious.

"Yes."

"How? *Why?*"

Leaning forward, she clicked on the files just behind her picture and bio. "Scott and Tim added an ingredient to my lotion. They let me think it was a texturing element but they lied. It's atom-sized transmitting microchips. It's genius, really, if you think of the implications. A heart patient, for instance. With the micro-transmitters in place, it would assist doctors in treating their patients. You could change a dose without ever having to see the patient, or even just monitor someone from long distances, allow them to live their lives, calling them in only when they were in danger, or—"

"Maggie."

She broke off and sighed. "Okay, I know. Gross invasion of privacy."

"You think?"

"Yes, of course. Not to mention completely illegal. But why the secrecy? Why didn't they just tell me? It's amazing."

"Gee, I don't know, maybe because of the *illegal* part?"

"Well, there's that," Scott said, coming into his office, twirling his keys on his fingers. He saw the computer windows up and his mouth tightened. "And for what it's worth, I wanted to tell you all along."

Tim shoved him aside and came in behind him. "But I didn't. And as for the so-called stalking—about which, FYI, I prefer to use the word surveillance—we simply needed the vial back, before you figured out what we were up to."

"But you gave it to me," Maggie reminded him.

"Yes, and once we realized what it could do, how intrusive it was, we needed that vial back before you understood what we'd done."

Maggie shook her head. "So the tire—"

"Was to slow you down so Scott could get to your apartment and retrieve the vial. We'd tried your office but it wasn't there."

"We didn't mean to scare you," Scott broke in, with apology in his voice. "But we knew we had to destroy it, before it got into the wrong hands. Now that you know what it is, you can understand that, can't you?"

"What hands could it have fallen into?" she asked. "I didn't even know what I had."

"No, but others did. Alice, for instance. She was here working late the night we discovered what we'd done."

"Alice is just an intern. She wouldn't—"

"Don't be naïve," Tim snapped. "This stuff is worth millions. People have died for far less."

At that, Jacob shifted closer to Maggie and reached for her hand. "No one's dying."

"Oh, no, don't worry." Scott lifted his hands. "We don't want to hurt you, either of you. We just want the lotion back, Maggie, that's all."

Slipping her hand into her pocket, where she had the vial, she shook her head. "I used the last of it this morning, it's all gone."

"You're lying." Tim didn't look quite as congenial as his brother. "Okay, here's what you're going to do. You're going to hand it over."

"No, *here's* what we're going to do," Jacob said evenly. "We're going to leave. Come on, Maggie." He pulled her with him around the desk, heading toward the door, but two things happened simultaneously. Tim stepped in front of the door, which opened, hard enough to knock him to his knees.

And then Alice entered. She lifted a gun and pointed it directly at Maggie.

10

"New plan," Alice said, with a sweet smile, the gun on Maggie, whose heart had all but stopped. "*I* get the lotion. Any objections? None? Good."

"Alice, what the hell is this?" Scott demanded.

"Oh, I forgot to mention. See, I need the lotion to catch my lying, cheating, soon to be ex-boyfriend in the act. Hand it over."

No one moved, and Alice shook her head. "Okay, listen up, people! I'm PMSing and hormonal, and when my grandma discovers I've borrowed her heat, she's going to go postal. So hand over the lotion pronto or I start taking out kneecaps, Soprano-style."

Tim pointed at Maggie. "She's got the vial."

Maggie gasped. "I do not."

"Yes," Scott said. "You do. We know you do because you clearly used the lotion and now you're trackable. You're on that screen right there, sending us your signals, see?" To show Alice, he twisted the computer screen around, pointing to the heart monitor. "This is Maggie."

Alice squinted at the screen. "How do I know?"

"Look at the history." Tim leaned over his brother and clicked a few keys on the keyboard. "See, look. She's all work and no play during the day. Now look at her nights—quiet, every single one. Typical boring scientist life—"

"Hey," Maggie said.

"Sorry, but it's true—" Tim broke off with a frown. "Wait a minute."

"What?" Alice demanded, staring at whatever they were looking at. "What's that?"

"She had sex." His fingers sped over the keyboard. "Here in this building." His head whipped around so he could look at her. "Jesus, *you had sex here?*"

Maggie did her best not to look at Jacob. "You want to discuss my sex life, now? With a gun on us?"

"Alice," Tim demanded. "Put the gun down."

"Not until I get that lotion!" Alice was looking quite unstable. She gestured the gun towards Maggie. "Hand it over."

Oh, God. If she handed over the lotion, someone might be able to eventually reproduce it, and that couldn't be allowed to happen. "Did you know Mary Stuart became the Queen of Scotland when she was only six days old?"

Alice cocked her gun. "Maggie, I swear to God, those quirky little facts were cute, oh . . . never. Okay? So please, shut up and *give me the lotion.*"

"Honey," Jacob said, squeezing Maggie's fingers, giving her a long look. "Give her what she wants. Give her the lotion."

Maggie stared at him. *Honey?*

"The jig is up," he said quietly. "So just give her the lotion. *Honey.*"

Honey. Of course! The honey lotion in her lab, the one he'd slathered on her and lapped off her breasts. "Right," she said, trying not to be disappointed that he wasn't calling her honey. "You're right. I'll go get it, but you're coming with me."

"Fine," Alice said, through her teeth. "But do it fast. While you're gone, Scott's going to make me a copy of the software required to go with the stuff." She waved at the windows. "Because I'm going directly to the asshole's apartment, putting the lotion on him, and catching him in the act of fucking his lab partner, and I'm doing that today, so hurry the hell up."

"Go," Tim said to Maggie and Jacob. "Quickly."

"And remember I can see your heart rate on the screen *and* your location, so no running away. And no more sex. No one gets any more sex until *I* get sex!"

"Maybe we should add Midol to the lotion," Jacob murmured into Maggie's ear, as they ran into her office, where she grabbed her honey potion. Turning back, she saw Jacob hitting 9-1-1 on his cell.

"She's got a gun—"

"Just get the honey lotion in a vial."

She did just that, her gaze on Jacob speaking quietly and quickly to emergency dispatch, looking so big and tough and . . . hers, dammit. If something happened to him she'd never forgive herself. She put a stopper in the new vial. "Okay, let's do this. But once she leaves with this vial, you're out of here. It won't fool her for long."

"We're *both* out of here."

"Deal." Her voice cracked a little, and she dropped her gaze, staring at his chest. "I couldn't handle it if anything happened to you, Jacob. I really couldn't. Listen, I know I totally took advantage of you with that whole Mr. Wrong thing—"

"Whoa. There were *two* of us making that decision. I wanted you, too."

"We're different."

Irritation flashed across his face. "We've discussed this, Maggie."

"You know what I mean."

"Did you know if you had enough water to fill one million goldfish bowls, you could fill an entire stadium?" he asked.

She blinked. "Um, what?"

"Yeah. And if you flew from London to New York by *Concorde,* due to the time zones crossed, you would arrive two hours before you left."

She let out a low laugh. "What are you doing? Did you look those up for me?"

He held up his hand. "One more. I don't want this to be a one-time thing."

Her amusement vanished as fast as it'd come. She swallowed hard but the sudden lump of emotion wouldn't go down. "Jacob."

"It's so much more for me. It's always been more. I'm not sure exactly when it happened, whether it was the way you look at work when you're concentrating, with your wild hair and fascinating brain, or how you make me smile all the time, or maybe it's that you always have a pen behind your ear—"

"What? I don't—"

Reaching over, he pulled a pen out from behind her ear.

"And your neck?" he whispered. "*Always* smells amazing. And then there's the way you look first thing in the morning, when you open your eyes and see me."

She let out a surprised laugh. "That was once."

"Yeah, but we can fix that. And then there's your laugh, that goofy, self-conscious laugh. It melts my damn heart every time. So you should know, it's not just a one-time thing, not anywhere close. I'm in love with you, Maggie."

Before she could respond, Alice screamed through the walls. "Why is your heart rate going up? Goddammit, are you getting naked?"

Maggie couldn't hear anything past the roar of her own blood in her ears, and those three words still echoing between her ears.

He loved her.

Loved her . . . "Jacob—"

"Maggie!" Tim yelled. "She's going to start shooting. Get back in here!"

"Come on." Jacob led her back into Scott's office, and Maggie, her heart still racing over what Jacob had just said, handed the vial over to Alice.

"Wait." Tim was staring at the vial.

Maggie froze. Obviously, the color was off, and he knew it. She locked gazes with him, holding her breath.

"You had a lot left," he finally said.

"Yeah. I did." *Crap*. Maggie turned to Alice. "You know how illegal this is, right?"

"Yes, because waving a gun in your face isn't illegal at all." Alice jammed the vial into her pocket and pulled out a fistful of cuff ties from her other. "Look, I'm sorry, all right?" She cuffed Scott to his filing cabinet and Tim to the desk. Then she came up to Maggie and Jacob, and after a hesitation, hooked them together. "For you," she whispered to Maggie. "Because he looks to be a keeper, someone you'd never need this lotion for."

Jacob didn't say a word but there was a muscle ticking in his jaw.

"Don't do this, Alice," Maggie begged her. "It's not too late to—" She broke off when Jacob jerked his arm—and therefore hers as well—hitting the button on Tim's desk that activated the magnetic couch.

The couch shot straight up from the floor, coming to a hover about two feet above the carpet, causing a handful of objects to instantaneously fly through the air as if hurled by a sling-shot—like Scott's phone, which nearly hit Tim, and . . . the gun, which was yanked right out of Alice's hands.

It slapped hard to the couch and stuck there.

"Dammit!" Alice yelled as Tim used his leg to trip her to the floor. Still attached to the filing cabinet, he slid down and sat on her.

"Hey!" she yelled, struggling. "I'll sue you for sexual harassment!"

"I'm gay," Tim informed her dryly. "I'm more likely to sexually harass Maggie's hottie than you, trust me."

Maggie stared at her "hottie"—the one who loved her—her free hand clutching her heart, because it had only just now started beating again. "Did you did mean it?"

Jacob's eyes softened, and some of the tenseness left his

body as he lifted his free hand and cupped her face. "Yes, I meant it."

"Oh, God. I love you, too." Her throat was so tight she could hardly speak. "For so many reasons. You say what you think and you do what you say, and you've got more logic and common sense in your pinkie than my last five dates combined."

"Hey," Scott said, insulted.

Maggie ignored him. "I think you're the smartest, funniest, sharpest, smartest man I've ever met."

"I could have said what I thought and what I feel," Scott muttered to Tim. "I could be solid and loyal."

Jacob pulled Maggie close. On Scott's desk, her heart monitor was still going nuts. With her free hand, she pulled the vial Tim had given her out of her pocket and smashed it to the floor. "That was the last of it," she told her soon to be ex-bosses. "I realize you can make more, but if you do, know this—I'll turn Data Tech over to the FDA, the DFA, the CIA, and the DEA, and whoever else will listen to me."

"You're bluffing," Tim said. "Your work is your life. And without us, you won't get funding."

"I'll wait for the right funding, I'll find it eventually."

"It could take years."

"Maybe." She looked at Jacob. "But I'll wait. My life is no longer just my work."

His eyes were full of affection and heat, lots of heat. "I like the way you think," he said, as pounding footsteps came down the hallway just outside the door.

Knowing it had to be the police, Maggie linked her fingers with Jacob's. "This is going to get messy, and might take some time to sort out. After which, I'm going to be unemployed." She winced. "Merry Christmas to me."

"I love messy. And I love you. As for the unemployed at Christmas, don't worry, I have an in with Santa. Have you been naughty or nice?"

"Nice."

"Well, we'll have to work on that," he murmured, just as the police burst through the door.

It took several hours to sort everything out, but eventually, Alice ended up in jail, Tim and Scott lawyered up, and Maggie and Jacob were free to go. Maggie walked out of the room where she'd been questioned and found Jacob waiting for her.

He looked into her face and slowly held up a little bough of mistletoe over his head.

She couldn't help but smile when she looked at him. "What's that?"

"A hint of what I want from you."

"And after the kiss?"

"More."

"More?"

"I want it all, Maggie. And I'm hoping you do, too."

"Yes." And she walked right into his waiting arms.

CAN YOU HAND ME THE TAPE?

1

"I need to talk to you."

Asking anyone for help made Natalie Pritchard uncomfortable. Asking *this* guy for anything made her downright twitchy.

Spencer Donovan stopped in the middle of shrugging out of his overcoat. "What are you doing here?"

She would have been offended by his tone except she'd asked herself the same question about forty times on her walk from the courthouse to Spence's office. Her current sorry situation kept her distracted and off balance, which explained why she stood in the middle of the room with melting snow dripping down her chin and not a clue about how to begin her story.

"I followed you," she said, just jumping in instead of overthinking the situation.

"From the garage downstairs?"

"From the courthouse." Over several blocks, through security in the lobby, up fourteen floors, past his assistant, Sue, and into the private office suite. She now knew Spence was not an easy man to stalk.

"That's almost two miles," he said.

He acted as if the feat were impossible. And, since it had felt more like ten miles, all of them straight uphill with ice blocks for feet, she could understand his confusion.

"A bit more than two actually."

"That explains the shoes."

She glanced down at the hiking boots. They made her feet look like she wore a size fifteen or whatever size giants wore. "They don't match the outfit but they kept me from falling down on the way over here."

"It's snowing."

His comment was not exactly news. "Mixed with freezing rain. Yeah."

She'd lost feeling in her face ten minutes earlier. The freezing temperatures in Washington, D.C. wiped out all of her nerve endings and left behind only a wet, shivering mess. At that moment strands of her hair stuck to her face. She counted the lack of a mirror in the room as a small mercy.

"Did Charlie send you in to talk to me?" Spence's dark brown eyes glanced past her and out into the empty hallway of the flashy office behind her.

Charlie Adams. The very big, very nasty, and very annoying reason she now stood in a puddle in front of Spence's desk.

"Why would you think that?"

"Charlie's tried everything else to piss me off during the last two weeks. It was only a matter of time until he used you." Spence sat in his oversize black leather chair.

His words sunk into her brain. "No one uses me . . . and why would my coming here tick you off?"

"Yeah, I wonder."

She ignored the slam. "Are you and Charlie fighting?"

"That's an interesting way to put it."

Lawyers and their control issues. "Fine. How do you think I should say it?"

Spence leaned back as he let out a long exhale. "We're dissolving our law partnership. Charlie wants the office space and most of our clients. I want him to have neither of those."

"Sounds like a fight to me."

Spence motioned for her to take a seat after she closed the door. "It's fair to say we passed from a simple fight to a probable court case weeks ago."

"Ohhh."

More like *ugh*. She needed Spence to reason with Charlie. Hard for that to happen if the knuckleheads were busy trying to destroy each other.

"Are you going to sit?" he asked.

"I think I'd better."

"It sounds as if Charlie forgot to share all the dirty little details of our partnership implosion with you."

Sharing was not something Charlie did. Not with her. Not ever. "Meaning?"

"You two are going out," Spence said as he brushed the last remnants of melted snow from his dark brown hair.

Were. They were well into the past tense stage, and she could not be happier.

"As such, I assume you talk." Spence stopped fidgeting long enough to show an interest in the conversation. "Right?"

Absolutely wrong on both theories. No dating. No talking. "That's why I'm here."

"Need love life advice?" Spence chuckled but his smile faded when she failed to join in the fun. "Look, Charlie served me with a list of demands this morning. As you can imagine, having his girlfriend show up the same afternoon makes me skeptical."

"I thought law school did that to you."

"So we're back to that."

"What?"

"Name-calling."

Yeah, telling him he was lower than a bloodsucking parasite one day and then asking for his help the next probably did not qualify as her best strategy. "I was angry with the way you handled your client in court."

"You hid that well," he said with enough sarcasm to freeze the remaining warmth right out of her.

"Can we get back to the topic at hand?" she asked, even though she dreaded the conversation.

"Which is?"

"You."

"Okay, I'll play along." He took a shiny black pen out of the chest pocket of his blazer and tapped it against his desk blotter. "What about me?"

"I need your assistance."

A smile tugged at the corner of his mouth. "I bet it kills you to say that."

"Pretty much."

"Since you admitted it, I'll be civil."

"Thanks."

"Is this help about anything in particular or just in general?"

"A problem."

"Some specifics would help right about now." He grabbed his yellow legal pad.

"That's the hard part."

"Nat, I understand things happen," he said as he switched to serious lawyer mode. "It's easier to just say whatever it is so we can figure out how to resolve the issue or get rid of it."

He made it sound so simple. No wonder businessmen paid big bucks for Spence's representation and petty thieves begged for him to be assigned to their case as free counsel.

"You know that whatever we discuss in here stays in here. I guarantee confidentiality. Nothing will seep over into our professional relationship," he said.

"I figured as much."

"Let's try it this way. Are you in trouble?" He flipped his pen between his fingers.

"Sort of."

"The legal kind?"

"The personal kind."

The color seeped from his face. Nothing made a man squirm

faster than a woman with a problem. Unless it was a "female" problem, then they just panicked. Nat was tempted to suggest she had one of those just to see how many colors Spence's cheeks would turn before he passed out.

"Am I the one you should be talking to about this? I'm an attorney, not a counselor or specialist." He did not loosen his shirt collar but from his hard swallow she guessed he wanted to.

"You're the only one who can help."

"What about talking to Charlie about this?"

"I'm here because of him."

"Yeah, I'm definitely not the right person for this." Spence grabbed his Rolodex. "Let me find you someone who—"

She slid her hand onto the desk, just inches from his. "It has to be you."

"Nat, this is a bad idea."

"Please."

Spence stopped hunting for a number and started whipping his pen between his fingers with enough speed to create electricity. "Charlie's your boyfriend."

"Not anymore."

Spence flicked the pen so hard it flew across the room and bounced against the law school diploma mounted on the wall.

"I can get it," she said.

"Leave it." Spence closed his eyes for a second. When he opened them again, the color had changed from chocolate brown to near black. "When exactly did this big breakup happen?"

Not soon enough to save her from trouble. "It doesn't matter."

"I bet it does to Charlie."

"We ended our relationship for good two weeks ago."

Right after that she relegated Charlie to the *huge mistake* pile of men in her past. Something she should have done months before.

"We?" Spence asked.

"Me."

Spence nodded. "That explains why Charlie's even less agreeable than usual."

She could not afford to let Spence seek out reasons *not* to help. "Don't blame me for whatever mess you're in with Charlie."

"I didn't."

"You were going to."

"That's not . . ." Spence flashed a small grin. "Okay, maybe I was, but your timing is suspect."

"I'm still not taking the blame."

"You dumped Charlie about the same time he started making impossible demands in our firm's dissolution, wanting more money and generally being a pain in the ass."

As far as she was concerned, Charlie acted like an ass most of the time. "Which one of you wanted the breakup?"

Spence frowned. "Of the partnership?"

"What else would I be talking about?"

"You made it sound like dating."

"Seems as if ending a business arrangement with Charlie is just as painful."

The harsh lines around Spence's mouth softened. "Look, I know Charlie can be tough. Mean, even. Are you okay?"

More like very not okay. "I will be."

Spence blew out a long, ragged breath. "Tell me what you need and what I can do to help."

"Charlie has something of mine."

Spence tapped his fingers against the legal pad. "That's easy enough to resolve. Is it jewelry?"

"No."

"Dishes?"

She wished. "Nuh-uh."

"Electronics? A car?"

"No and no."

"Give me a hint."

Here came the hard part. The embarrassing, she-should-know-better part. "It's personal."

"Like clothing?"

The exact opposite, actually. "A tape."

Spence stopped tapping. "Video or audio?"

"Video."

"Why do I think you're talking about something other than a movie?" Spence's mouth moved but every other part of him remained frozen.

"As far from it as possible."

"Just how far?"

"It's a video."

"I got that part."

"Of me."

His skin grew even paler. "And?"

"I'm naked."

2

Spence forced his gaze to remain locked on Nat's face. No way he could let his eyes wander after that comment. One sweep down her body and she would kill him. No doubt about it.

But, man, it was tempting.

"You mean you . . . that you . . ." He was not sure how to finish the sentence, so he let it hang out there all by itself.

"Me. Naked."

"On video."

"That's what I said. Yes." She picked that moment to stand up and take off her coat. The disrobing revealed a slim red turtleneck and black short skirt on a curvy body Spence had never noticed until that moment.

How the hell was a guy not supposed to sneak a peek now?

From her scowl, he knew she had picked up on his weak attempts at not looking. She returned the favor with one of those disapproving frowns he saw from her so often.

Good thing that big desk sat between them and hid most of his view of her lower half now that she sat back down. Made gawking a bit tougher. Which likely extended his life by a few more minutes.

"Did you want to say something?" she asked.

"Uh, no."

"To ask me something?"

About a thousand things, most of them centered on the naked part of her story, but he was smart enough to refrain from venturing there. "I figured there was more to your video story. That you weren't done talking yet."

"I don't think you need all of the details."

"One or two might help."

"You get the main idea from what I've said."

Oh, he had all sorts of ideas. The woman who fought him to the death at work and played the quiet girlfriend to his soon-to-be former business partner in private always confounded him. Now she took on a new dimension. A naked one.

Spence rarely thought of probation officers as sexy or seductive. Probably had something to do with most of them being male, but his mind never went there with Nat either. Or, it never did before right then. Now that was the only place his mind *would* go.

They met in the courtroom all the time when one of his clients got probation as part of a sentence or when the Parole and Probation Office had to provide a report before sentencing and she came as the representative. But all of that was professional. This tape thing brought a whole new meaning to that old adage of picturing your audience naked.

Spence wondered how, for the next moment or two, he was going to do anything else with Nat in the room. He cleared his throat and tried to wipe his mind clear of all disrespectful thoughts.

"Okay, this is not a big deal. We're adults."

"I thought so until two minutes ago. I'm not so sure now," she mumbled.

"No, really. You made a sex video. So what?" Her naked on tape amounted to a big "what" in his book, but he shrugged and pretended otherwise.

"What did you just say?"

Damn, she wanted him to repeat it. "You made a sex—"

This time she jumped out of the chair. "I meant, what are you talking about?"

"The tape."

"It's not a sex tape."

Thank God. "It's not?"

"Of course not." Energy pulsed off her but she managed to sit back down anyway.

"But you said—"

"A tape." She pulled the neck of her sweater up high enough to choke herself.

"You, uh, mentioned something about being naked."

The material hovered just under her mouth now. "That doesn't mean porn."

"Who said porn? I thought you were talking about a private video."

"Stop talking."

He should. He knew he should. "All I was saying was that it—"

"Stop." She dropped the sweater and held up her hands. She may have closed her eyes in frustration but he was too busy trying not to say anything stupid to fully appreciate all of her angry gestures.

"The tape is just of me."

"What are you doing on it?" The question slipped out before his internal filter could catch it.

"Excuse me?"

"Forget I asked."

"I intend to."

"Why me?" And by that he meant: How did he get stuck with this conversation?

"I couldn't go to the police. I deal with those guys all the time at work and the idea of them seeing me . . . or what they would say. Well, you know."

He did except for not understanding how he somehow got chosen for this conversation. "Sure."

"That left me with very few options. Only one, really."

"Me."

"Yeah."

Spence looked for another pen in the hope that concentrating on taking notes would help him from concentrating on Nat. "Is someone threatening to disseminate the tape?"

"I hope not. The holidays are going to be horrible enough without having to worry about that."

He was not sure what the comment meant, so he focused on the tape. "Who has this tape?"

"Charlie."

The situation went from bad to untenable. "What did he say?"

"When?"

"When you asked him to give you the tape back."

"I didn't."

Spence suddenly missed talking with his criminal clients. They lied but at least most of the lies made some degree of sense.

"I'm thinking we should start this whole conversation over again," he suggested.

"I didn't ask Charlie because he doesn't even know he has the tape."

"Believe it or not, that explanation does not clear things up for me."

She sighed and frowned and mumbled about him being slow all at the same time. "I made the tape for him as a Christmas present. I didn't wrap it yet because I was watching it."

Something exploded inside his brain. "You were what?"

"He walked in while I was . . . well, that's not important. I hid the tape in the mess on the coffee table. Then, when—"

"Hold up a sec."

"When we fought, he grabbed up all of his paperwork and materials for his big murder case that just ended and unknowingly took the tape with him."

"You didn't show him the tape?"

"Of course not. It's not Christmas yet."

Sure, right. That made sense. At least as much sense as the rest of the discussion made.

"But Charlie knows about the tape." Spence decided to make a statement rather than ask a question since her answers were not helping at all.

"How could he?"

"So, if this happened a few weeks ago, why the big rush to get it back now?"

"Charlie's case just got appealed. That means he'll be digging around his case box soon. Probably within a few days."

"So, is this really a tape or is it some sort of disc?"

"No. A tape. I used an old recorder. It's all I could find and I needed to mount it."

Spence started to think this whole scene might be a joke. "What the hell is on this tape again?"

"Me."

"Naked. Yeah, I got that part. What else?"

She glanced at the closed door to his office. "I'd appreciate it if you didn't yell."

"This is my office."

"And Charlie's is just a few doors down. The goal is to keep this from him."

Spence dropped his voice to just above a whisper. "How are you going to do that?"

"We're over. Charlie never needs to know the tape existed."

"I don't understand how you plan to get it back without asking Charlie for it."

"Simple." She smiled. "Take it."

"You've got to be kidding."

"That's why I need you."

"To bail you out of jail when this idiotic plan goes to hell? And it will. I rarely give guarantees, but this one plan is headed for failure."

"Your job is to grab the tape from Charlie without him knowing."

"Let me get this straight. You want me to steal the tape." He said the phrase nice and slow, allowing her plenty of time to rush in and deny.

"Stealing is a strong word."

"How do you feel about the word insane?"

"The tape is my property."

Spence got more confused by the second. "It was a gift for Charlie and he has it."

"Only by accident."

Spence rubbed his temples. "I'm sorry I came to the office this afternoon. I should have kept on driving."

"I would have come to your house."

"Breaking and entering? Happy to know your life of crime isn't limited to theft and burglary."

"I don't have much time. I'm desperate here." She rubbed her hands together as if to prove her point.

"And what do I get other than the potential of jail time and the promise of public humiliation?"

"How about the satisfaction of helping someone in need?"

"I do that every single day." He also wondered if this new headache was a permanent thing.

"Right. Because you're such a good guy."

She had crossed into false flattery. "Maybe I should remind you how you called me a bloodsucker a few days ago."

She had the decency to look uncomfortable. "Yeah, about that—"

"And I believe you referred to me as a humorless pig last week."

"Prig."

"What?"

She waved him off. "Never mind."

If only. Hell, he wished he could forget this whole conversation, but he doubted that was ever going to happen. Her comments about being naked were imprinted on his brain.

"I still don't understand why you picked me." He asked because he really wanted to know what he did to warrant this duty so he never did it again.

"Honestly?"

"Now you do sound like a client."

"You help them. Why not me?"

Her logic made his head pound.

She let out an exasperated exhale when he didn't jump in and agree. "Fine. Do you want to know the real reason?"

"Definitely."

"Because you don't care."

She managed to lose him again. That made about fifty times during the course of this conversation. "About what?"

"The tape's contents."

Never was a woman more wrong about an issue. "How do you figure that?"

"We've known each other for two years. You've never shown one bit of interest."

He would have said something if he knew what the hell to say to that.

"And," she continued, "despite our differences, my sense is that your internal honor code would prevent you from taking a look just out of curiosity."

"With all of your cryptic comments about this tape, you think I'm not intrigued about what's on it?"

"That's different from being interested. You wouldn't show the tape to anyone or try to take advantage of me."

"The last part is true." The rest was pure crap.

"You don't care about what I look like without clothes on."

There's where she got confused. "How did you come to that conclusion again?"

"I can tell."

"Which goes to show how little you know about men."

She blinked a bunch of times. "What does that mean?"

"I don't know a lot of men who would pass up a chance to

see a woman naked." None, actually. Did not matter what she looked like. Men were curious.

"That's not true." She bit her bottom lip. "Is it?"

"It is."

"But you won't look."

"I don't know why you think that's the case."

3

The door opened after a loud knock. In walked the one person Nat did not want to see. Ever.

Dirty blond hair, brown eyes, broad shoulders, and an ego the size of a football stadium. Charlie Adams entered every room as if he expected all eyes to turn to him. Being over six-four with rough, handsome looks, most people took notice. Until Charlie opened his mouth. Then they got annoyed.

His courtroom skills and ability to wow a jury qualified him as a fine attorney. People who dealt with him on a peripheral level viewed him as charming. Those who knew him well referred to him as a blowhard. Nat considered him a nightmare.

Charlie wasn't abusive or unfaithful, but their combination as a couple had proven toxic for her. Over time he'd balled up her self-esteem and chucked it in the garbage. She started losing weight to please him. That accounted for the first twenty pounds. She owed the last twenty-five to stress.

As much as she wanted to hate Charlie, she knew he only deserved part of her anger. She'd earned the rest. She'd stayed too long, put up with too much, and expected too little.

For a strong woman working in a tough environment, when

it came to Charlie she acted like the fat girl standing alone on the school playground waiting to be picked last for a team. No matter how hard she tried to kick that chubby girl out of her head, she hung around and messed up everything.

Spence stood up, all traces of civility gone. "Did you need something?"

Charlie ignored the question and focused on her. "Sue said you were here."

"I'm meeting with Spence."

Spence moved around his desk to stand next to Nat's chair. "We don't need company."

For the first time, Nat noticed the men's strained interaction. Due to his size, Nat always viewed Charlie as the leader and more powerful of the two. Now she knew she had that wrong. Spence might be a few inches shorter, but his shoulders were just as broad and his demeanor struck her as equally unbending, maybe even a bit more imposing.

Spence came off as a cleaned-up, less pushy version of Charlie. And Spence had the better courtroom record. A fact that pissed Charlie off and made Nat smile.

"Last I checked, my name is still on the door," Charlie said.

"I'll go scrape it off if that will get you out of here faster." Spence grabbed his scissors. "Just say the word and Donovan & Adams becomes Donovan."

"I'm talking with my girlfriend."

A muscle in Spence's cheek twitched. "The way I hear it, she dumped you."

Time to stand up and put an end to the male madness. Nat shoved out of her chair and stepped between the two men. "The testosterone show, while impressive, isn't helping."

"What the hell are you doing here with him?" Charlie demanded.

Shouting. Yeah, Charlie was great at shouting. "It's business and you're interrupting."

This time Spence angled his body in front of hers in what Nat assumed was a protective stance. The move filled her stomach with a sudden lightness. At five-eight, and as someone who'd spent most of her life about sixty pounds overweight, men did not rush to her rescue. Everyone assumed she could handle any physical threat. In the biggest insult of all, people probably thought she'd just sit on anyone who tried to hurt her.

Being the opposite of petite resulted in never being cherished or shielded the same way as thinner women. Some of her tiny friends viewed the male protective instinct as sexist. To Nat, it related to attractiveness and being worthy of affection and to all the things she wasn't. The male reaction was normal, healthy, and not something she ever had the opportunity to either enjoy or find offensive.

"What the lady is saying in a nice way is, get the hell out of my office," Spence said.

"You looking to taste my leftovers, partner?"

"Don't talk about Natalie that way. Ever."

"She's a bit too smart and a bit too *big* for you, isn't she?"

She refused to wither from Charlie's nastiness but stayed behind Spence's broad shoulder anyway. "That's enough, Charlie."

"More than enough. Apologize to the lady," Spence said.

"Nat and I understand each other. You can't do the things we've done together and not." Charlie winked after he made the comment.

She did not know if Charlie wanted to hurt her or show off to Spence. Either way, she wanted Charlie out. And had a sudden need for a shower.

"You'd think you'd have the decency not to be vulgar, what with all that intimacy you've shared." Spence took a final step toward Charlie. "And this is your last warning. Get out of my office."

"Whatever you need." Charlie glanced over at her. "Stop by to see me before you go."

Spence shut the door in Charlie's face before he could wink a second time. When Spence turned back around to face her, his red cheeks spoke to his fury.

"If you stop by his office . . ."

The tightness in his voice intrigued her. "Yeah?"

"Just don't."

Her anger rose over Spence's demand but she tamped it back down. "No problem."

"What the hell did you see in him?"

"It was one of those things."

Spence continued as if she had not spoken. "Why would you go out with a guy who spoke to you that way?"

The questions stung. Each word knocked against her wounded self-esteem, making her feel even more dumb and less sure of her ability to judge the men in her personal life.

Not that she had many men in her personal life. One socially backward guy in college, a quiet accountant without a personality in her early twenties, and one handsome lawyer with a high jerk reading in her present. Pretty lame dating life for twenty-nine years on the planet.

"I could ask you the same thing. Why would you partner with the guy?" she asked.

The harsh lines in Spence's face eased. "I've wondered about that myself."

"Come up with an answer?" If so, she might use the excuse, too.

"He's a good lawyer. I thought I could—"

"Change him?"

"Refine him." Spence balanced his head against the door. "Sounds stupid, I know. It's just that Charlie has more potential and raw talent than any other criminal defense attorney in D.C."

"You make it sound as if you're a hundred years older than Charlie."

"Most days I feel like it. Charlie might be thirty but he acts younger. The five years between us stretched pretty wide most weeks."

"So, I'm not the only one who has been the target of Charlie's more juvenile side?"

Spence stared for a second before looking away. "Let's get back to your plan about the video."

Spence brushed past her on his way to fetch his flying pen and sit back down. Nat knew an intentional change of topic when she heard one. Spence's demeanor had morphed from angry to disinterested with one question. His face wiped clear of expression and his eye contact wandered.

Something she said caused the change. She just did not know what it was.

"Spence?"

"Please don't talk about being naked again. A guy can only take so much in one afternoon."

Nat did not fight a smile. "I promise."

"Thanks."

"About Charlie—"

Spence tapped the tip of his pen against his desktop. "We're done talking about him in terms of your relationship and my partnership. Agreed?"

Now there was a offer she did not want to accept. Not until she knew more about the partnership dissolution. Why had the relationship turned sour and what was behind Spence's reluctance to talk about all of it.

"Nat, do we have a deal?"

"Fine." Not fine but acceptable for now. "So, how are you going to get the tape from Charlie's house?"

Spence flipped back a few pages of his legal pad until the one in front of him did not have any writing on it. "This is your plan, not mine."

"Well, yeah, but you're going to be the one doing the actual stealing."

"I thought you didn't like that word."

"You know what I mean."

"Unfortunately, I do."

"So, what will it be?" She rubbed her hands together as she dropped back into the chair. "Some sort of break-in, or are you going to ask Charlie if you can come over and then some-how sneak it out?"

"You're still not getting that part where I don't have a plan."

"Why not?"

"Because I just heard about this idiotic idea forty minutes ago."

"Oh."

"And I haven't agreed to help."

"But you will." She knew he would.

"Look, Nat. I know you're nervous. I know you're worried Charlie will find the tape and do something irritating or inap-propriate with it before we can retrieve it."

"Among other things."

"I get all that."

"Then come up with a plan."

Spence's eyebrows inched up. "Anyone ever tell you how bossy you are?"

"No." Never, actually.

She had been called sweet, told she had a pretty face—which she knew to be code for "fat but not ugly"—and other-wise been the one to keep the peace. Something about Spence brought out the fight in her. She argued with him, even called him a few names. With Spence she felt feisty and challenged, frustrated and angry.

"Guess I'm the only one you refer to as a bug," he mum-bled.

She knew that parasite comment would be a problem. "You've called me some names, too."

"Referring to you as a do-gooder is a fact not an insult."

"What you've called me is 'a do-gooder with no sense of the real world.' " She cleared her throat. "And talk about cyn-ical."

"You'll see. After a few more years in this business you'll become less invested in the idea of getting emotionally at-tached to the criminals and more convinced that rehabilitation is not a reality for most of them."

She treated him to her best exaggerated eye roll. "If you hate them all so much, why aren't you a prosecutor?"

"I was one at the beginning of my career and didn't hate the criminals then." He passed the pen from one hand to the other. "For the record, I don't hate them now either."

"You changed sides to make more money." And from the courthouse gossip and the high-end office space, she knew Spence made a lot of money.

"You're against people earning a living?"

As a D.C. employee, she made enough to eat and pay rent. She did not begrudge anyone who wanted more financial security than she enjoyed.

"I wasn't making a judgment."

"You didn't ask, but so that you know, I'm a criminal defense attorney because I have a belief in the system and the idea that everyone, even the morons and the most evil, deserves a fair trial and competent representation. Being a prosecutor did not serve that purpose. Not for me, so I changed sides." He grinned. "Making more money is just a bonus."

His honor ran deep. She hoped his stealing skills were just as strong.

"So, when do you think you'll have a plan to get the video back?" she asked for what felt like the fiftieth time. Would it kill the guy to give her an answer?

"So, we're done dissecting my motives?"

No, but she would do that in private. "Yeah."

"Good." That smile grew even wider. "And, I don't know when I'll have a plan."

The man was not understanding the extent of her predicament. "I need the tape. Now. Yesterday, in fact."

"You've made that clear. What I need is ten seconds to come up with a plan."

"Fair enough."

"I thought so."

"I'll start counting." She could be reasonable. She glanced at her watch to start his countdown.

"Don't time me." He chuckled. "First, I'll require a few more minutes to figure out what I want in return for this dangerous caper."

She dropped her hand to her lap. "I thought you were doing this to feel better about yourself."

"You thought wrong."

"You should consider it."

"I feel fine about my charitable works, but thanks."

She straightened her spine. "What do you want in return?"

He took his time leaning back in his chair and folding his hands behind his head. "Once I figure that out, I'll let you know."

"That's not fair."

"That as good a deal as you're going to get."

4

The next afternoon Spence sipped on flat club soda from a plastic cup as he watched a bathroom door. He had done a lot of strange things in the courthouse lobby. Even for him, staring at the ladies' room for minutes at a time registered as odd.

"Something wrong?" his assistant asked as she walked up behind him.

"Everything."

"You're missing the party." Sue delivered her comment in a loud enough voice to carry over the taped Christmas carols blaring on the courthouse loudspeaker.

Between the rumble of the crowd and squealing strains of "We Wish You a Merry Christmas" bouncing off the marble floors and walls, Spence wondered if his hearing would ever return to normal.

"Uh-huh."

"Are you listening to me?"

"Of course." But mostly he was watching the door.

Nat had walked into the bathroom more than ten minutes ago. Spence expected a speedy exit. Instead, Nat had set up house in there.

"You do know this is a party, right?" Sue asked.

"That explains the people, the food, and the insipid chatter."

The party amounted to a professional "mandatory good time" he did not want to attend. He appreciated the courthouse staff and their hard work. That did not mean he was in the mood for a few hours of standing around in his suit pretending to have fun after a long day of hearings and conferences.

"Ho, ho, ho to you, boss."

Spence snapped out of his trance and glanced at Sue. The red Santa hat dwarfed her head and fell down to the top of her dark glasses. At fifty, five-two and about two hundred pounds, Sue did not need the strange getup to attract more attention. Her scratchy two-pack-a-day voice didn't exactly inspire holiday cheer either.

"That's a good look for you," he said.

"It's festive."

"If you say so."

Sue traded a fresh drink for his flat one.

"Thanks," he mumbled as he watched a married judge engage in a bit too much touching of his unmarried clerk.

"You should mingle. This is the official courthouse holiday party, after all."

"Your point?"

"I know you're upset about Charlie—"

"This isn't about Charlie." Spence hated that everything in his life revolved around Charlie lately. Even his relationship with Natalie depended on a Charlie issue this week.

So far as Spence could tell, Charlie ruined everything he touched. He was a good attorney, possibly even a great one. It was the way he treated people that left Spence cold.

"Then why are you standing alone in the corner when all of those young available women are waiting around for you to give them a little hello?" Sue asked.

Spence saw a group of courtroom clerks hovering close behind Sue as they giggled and stared. Being available and successful made him a bit of a single-woman target. While flattering, that sort of short-term hookup just was not going to happen. He preferred being known in the courthouse for his legal talent rather than his bedroom skills.

"I think that tall brunette has mistletoe," Sue said.

"Save me," he whispered, and meant it.

"Why should I?"

"How are you going to feed those three cats of yours without a paycheck?"

"Please." Sue snorted. "I've been working for you for years."

"Trust me, I know."

"This is the longest dry spell I've ever seen for you."

A man deserved some privacy in that area. "I'm discriminating."

"You're distracted."

The object of his distraction stepped up beside him. He did not have to look over to see her. He could smell her. That light floral scent he associated with Nat hit him before she moved into his line of sight.

"Hello, Sue," Nat said in a warm voice.

Sue grabbed Nat in a bear hug. "You look prettier every single day."

"How can you tell when you're squishing her like that?" he asked.

Sue talked right over him. "Probably has something to do with getting rid of that no-good boyfriend of yours."

"Sue." Spence said her name with enough warning to let her know not to travel down that path right now.

"Thanks." Nat leaned in close to Sue. "And you're right."

Nat treated Sue to a huge smile. One so genuine and caring that Spence stopped staring at Nat's slim navy skirt and the shapely legs beneath it to focus on her face.

He remembered her as having sad eyes and a friendly personality. Well, friendly to everyone but him. But something had changed. A certain frailness still lingered on her face but all of a sudden he associated Nat with something more than a nice personality. Maybe it was a new haircut, or . . .

"And you're getting so thin. Too thin. Isn't she, Spencer?" Sue elbowed him in the side.

"*Umpf.*" He rubbed the injury. "What was that for?"

"Make some conversation with the nice lady."

"Hard to do that when I can't breathe."

"She's losing too much weight. Tell her." Sue did it for him. "Natalie, honey, there is such a thing as too skinny."

"I am far from that."

Spence let his gaze wander over Nat's shape. He'd heard the whispers in the courthouse about Nat losing weight. The petty talk about why and how much Charlie must like the change.

Seeing Nat now, the trim waist between all those curves, he noticed just how much weight she'd lost. This was not a matter of a few pounds. She'd lost a lot.

"How much?" he asked the question on his mind.

Apparently it was only on his because Nat's eyebrows drew together in complete confusion. "What?"

"Spencer Donovan." Sue whacked him on the arm. "That is not the kind of question you ask a lady."

"Sue, do you mind if I steal Spence for a second?" Nat asked.

"You can have him until his attitude gets better. Unbelievable." Sue shoved him in Nat's direction. Any harder and Nat would have been wearing his drink.

"I don't want him that long," Nat said. "Just for a few seconds."

He ignored Nat's comment and focused on Sue. "I hope you weren't counting on a Christmas bonus this year."

"The office is rough enough without this one grumbling all the time." Sue hitched her thumb in his general direction.

"You're fired."

"Oh, please. You'd be lost without me." Sue grabbed the drink out of his hand.

"Hey!"

"I'll be at the dessert table when you're ready to take me back to the office. Apologize to Natalie first."

Sue turned and left. Spence thought he noticed a bit of a spring in the older woman's usually heavy step. Made him wonder if someone had spiked the bright red punch.

"Maybe I should take her to someone else's office. Want her?"

"She's in rare form," Nat said with the wide smile still in place.

"Sue loves Christmas," Spence said.

"You don't?"

He did. Family, food, playing with his nieces. "It's a day."

"Wrong."

"Did someone change the calendar and not tell me?"

Nat chuckled. "It's a feeling. One that's much bigger than a date or a time or a few hours spent opening packages."

"Hours? How many gifts do you get?"

"People like me."

"Says the woman who wants me to steal for the holidays."

"Speaking of that. Did you come up with a plan yet?"

And people thought he lacked the holiday spirit. Nat had only one thing on her mind and it did not relate to the party or the three clerks watching her and whispering. "No."

"What is taking so long to get this done?" she asked through gritted teeth, all signs of a smile now gone.

"We talked less than twenty-four hours ago."

"I need that tape back immediately."

"So that's why you keep saying the word now."

She pinched him. "I'm serious."

"And I'm sick of getting smacked around by the women at this party." He glanced around to make sure there was no one else waiting to take a turn.

"As if that's a new thing."

"Insulting my way with women is not going to make me go any faster."

"Oh, please." She gave him one of her dramatic eye rolls. "I've heard all about you and your women."

According to Sue, he didn't have any women. Interesting how two women could see the situation so differently. "Care to fill me in?"

"Charlie told me all about your conquests. How pretty the women were. How smart and thin." Nat waved a hand in the air in a dismissive gesture, but her serious tone suggested she was much more invested in the conversation than she wanted to be.

"I see Charlie made being a jackass a full-time job," Spence mumbled.

"What does that mean?"

"Why would Charlie think you'd care about my dates?"

"He lived vicariously. He was stuck in a relationship with me. You were out leading this wild social life—"

"Wild?"

"—and he wasn't."

Spence hated the way she described their parallel lives. Her preoccupation with weight loss did not sit well with him either. "How much weight did you lose?"

The question made her eyes pop. "Why?"

"Just wondering."

"It doesn't matter."

For some reason, he thought it did. "Twenty pounds?"

"Forty-five."

"That's the equivalent to the weight of a kid. Are you sick?"

"I'm impatient."

"I hadn't noticed that about you."

"Spence, really." She shifted in front of him, blocking his view of the rest of the party, and dropping her voice low enough for only the two of them to hear. "When are you going to get the tape? I need to know."

"I haven't even figured out *how* I'm going to get the tape."

And that was the truth. Walking into his estranged partner's house and taking a look around was not a feasible solution.

Breaking in was not going to happen either. Spence knew he had to find another way, and one that would not tip Charlie off. While Charlie did not treat Nat well, he did not want anyone else near her either. That meant Spence had a whole wall of furious male to get through in order to retrieve the tape.

"We need to come up with something smart and workable," she said.

"Maybe food will help. There are these blobs of something being passed around on trays. Sue said they were crab. I don't think—"

Nat's jaw dropped. "What are you talking about now?"

"Getting something to eat."

"Forget the party."

"That's kind of hard when about twenty people are watching us talk." A slight exaggeration, but it got the intended result.

Nat spun around to look at the rest of the crowd. Some stared. A few hid their curiosity well. Others, not so much. Most had the grace to look away when Nat returned the stares.

Spence did not bother to get angry with being in the spotlight. He understood the interest. The D.C. legal community was a small one. Seeing him talk with his estranged partner's former girlfriend supplied the right amount of intrigue to get everyone wondering and talking—the two things he hated when they were directed at him.

"Man, people are nosy," Nat muttered under her breath.

"They're probably hoping Charlie will show up and cause a scene. Nothing says happy holidays like a fist fight."

"Is Charlie coming tonight?" She looked horrified at the idea.

Spence felt the same way but did not let the concern show. "How should I know?"

"We'll talk fast and get out of here."

He was all for the leaving part of her plan. "If you think that will help."

"I got it." The panic left her eyes. "Here's what we'll do."

He still held out for finding some food. "This sounds bad."

"We need to meet in private."

Worse than bad. "Right. That should cut down on the speculation and gossip."

"What are you doing after the party?"

Since she'd missed his last attempt at sarcasm, he tried again. "Moving out of the country."

"I'll come to your house."

Where the hell had that come from?

"Nat."

"We'll figure out what you need to do and when."

"Natalie."

"And finalize everything."

Wait a second. "What if I have plans?"

She gave him a blank stare as if that possibility had never occurred to her, which was true but insulting. "Do you?"

He should lie. Say he did and get out of this situation. Put off the tape discussion for a while longer. Stay the hell away from her and any situation that put them alone together. "Well, no."

"Then it's set. I'll be over around seven."

5

Two hours later Nat stood outside Spence's front door, wondering what made her throw down the ultimatum and insist on coming to his house. The whole time she dated Charlie she never made it into Spence's place. The men worked together but did not socialize, so having an excuse to see how the famous bachelor criminal defense attorney lived did not materialize. Nor was she interested in seeing inside Spence's private life until right then.

Now that the opportunity arose, she was curious. And she could not be more shocked. The three-story townhouse near Capitol Hill was not what she'd expected. A condo bachelor pad, yes. A brick-front family home, no.

Before she could knock, the front door flew open. She could not figure out which was more disconcerting—the cozy home or seeing Spence wearing blue jeans and a slouchy navy blue sweater. She always assumed his casual attire consisted of a novelty tie. That he wore suits to bed or something.

"Why do you look like that?" he asked.

Not the most flattering question ever, but she had heard worse things said about her. "You don't like the black pants?"

His gaze moved over her body, slowing the lower he went

238 / *HelenKay Dimon*

and causing her skin to flush in return. The unexpected warmth hit her out of nowhere and refused to leave.

She snapped her fingers in front of his face to get the attention away from her body. "Hello?"

"I meant the sour expression on your face."

"Oh." Now there was a flattering comment. Sour?

"Come in so we can get this over with."

"What a lovely welcome."

The next snide comment died in her throat. Seeing the gleaming dark hardwood floors, beige couches arranged around the fireplace and a huge decorated tree stole her ability to talk. Spence lived in the house she dreamed of owning. Simple lines, open floor plan, comfortable furniture, and a touch of homey warmth.

"Do you have a girlfriend?"

He ran into one of the sofas on the way to the kitchen. "What?"

"This place."

He rubbed his upper thigh. "What's wrong with it?"

"Nothing."

He slipped behind the counter and grabbed two wine-glasses from a cabinet to his left. "Have you been out walking in the cold again?"

"I used a car this time."

"Good call."

"You live alone?" she asked, tying to fit all the pieces she knew about him with the inviting family room in front of her.

He set the glasses down with a *clank* on the marble kitchen countertop. "Nat, with the courthouse gossip, you'd know if I were married, engaged, or dating anyone seriously."

"Sure. Right."

"Hungry?"

Always. Something in addition to the crackling fire smelled fabulous. She dropped her winter coat on his love seat and followed him back to the breakfast bar. "What do you have?"

"I ordered pizza."

Pizza. Her downfall. The combination of cheese and dough zoomed right to her thighs and took up perpetual residence. Even forty-five pounds later, the evidence of her love of carbohydrates remained right there for anyone who saw her naked, which was just about no one unless that tape got out.

"I made a salad to go with it."

"You can cook?"

"Yeah, but with the time crunch all I did was open a bag, pour it in a bowl and add dressing. It's not exactly fine dining."

"That's more skill than most."

"Now you're frowning." The smile on Spence's face suggested that he found her discomfort amusing.

Good one of them found the situation funny. "I'm not hungry."

"We're not talking unless you eat."

"Excuse me?"

"Sue's right. You're too thin." He popped the top off a bottle of red wine.

Now, there was a phrase she'd never heard in connection with her own body until today. Now she had heard it twice. "I'm about ten pounds overweight."

"Says who?"

Charlie. Her doctor. Every designer who mocked her by making slim-fit and one-size-fits-all clothing. "Me."

"That's ridiculous."

She snorted.

"What?" He slid a glass in her direction.

"How many bigger women have you dated?"

"How did you losing weight become an indictment of me?" he asked.

The one thing she could not tolerate was how people said weight did not matter, then lived their lives as if it did. "Exactly zero, I bet. No woman over a size four, would be my guess."

"I don't know a thing about women's sizes except that you're not a bigger woman."

"Well, I'm not small."

He put down his glass. "How the hell did we get on this subject?"

"You and your pizza."

"You're anti-pizza?"

"It's fattening."

"Everything is if you eat a pile of it."

Now he sounded like a weight-loss mantra from one of her old classes. "I'm here about your plan to lift the video from Charlie's house."

He came out of the kitchen area and joined her at the breakfast bar. "Did Charlie say something about you being too big?"

"This isn't—"

Spence slapped his palm against the bar and leaned in close. "So, that's a yes."

"Charlie wasn't wrong." He just didn't have to mention her negatives every five seconds.

"The man treated you like shit."

"He was a little insensitive." And how did she end up defending Charlie? This happened every single time someone made a comment. She jumped in and rushed to explain Charlie's actions as if that was her job or goal in life.

Defending the indefensible and the hurtful. That summed up the last month of her relationship with Charlie.

"I know all about it, Natalie."

"What?"

"I overheard."

No, no, no. Dread filled her stomach. "What?"

"The things he said to you."

This could not be happening. "Charlie didn't say anything bad."

"He just never bothered to say anything positive or supportive or flattering."

The memories rushed back over her. Charlie had told her to "keep up the good work" when she started to lose weight. Then he found a chart and pointed out what her weight should be and that she needed to work harder. When she tried to make him understand how hurtful his words were, he laughed off her concerns.

Spence leaned down on his elbow. "He let you believe you were lucky to have him. Convinced you how you did not deserve better treatment."

"How did you hear that?"

Spence's gaze left hers. "It doesn't matter."

"It certainly does."

Spence stayed quiet as if some battle was playing out in his mind. Finally, he blew out a breath. "Look, Charlie didn't just say those things to you, Nat. He made small comments, said shit around the office all the time. Sue and I heard all about how you were lucky he wasn't the kind of guy who cared about weight. When, of course, he was."

A flash of dizziness threatened Natalie. She wanted to be strong, act like the hateful words did not matter, but she was too busy trying not to throw up, to guard her reactions.

Spence brushed his knuckle under her chin in a gentle touch. His dark eyes glistened. Christmas music played in the background. Two more seconds and she'd make an ass of herself and throw her body into his arms while she mourned the death of her self-esteem.

"We should work on our plan," she said as she broke away from his touch and the strange spell his words wove around her.

Detaching emotionally was not enough. She had to move. Put up a barrier of ten feet between them, so she grabbed her glass and walked over to the tree. The white lights glowed, making the gold balls shine and twinkle.

"My sister," Spence said from behind her.

"What?" Nat turned around in time to watch Spence breach her ten-feet rule. He had gotten to within three.

"My sister and her kids came over and helped with the tree."

"You have a sister?"

"Two." His mouth kicked up in a smile. "And parents."

"Oh." Of course that made sense on some level.

"You think I fell to Earth in a spaceship?"

"Kind of." The explanation would answer some of her questions about him.

"I arrived the usual way. If you don't believe me, ask my mom. She has some long, dramatic story about being in labor for twenty hours."

From his smile Nat knew the story was one of those passed down at family gatherings and every birthday party since he was born. She envied him. As the only child of a working mom, Natalie's memories of family times were few. Her mom did the best she could, when she was around, which was never.

Which began Nat's lifelong love of food. She understood the origins of her emotional eating. Eating to fight off loneliness and insecurity. That did not mean she had conquered the problem.

"You never talk about family," she said.

"Do we ever talk about personal things? Up until now, I mean."

She shrugged. "I guess not."

And why did that feel like a loss? With Charlie, talk turned to work and football. A relaxing evening at home by the fire was not his thing. He liked beer and parties and eating and all the things Nat tried to make low priorities in her life.

"I never think of you as a family man," she said.

"Too busy thinking of me as a parasite, huh?"

"I'm sorry about that." She dragged her finger along the rim of her glass.

"Sorry, or sorry I keep bringing it up?"

"Yeah, mostly that second one." She laughed then. She had not laughed in quite some time, so it felt good. "But, I do apologize for insulting you."

"All's forgiven." He held out his hand as if to shake on it.

The innocent gesture should not have fazed her. A simple agreement between business professionals and then they could move on. Happened every day in the courthouse. So why did the idea of touching him make her stomach jump around and her muscles feel heavy?

"Maybe all's not forgiven, then?" He continued to hold out his hand.

"Of course it is." Against every nerve in her body screaming for her to run, she slipped her palm against his.

One minute he stood there smiling with her hand folded in his, the next the corners of his mouth fell into a flat line.

"What's wrong?" she asked, but she knew.

The lights, the music, the warmth of the fire. Something strange zinged around the room. Something dangerous . . . and dumb.

She swallowed. "We should—"

He used his hold on her hand to pull her close. All that passed between them was a touch of their fingers. All that separated them was a few inches of heated air.

"I'm about to do something crazy," he said in a deep, husky voice that sounded more excited than nuts.

"What?" But she knew. All women instinctively knew when this moment arrived.

He tucked her hand against his stomach and held it there with his. "This."

His head ducked and his lips met hers. The kiss lasted about a second. A warm mouth and the punch of his aftershave mixed, then he lifted his head.

"I don't think—"

When his mouth dipped again, he caught her in mid-sentence. This time the kiss was not short or sweet. His lips were soft and smooth. The kiss skipped over light to burn deep. It caressed and inflamed, setting off a tiny explosion behind her eyes.

She fought to keep her eyes open. To watch him and stay detached. That was the theory. The reality included a whimper that turned to a groan.

So much for staying tough and uninterested.

Just when she gave in and pressed her open hand against his sweater and grabbed a fistful of material, he broke off the kiss. From his wide-eyed expression, she knew he was as surprised as she was.

She felt something else. Doubt and anger at herself and him. The guy barely acknowledged her except to disagree with her in the courtroom, and now he had his mouth all over her. Amazing what losing a few pounds did for a woman.

And how sexually interesting she became the minute she broke up with Charlie, the guy with whom Spence just so happened to be engaged in battle. Having anything to do with Charlie was bad enough. Being a pawn in his testosterone battle with Spence did not interest her at all.

"How much did you drink at the courthouse holiday party?" she asked in a half-hearted attempt to make a joke.

"Sorry."

Not the response she expected. "For the kiss?"

"For not having you put down the wine first."

"Why?"

"You spilled it all over the tree."

6

Spence watched the red liquid drip off the branches and land in dots on his shiny hardwood floor. The sight scared Nat enough that she dropped her glass. The shattering crash followed by flying glass made them both jump.

"Oh, my God!" She fell to her knees, crunching pieces beneath her.

"Don't do that."

"I'm so sorry." She started picking up the tiny shards of glass.

"It was an accident." He lifted her up by the elbow to keep the injuries to a minimum. He could clean up red wine. He did not want to clean up blood.

"If you have a mop, I can get that up."

She acted as if no one ever broke a glass in his house before. His nephews broke something on every visit. No big deal. "You can sit down."

"Spence—"

"Sit." He took her by the shoulders and plopped her on the couch. "Do not move until I make sure the glass is gone."

"I can help."

"No."

He jogged into the kitchen and picked up some towels and

a small vacuum. By the time he got back to the tree, she was back on her knees separating pieces of broken glass from the tree branches.

"You don't listen all that well, do you?"

"And you don't accept help, so we're even."

He resigned to having assistance. She mopped. He vacuumed. They had the mess cleaned up in a few minutes.

He started to stand up until he noticed she'd remained on the floor, staring up at the tree.

"You okay?" he asked.

"Why did you kiss me?"

Because the need swamped him. Because he wanted to taste her. Because for that one second he did not want to do what was right or what was expected.

But none of that excused his actions. She just recently broke up with Charlie. She was trying to find her feet again after a bad relationship. And, she needed his help. In the history of bad-guy moves, the kiss ranked right up there.

"I'm sorry." he said.

She finally looked at him. Light from the tree bounced off her big green eyes, making them sparkle. Her clear skin took on a pink hue in the firelight. He'd always described her as cute. In that moment, he saw her as beautiful.

"You didn't answer my question, Spence."

He'd lost track of what he was supposed to answer. "I thought you were being rhetorical."

"I asked why."

And from the stern look on her face he figured she was determined to get a real response. So, he gave her one. "I wanted to."

"You never have before."

"You were taken before."

She frowned and looked away. "Sounds like an excuse to me."

It was. A rotten one, too.

"Let me ask you something else."

He was tempted to say no. "Shoot."

"Why did you stop?"

She had him stumped there. He could blame the wine, the bad work party from earlier, or being hungry. But none of those captured the truth. He'd stopped because he thought he should.

"I wasn't thinking," he said because the statement included a kernel of truth.

"Since when did kissing and thinking become linked?"

"Okay. If you must know, I shouldn't have kissed you. When I remembered that fact, I stopped."

"If I didn't know better, counselor, I'd say you were trying to protect me." Amusement filtered beneath her words.

"That's not like me."

She tipped her head to the side and shot him the sweetest smile he had ever seen. "I used to think so."

"A lot of people actually like me, you know."

"Women."

"Women being people, they are included in that group, yes." He went from crouching to sitting on the floor next to her. "Some even think I'm a decent guy."

"Just a bit cool when it comes to your clients' personal lives."

This was not the first time she'd issued that complaint about him. She'd whined about him being detached and aloof. "It's my job to represent them, not love them. You can get too close."

"How close is too close?"

"Depends."

"On what?" She scooted over until her shoulder touched his.

The temperature in the room skyrocketed and took his internal temperature along with it. Simple words, but he knew she was asking something quite complex. "I'm not sure yet."

He leaned back against the sofa and shifted her body until it rested against his. Her shoulder touching his chest. Her hair brushing across his cheek. He could smell her, feel her. Hell, if he licked his lips, he could taste her.

The whole situation was nuts. Just a few days ago she was yelling at him for not caring enough about his clients, and then came the tape and now this.

"Did you think of a plan yet?"

And with that, she broke the mood.

He laughed, full and deep until he could not laugh anymore. Laughed until he coughed. "Unbelievable."

She sat up and reached around to tap on his back. "You okay there, sport?"

"You have a one-track mind."

"I have a problem that needs to be solved. You said you'd help."

"And I will."

"When?"

"How do you know I'm not working on a plan as we sit here?"

She looked up at him with a mixture of hope and surprise. "Are you?"

"No." Not even close.

She shoved against his shoulder. "Spence, I—"

"Need this done yesterday. Yeah, I know."

"No, not that."

"What?"

"The kiss."

She seemed determined to dissect and analyze what was, to him, a natural move. "It wasn't a big deal, Nat."

Her face fell. "Oh."

When he saw her reaction, he knew he had to fix the hasty comment. "That came out wrong." Really dead-ass wrong.

"No, I understand." She moved away from him. A subtle shift but one that separated them. "I do."

"You clearly don't."

"It was a moment."

"That's true."

"Nothing big." She waved her hand in the air.

He saw the nervous gesture for what it was—a poor attempt to hide her discomfort. He'd done this to her. She was so tough in so many ways that he forgot to weigh his words when it came to personal matters.

"And you didn't mean for it to happen," she said as she slid her butt across the floor and a few more inches away from him. If she kept this up she'd be sitting outside.

"Oh, I meant it."

She stilled. No scooting or running or pretending to fidget as she shimmied away from him.

He took advantage of her temporary stupor and the accompanying quiet to make another move. He slipped his finger through her belt loop and pulled her back against him again.

"Spence!"

"It was not a pity kiss or a strange case of curiosity." His mouth waited right above hers. "Understand?"

"What was it, then?"

"Need. Desire. Your normal sexual attraction stuff."

"But you—"

"Never made a move on you before. Yeah, I know. I'm a dumb-ass." The woman refused to recognize her positive qualities or give him any credit for noticing them. Breaking through the doubt would be a challenge.

"I won't argue with that, but I was going to say that you don't even like me."

"Let me show you something."

He did not wait for her agreement. He swooped in. With his lips over hers, he treated them both to a deep, inviting kiss. He lingered over her mouth, tasting every plump inch. Coaxing until she kissed him back with equal enthusiasm.

Slow and deliberate, he lowered her until her back touched the floor and his arms surrounded her. His fingertips caressed her cheek as his lips tasted her soft skin. Never breaking contact, his mouth hovered over hers, deepening his touch with each kiss.

When he lifted his head, her lips were puffy and red and her eyes soft and loving. "Hi."

"Hi," she said with a rough, seductive voice.

"Now do you believe I like you?"

She treated him to one of her sly smiles. "I'm starting to."

"Are your ready to try the pizza?" He continued to hold her. He realized he would be happy to hold her all evening.

"Depends."

"On the toppings?"

"On whether you're going to tell me how you plan to steal the tape back?"

"Not yet." He placed a quick, hard kiss on her mouth. "But I am going to eat something."

Her shoulders fell. "That's it?"

He sat back up and brought her with him. "Not just food. I'll probably have some more wine, too."

"You talk about desire and kiss me, and now you're ready to eat?"

"I'm a complex guy."

"And a hungry one, apparently."

"Now you're getting it."

7

Natalie made it the whole way to three o'clock the next day before seeing Spence. Not that she'd planned the time away or that he had the decency to stay out of her head in the interim. Oh, no. By the time she'd left his house the evening before, she had eaten a piece of pizza and two bowls of salad and not heard one word about the tape.

But she did get two more kisses. One quick and sweet, while she put her dishes in the sink. Another long and lingering after he walked her to her car and clicked her seat belt closed.

He had her hot and hanging on the edge. No man had ever bothered her this way. *This* man should not have any effect on her. He was way out of her league. Like, in a different ball park on another planet.

Nothing from their past suggested an attraction. If he wanted a conquest or subconscious shot at Charlie, he could look somewhere else.

But none of that explained why she stood outside his office door at two-fifty-nine with a gift in one hand, and a question on her tongue. The confusing feelings for him bouncing around inside her did not bode well either.

"Go on inside." Sue sat at her desk outside Spence's office and made a shooing motion with her fingers.

"The door's closed."

"That because of Charlie and his . . . well, forget that. Spence won't mind seeing you."

Charlie. Nat blamed Charlie for all of this. Without dating him, without that damned tape, she would not have come to Spence. They would have continued with their antagonistic, reluctant-respect-type of relationship but never ventured into kissing. Then she would be able to think of something other than kissing Spence. An impossible thing to accomplish at the moment.

"I can come back later," Nat said.

"Nonsense." Sue hit the phone intercom. "Boss? Natalie is here for you."

Sue sent her a smug smile when Spence said to send her in. "See?"

"We don't even like each other, you know." Nat said the words just to make sure Sue did not get the wrong idea.

"Uh-huh."

"Really."

Sue stared at the gift in Nat's hands. "Sure looks like you feel something other than dislike for each other."

"We're working on a project."

"Then get inside and get to it." Sue went back to staring at her computer screen.

Nat refused to explain it all again. It would not help anyway. Sue would think whatever she wanted to think, just like the clerks at that courthouse holiday party had thought whatever they'd wanted—which was that Nat had ventured a bit too close to Spence. She'd gotten the hint from the scowls this morning and the fact that two of the reports she'd filed were now missing somewhere in the loose papers of the courthouse.

"He's waiting," Sue mumbled without looking away from the screen.

"Stop pushing me."

"Just doing my job. And, no need to knock. He knows you're coming."

Despite Sue's comment, Nat tapped once on the door before opening it. Spence sat at his desk, smiling and watching the door. Dressed in his dark suit and bright red Christmas tie, he looked anything but serious. And a bit too delicious for her to ignore.

She walked up to his desk and dumped the wrapped box on it. "Here."

"What's this?"

"A Christmas gift."

"Christmas is next week."

She wondered if it would kill the holiday mood to slap that silly grin right off his face. "I'm early. Sue me."

"And a bit grumpy, I see."

A state that was totally his fault. A bit of touching and kissing and he had her insides all balled up and twisted.

"I was going to give it to you next week, but I needed something to lighten your mood now." A bribe of sorts.

"You have my attention." He fingered the big white bow on the red package. "Because?"

"A couple of reasons."

"Give me one."

She unloaded the worst. "I had to hit the Cassidy kid with a VOP this morning."

Spence's hand froze on top of the package. "You violated his probation the week before Christmas?"

And she felt like crap about the situation. "I didn't have a choice. He got caught with drugs again."

"Damn it, Nat. The kid's home life is a mess. Couldn't you give him a break? Maybe issue a warning or come up with something less severe?"

He could not have surprised her more if he'd jumped out the window and tried to fly. "Since when do you get all emotional about a client's personal situation?"

"That's not fair."

"Spence, I've asked you a hundred times to help with clients before they go too far and land in trouble a second, third, or even fourth time. You always tell me that they're grown-ups and have made their choices. That we can't hold their hands forever."

"This is different. Cassidy is a kid with an addiction problem."

"Which is why he'll be back in a live-in program before he loses complete control. Christmas or not, I had no choice." Which was the truth. She debated putting off the inevitable, but the boy needed help fast.

Spence acted as if he was going to say something. Instead, he closed his mouth and sat back in his chair. For what felt like hours, he sat in silence.

"Fine," he finally said, through clenched teeth.

"Spence—"

"Let me see the gift." He grabbed the package and tore off the bow.

"Good thing it's not alive."

"Sorry." He gentled his touch.

He got the paper off and flipped open the top of the box to lift out a wineglass.

"There are four. Didn't seem right to only buy one since I couldn't find a match to the one I broke."

"You didn't have to replace the glass."

"I wanted to."

"Well, thank you." His smile returned, a bit strained but still there.

"You're welcome."

She nibbled on her bottom lip as an awkward quiet filled the room. She refused to ask again. She was standing there. He should just fess up about whatever plan he'd concocted for stealing the tape without her having to beg.

"Well?" he asked.

"What?"

"You haven't asked me about the tape in the almost ten minutes since you've been in my office. That could be a record."

She flattened her palms against his desk. "I can be patient."

"That is not my experience."

"Maybe I was too busy being impressed with your show of compassion for Joe Cassidy."

"Whatever you say."

"See, I knew it. You care even though you pretend you don't." She clapped her hands in triumph. "You know what that makes you?"

"A girl?"

"I'm going to pretend I didn't hear that sexist remark."

"I can talk louder," he said.

So could she. "It makes you a decent guy."

He screwed up his face in a look of horror. "That's a shitty thing to say."

"What are you talking about?"

"Decent guys never get chicks."

"Sorry to ruin your future chick-chasing plans, but it's true."

"Well, hold onto that thought." He moved the box with the glasses to the credenza behind his desk. "You may not think I'm such a great guy in a second."

Now she knew why he'd taken the box out of her reach. So she could not use the glass as a weapon. "You're not going to help me with the tape."

"What?" Confusion crossed his face. "Of course I am. I promised."

Relief raced through her with a powerful push. "So?"

"I've decided what I want in return for my help."

Time to sit down. She dreaded this moment. "My gratitude?"

"I was thinking of something more long-term and memorable."

"I'm ready."

"The tape."

"You want my tape?" The idea appalled her. She wanted the tape ripped into little pieces and destroyed by fire.

"Nope."

The relief did not come back but she no longer wanted to push him out the window. "Then what?"

"I want to see what's on the tape."

Wasn't that what she'd just said? "I don't understand."

"A private showing."

"You'd better be kidding."

"You were willing to do . . . whatever . . . for Charlie. What I want is to see you."

"You're about to see my fist. Will that satisfy you?"

"What's on the tape?"

"Spence, we've been through this."

"You expect me to put my safety and ethics on the line. The least you can do is answer a clear-cut question about the tape's contents."

"Okay. Me."

"You told me that part already."

And she did not want to say anything more, but his argument made sense. She was asking a lot without providing any information. It was just so embarrassing. So stupid.

"Why in the world are you asking for this?" she asked.

"Because I want you. I thought I'd made that clear last night."

In her view, everything had gotten very muddy last night. "No."

"We kissed. You spilled wine. Any of this ringing a bell?"

"I'm not part of the deal."

"This is separate." He shrugged. "Sort of."

"No, this is about getting one up on Charlie." The realization made her both furious and sad. She'd started opening up, seeing Spence in another way, and the door clamped shut. She felt the loss down to her feet.

"This doesn't have anything to do with Charlie." Spence got up from his chair.

She was faster. She made it to the door before he could catch her. "Come up with another form of payment."

"You're taking this the wrong way."

She held onto the doorknob as if it were the only thing holding her upright. "There isn't a good way to take it. I'm desperate, but I have my limits. The main one is that you leave me out of your office squabbles."

Nat opened the door and rushed past Sue's desk. She tried to stay calm, but she ended up running to the elevator. She did not want to be friendly or answer questions or engage in mindless chitchat.

She felt Sue watching and heard Spence's door opening. All Nat wanted was to be on the elevator and out of the building. She did not see anything or notice anyone.

Until she stepped in the car and walked right into Charlie.

8

Spence stepped out of his office and faced off with Sue. "Where did Natalie go?"

"She looked upset," Sue said in an accusing tone.

"She's fine."

Sue tucked a pen behind her ear. "What did you do to her?"

"Nothing."

"*Hmpf.* Ever think that could be the problem?"

He did not have the time to debate his relationship with Nat. He had done enough to screw that up on his own. He wanted to use the tape to show her that her body was beautiful and not something to hide or be ashamed of. Instead, he'd sounded like a letch and had scared her off. Worse, he'd pissed her off.

"Did she take the elevator?" he asked.

"Yes."

Spence took off in the direction of the elevator bank.

"Charlie is with her," Sue called after him.

Spence stopped in mid-stride and turned around. "She left with Charlie?"

The idea made him furious and sort of sick inside. Not being

260 / *HelenKay Dimon*

with him was bad enough; going back to Charlie and his indifferent treatment was worse.

"That's not what I said." Sue took her time making her point.

"What did you say, then?" He glanced at the elevator. "And make it quick before I miss her."

"She got on."

"Yeah? And?"

"Charlie was in there." Sue lowered her glasses to look at Spence straight on. "Now they're in there together."

"I'll take the stairs."

"Happy to hear you're finally talking sense."

"I was going to call you today," Charlie said.

As if she needed another reason to disconnect her telephone. "I'm not there."

"Where?"

"Wherever you were calling."

Nat moved to the very front of the glass-walled car and kept her back to Charlie. Being in the confined space with him raised every defensive cell in her body—put them on notice to get ready to fight.

"You visiting Spence again?"

"It's a case, Charlie."

"Sure." Charlie nodded.

"Believe whatever you want."

"Did he invite you there for a meeting? Tell you he had some information for you? That's how he works, you know."

"You've got this all wrong."

"He starts out subtle. Reels you in. I've seen it a million times. He's smooth, I'll give him that. Women looking for a bit of attention fall fast."

Nat dissected his words. Just last week, the suggestion of her being lonely and desperate would have rung true. She would have taken his comment as a shot at her. Being away from those biting remarks had dulled their impact. She did not understand

Spence's motives, but she knew she was more to him than an ego stroke.

"Don't kick yourself. All types of women fall for Spence's lines. It was inevitable, what with everything going on, that you would take his flirting too personally," Charlie said.

She glanced up and saw Charlie's reflection in the glass. Anyone else would come off as relaxed, slouching against the back wall with his arms folded across his chest. Charlie looked ready to pounce.

"He uses clients as an aphrodisiac. Talks about them, plants the seed about what a good guy he is, then moves in." Charlie continued to press his case.

She knew from experience Spence did not rely on those tricks. The man could seduce and kiss. No need for subterfuge there. So she let Charlie talk. Let him think he was scoring points. When, in reality, he just dug the hole deeper.

She had to fight off the urge to laugh, or at the very least, smile. For once, Charlie's words bounced right off her. The syllables did not chip away at her self-esteem or make her feel worthless like they had in the past.

And it felt great. The progress empowered her, flooded her with a sense of security and self-respect. For the first in a long time, she did not spend every minute with Charlie thinking about her weight or how she looked in an outfit or be on guard about what he might say.

"It's scam, but it works for him." Charlie chuckled as he warmed up to his lame story. "The ladies can't get enough."

Two weeks ago she would have bought into Charlie's talk. She'd let him do her thinking and believed him when he insinuated she had all these failings that needed fixing.

Those days were gone.

She finally understood that Charlie's big talk and subtle slaps had more to do with how he felt about himself than about other people. "Why do you hate Spence so much?"

"I don't."

"You have a vendetta."

"He's not who you think he is." Charlie pushed away from the wall and stood right behind her. His gaze traveled along her neckline and his finger followed.

She pulled away from his touch. "Charlie. Don't."

"You're not falling for his lines, are you? You're smarter than that."

All of a sudden she was smart? Interesting. A few more minutes of this and Charlie might actually call her pretty. More than likely he would if he thought he had to in order to win his point.

"Have I told you how good you look these days?"

She glanced up at the floor indicator panel and saw she only had two more to go. "Almost never."

"Give me another chance, honey."

He dropped a kiss on her neck. She shivered, but not from excitement like she did with Spence. No, this was from distaste.

She'd shared something with Charlie once. Something unhealthy. She did not want to go there again.

"It's over."

"It doesn't have to be. We could spend a few nights together. See where we go and how we feel."

He wrapped his arms around her waist just as the bell chimed for the ground floor. She tried to step out, but he put his foot in the opening and held her tight.

"Does Spence make you feel like this?"

She tried to pry Charlie's fingers off her. "Let me go."

"Babe, he's using you to get to me."

Charlie'd voiced her biggest fear. Her hidden worry. "Spence is a friend."

"You don't want him like you want me." Charlie kissed her ear, then her neck.

"Stop." She tugged on his arms, but he would not budge.

"Relax, babe."

Panic filled her. Deep down she knew Charlie would not physically hurt her or force her. That if she screamed, the guys at the security desk would come running. But, for the first time, she did not want to be rescued. She wanted to fight back and take a stand. To show him she was good for something other than making him happy.

She tramped down on the inside of his shin.

Charlie let out a howl just as Spence came around the corner. Even out of breath and doubled over, Spence managed to outshine Charlie.

"You okay?" Spence asked, through sharp breaths.

"I am." She sidestepped Charlie as he jumped around the inside of the car, swearing his head off.

"Everything's fine," Spence shouted to the security guards on their way to the elevators as he waved them off.

"It is now," she mumbled, feeling very satisfied.

"Did he hurt you?"

Yeah, over and over again. "Not this time."

"Her? The bitch kicked me." Charlie's incredulous yell echoed in the lobby.

Spence took a threatening step forward. "I told you never to talk about her that way again."

"Spence, don't." She held onto his arm. "He's not worth it."

Charlie stopped shouting long enough to point fingers. "We were making out, then she hauled off and kicked me."

"We were not." The idea of being with Charlie again repulsed her.

"That's it." Spence took one step, and with one hit to the jaw, knocked Charlie to the floor.

Charlie squealed and grabbed his face. "What the hell was that?"

"An early Christmas present for Natalie."

Spence leaned into the elevator car and hit the button for the fourteenth floor. "Go recuperate in your office."

"You'll pay for this."

The door shut on Charlie's threat.

"I can't believe you hit him." Nat shook her head to loosen the shock holding her brain. "He is going to be furious."

"Nothing new there."

"He'll use this against you in the partnership dissolution. He may even bring charges." The possibilities were endless and awful.

"I don't care."

"Spence, this is serious."

He acted as if he could not hear her. "Did he touch you?"

"I'm fine." She grabbed Spence's arm when he punched the up button on the elevator panel. "And you're not going after him."

"It's my office. I have to go back sometime."

She said the first thing that popped into her head. The one thing she wanted but feared the most. "Come home with me instead."

He turned around. The red-hot anger seeped from his face as he stood there. "Nat, you don't owe me anything."

"It's my turn to make dinner."

"Are you sure?"

"Definitely."

He smiled. "I guess pizza's off the menu."

"So are donuts, french fries and everything tasty. You'll live."

"I'll take what I can get."

9

Spence tried not to touch Nat. On the drive over, on the elevator ride up to her apartment, all he wanted to do was put his hands all over her. So he held them behind his back. He was not an animal. He could refrain from groping her in public. Could wait ten seconds to make sure they both wanted the same thing.

Seeing Charlie with her had sent a rush of jealousy racing through him. An overreaction, Spence knew. After all, Nat had injured the guy. She clearly did not want Charlie anymore. Spence's mind knew all that. The other parts of him were not so forgiving.

Landing that punch helped, but the adrenaline rush would not die off. She had to fight Charlie off on her own, and Spence hated that fact.

"Here it is." Nat opened the door to her apartment and flicked on the light.

The small room reminded him of her. Warm and light. Books packed the shelves and a small crooked Christmas tree graced the corner.

The smell of her morning coffee lingered in the room. So

did the signs of her gift wrapping. He walked over and fingered the white ribbon that matched the one on his present.

"Let me get that." She grabbed the remnants out of his hand as she whipped around the room cleaning up and straightening everything.

"Natalie?"

"Yeah?" She turned to him with an armload full of unfolded sweaters, a glass, and a garbage bag.

"Put all of that down."

"I was just—"

He lifted the glass from her hand and put it on the kitchen counter. After that came the sweater, a shirt, and the bag of leftover wrappings. He kept unloading until her arms were empty and open.

"Your house is fine," he said.

"It's small."

Funny how she could recognize the apartment as small but still saw herself as this huge giant of a woman. "It's you."

"Messy?"

"Comfortable."

He took advantage of her empty arms and filled them with his body. His hands slipped around her waist like they belonged there. Feeling her fingers brush against his shirt and tangle in his buttons ignited a brushfire in his nerve endings.

Stepping up close, being wrapped in her arms, he could see the sparkle in her green eyes. Smell the scent of her skin. Watch her breath catch in her throat as she made eye contact and saw the determination in his face.

"Is this where you collect on my part of the tape deal?" she asked, in a small voice.

Her insecurity kept him from losing his temper. "This is the part where we forget about Charlie and the damned tape and everything but us."

"We should talk about this."

"No."

"No?"

He decided to take control until she was ready to believe she could be in charge. "Do you want me, Natalie?"

"Yes." No waffling. Just the truth delivered with bright red cheeks and shiny eyes.

"I want you, too."

"I'm not your type."

She refused to see their attraction as a mutual thing. "You're a woman."

"Last I checked."

He trailed his hands down her back until they landed on her backside. He squeezed.

"Spence!"

"From what I can feel, the answer is yes. You're all woman."

"But you like—"

He refused to hear another denial. "How about you stop telling me what I want and let me show you instead?"

"I'm just trying to warn you."

He hated to ask but wanted to know. "About what?"

"That I'm not the same as the other women you've been with."

"That's true."

Her head shot up but her mouth remained closed. For once.

"You're bossy, sexy as hell, and too stubborn to realize it."

"I was talking about the stretch marks and the extra ten pounds."

She was determined to ruin the mood. To push him away before he could reject her. He saw the tactic and decided to ignore it.

"Stop." He covered her mouth with his fingers. "Let me judge what I like and don't like in a woman."

"That's kind of what I'm afraid of," she mumbled around his hand.

Time for a grand gesture. He had not carried a woman in a long time. It was one of those moves best reserved for younger men with better backs. But if ever a woman needed a man to carry her around for a few seconds, it was Natalie.

He slipped his arm under her knees and put the other behind her back.

Her panic set in immediately. "What are you doing?"

"Taking you to bed."

"Spence, don't. You'll hurt yourself."

He lifted her into his arms without even a groan. "Which way?"

"This is ridiculous."

"I'll stand here all night if I need to."

"You'll need traction." When he continued to stand there, she rolled her eyes and pointed to the small hallway next to the kitchen. "There."

The apartment was small enough that he made the journey to the bedroom in about five steps. Stepping over the threshold he hit the wall switch with his elbow and saw exactly what he had fantasized for the last two nights—a bed. A queen-size bed filled with pillows and puffy bedding and all he wanted to do was throw her on top of it.

A wild need clawed at his insides. She deserved gentle. He hoped he could beat back the need coursing through him long enough to give it to her.

He set her on the bed and followed her down until he lay over her. "You're beautiful."

"You're strong." She skimmed her hands over his shoulders.

"Why, thank you."

"You didn't even break a sweat."

"I'm sweating, believe me. Hot and sweating. But my state has nothing to do with carrying you. It has to do with wanting to get you naked, then get inside you."

"What's stopping you?"

The husky invitation set the need in his gut spinning. "Be sure."

Her fingers slipped beneath his tie. The silk scraped against his collar as she pulled it out and it landed on the floor. Then she went to work on his buttons.

He wanted to be smooth and careful for her, but she was making that damn difficult. Her hands were everywhere. Roaming and undressing, caressing the bare skin of his chest while her mouth sucked against his neck.

Screw going slow. They'd go slow the next time. This time they would go with fast and frenzied. Variety worked for him.

He captured her mouth in a searing kiss. Lips, tongue, mouth. They all melded together in an explosion of heat and desire until all he saw was her.

And her hands kept moving. When he lifted his head, he was naked to the waist and her hands rested on his belt.

"Two questions," he said, through rough breaths.

"Make it fast."

"I like the way you think." To prove his point, he kissed her again. "Condoms?"

"In the nightstand."

He refused to think about how the condoms were once purchased for Charlie and grabbed for the box. "I'll try to go slow and—"

"Don't."

"No?"

She opened the condom package and held one out to him. "I want you now."

"That's all I need to know."

With the green light on, his hands did some traveling of their own. He lifted the sweater up and over her head. Desperate to taste her bare skin, he took only a second to admire her lacy black bra before reaching around to unhook it.

Her breasts fell into his waiting hands. So smooth and soft, like the purest silk. As his gaze wandered, her hands jerked as if she intended to shield her body from him. He refused to give her the chance.

He lowered his head and took a tip in his mouth. Licking and sucking, he tasted her. He rolled his tongue over her nipple and felt it harden. Smoothed his fingers over the firm roundness of her breasts.

He pulled back to see the wetness from his mouth glisten on her pale skin. "How can you think your body is anything but perfect?"

She let out a nervous giggle. "I'm too—"

"Perfect."

His fingers found the waistband of her pants. He watched her eyes cloud over as he lowered the zipper and slipped his hand inside.

He brushed his hand against the fluff of hair he found there, but the brief touch was not enough. He wanted to plunge his fingers deep inside her wetness. Feel her from the inside while he readied her body and brought her to orgasm.

He tugged her pants off before she could protest or give him a lecture on belly fat or some other annoying thing. He saw pink skin and the most adorable little roundness over her stomach. She was not a twig or all bones. She was a voluptuous, stunning woman.

He kissed her belly to let her know he found it as beautiful as she was.

"Spence . . ."

Not yet. The woman needed to be cherished. To have a moment be all for her. He vowed to give her that and moved down the bed until he sat between her upraised thighs.

Her eyes grew wide just as he dipped his head to taste her. His fingers pressed inside. Her scent filled his head. His tongue pulsed with the memory of her.

"Yes," she groaned, as her legs shifted on the bed.

The idea of a slow tortuous tasting appealed to him, but his body burned for completion. In just a few days he'd gone from liking her to not being able to think about anything but her.

"Tell me you want me," he mumbled, against her heated flesh.

"God, yes." She grabbed the comforter in her fists.

When her wetness flooded his hand, he moved back up her body, stripping his pants off as he went. With a rip, he opened the condom, then slipped it on.

He balanced his body over hers, touching skin to skin until she opened her eyes and stared at him. "Do you still doubt how much I want you?"

One of her hands drifted over his chin before winding behind his neck to pull him down for a kiss that gave him his answer and blinded him to every intelligent thought. Then her other hand landed on his cock and he lost the power of speech. Those fingers curled around him, pressed just hard enough to force a harsh exhale from his lungs.

"Damn." He brushed his nose over hers before capturing her mouth in another kiss.

"Spence?" Her head tipped back against the bed.

"Yeah, baby?"

"Come inside me."

That's all he needed. No more foreplay or teasing. His body took over. His hips flexed as he pushed just inside her. The gentle suction of her body around his broke him. With a long firm push, he entered her without stopping or giving in to the friction of her body against his. He filled her.

Her back arched off the bed, pressing her breasts tight against his chest. The feel of her body naked under him, around him, clipped the last hold on his control. He pulled out, then pressed deep again. Over and over, faster and faster, he plunged and retreated until her head pressed deep into the pillow and her body moved with him.

When her breaths rushed out and her hands clenched as hard as her internal muscles, he knew she was as close to the edge as he was. The spiraling tightness kept coiling inside him, stiffening every muscle until the pleasure bordered on pain. Unable to hold back, he pressed harder, went deeper, and his body let go.

His last memory was of a shout ringing around the room. He just did not know if it was hers or his.

10

Nat tried to remember when she'd last had sex that good. If she ever had sex that good.

"I can't believe you think you're fat." Spence mumbled his thought into the pillow beside her head.

She refused to talk about that subject now. Not when her body still hummed from their lovemaking.

"I feel bad for all those courthouse clerks. Those poor women do not know what they're missing."

He opened one eye and stared at her. "Funny."

"Who's kidding?"

He turned and pushed up on one elbow. With an ease she did not expect, he leaned in and kissed her. Then he kissed her again.

Despite what they had just shared, the idea of giving him the full frontal view made her a bit uncomfortable. She grabbed the edge of the blanket and pulled it across her body. She hoped he missed the action.

"Still shy?" he asked.

Nothing got by this guy. "It's a hard habit to break."

"I've been inside you and touched you all over. You really think a stretch mark is going to turn me off?"

"Yes." And she did.

"I am not as shallow as you think." He traced his fingertip over her lips. "I'm also not the emotionless parasite you make me out to be in your head."

Guilt washed over her. "Haven't I apologized for that?"

"A few times."

"Then can we forget it?"

"I have my reasons, you know."

The quick change of conversation threw her for a second. "For?"

"For how I conduct my cases. I used to get involved. Brought all of my clients' worries and concerns home with me. I spent hours trying to change their lives and ignored my own."

"Which explains why you're still single." She knew there had to be a reason.

"I thought I was doing something good."

She sensed a terrible story on the horizon. To encourage him to tell it, to get it out, she brushed the back of her hand against his bare chest. He grabbed on like it was a lifeline.

He lifted her palm to his mouth for a kiss. The gentle touch tickled and comforted her.

"I was assigned to this client who smacked his wife around. A guy who functioned at work, coached his kids' teams, and seemed like a good guy."

"I guess he wasn't."

"It happened years ago." Spence pressed her hand against his chest. "He would apologize. Went into an anger management program. We talked and talked about how he could make it up to his wife and be a better man."

"I'm not sure he could do either, but it was good of you to try."

Spence continued as if lost in the need to get the poison out of his system. "When he got out of the program, he violated the protection order. Went to her house and killed her."

Shock rumbled through her. She held the blanket to her

chest, but her focus stayed on Spence. It was her heart that ached for the woman and for Spence. "That's awful."

"The experience shaped me. Changed the way I practice. I learned not to make friends with clients. I represent them, give them advice, and refuse to live their lives." He shifted until he leaned against the headboard. "The feelings are there, Nat. I just have to handle these matters in a certain way if I want to survive."

How did she ever think of him as emotionless? He was a kind and decent man. He had shared a private piece of his world with her.

She wanted to give him back the same. She rested her head on his shoulder. Not seeing his face might make the telling of the story a bit easier.

"I made the tape for Charlie, but also for me."

Spence's hold tightened on her shoulder but he did not say anything.

"When you lose weight, you can't always see it. That's how it is for me. I see the same fat person I used to be in the mirror."

"Please don't call yourself that."

"Forty-five pounds has to show. I know that on an intellectual level."

"I guess that's something."

The next part was not as easy to tell. "Charlie wanted to make a tape. A sex tape."

Spence's body tensed. "I'm not sure I want to know this."

She did not want to tell the story any more than he wanted to hear it, but he deserved an explanation. He needed to understand who she was and why being with him was such a big deal for her.

Why she could not just be a means to an end in his fight with Charlie.

"I was too self-conscious. But, when I lost the weight, I thought, maybe."

"You don't have to tell me this. Honestly, I don't want to know all the details of your time with Charlie."

"I don't plan on going into detail on everything. Just this."

"He's not going to bother you again."

She heard anger in Spence's voice and hugged him closer. She appreciated the way out, but she could not take it. "I decided to try making a tape. I'd strip, try to be sexy—"

"You don't need to try. You're sexy just as you are."

"Uh-huh."

"It's natural for you . . . or do you need another demonstration?"

She poked him in the side. "I couldn't do what Charlie wanted but I thought I could make a gesture and maybe, just maybe, in the process, I'd be able to check it out and see if I noticed the weight loss."

"Which is why you were watching it."

"Yeah."

"That's better than the reasons I came up with."

"Which were?"

He laughed. "You don't want to know."

She loved the deep, rich sound of his voice. The eager touch of his hands. The way he listened and made her feel. There wasn't anything about Spence she disliked.

She knew she was falling in love with him. The thought should have sent her into a panic, made her feel awkward and exposed; but she experienced a different kind of emotion. A sort of strength that came from deep inside and spilled over into everything else.

That's why she had to be clear. She had to know.

She shifted around until she sat cross-legged, facing him. "I don't want to go back."

"To Charlie? You're not." Spence reached out and held her hand.

"To feeling the way I did with Charlie."

"Okay."

"With anyone."

Spence stopped smiling. "I'm not him, Nat."

She drew a design on the blanket with her finger as she worked up the courage to take the next step.

"What is it?" he asked, and then squeezed her hand in encouragement. "You can tell me."

"You only showed an interest in me after I lost the weight and after you and Charlie started fighting." She'd blurted it out in one fast sentence, but did not regret the words. They were true.

"That's not true."

"Come on, Spence. It's okay." It actually was. She understood physical attraction.

"How could that be okay with you?"

She skipped to the question she really wanted to ask. "What is this to you?"

"This?"

"Us."

He did not hesitate. "The start of something."

Falling for him jumped right to love with that answer. "I could gain it all back again. What then? What would you feel?"

"You're still stuck on your weight?" He dropped her hand. "Damn it, Nat. That was who you were."

"That's where you're wrong. It's part of me. And, if all of those pounds come back, all forty-five pounds or even more, what happens to your feelings, your attraction, then?"

"You still think I'm shallow. That I'll leave you for a thin woman."

She did not want to think it, but she did. "Can you blame me?"

"I blame Charlie."

"He did not force the food in my mouth."

"But he made you feel worthless." Spence got out of bed and tugged on his pants.

"And I let him."

"Look, I'm here for the long haul. I don't know how to prove that to you."

"Putting on your pants and acting as if you're about to leave is not the best way." He was taking the easy way out. Walking away and blaming her. Typical.

"I'm going, but I'll be back."

Sure he would. Two seconds after never, he'd walk back through her door and express his undying devotion. Right.

"Just go," she said.

He shrugged on his shirt. "I'll see you tomorrow."

"Uh-huh."

He leaned down and kissed her. "You want a Christmas miracle, I'll give you one. Your only job is to believe in me for two seconds."

"I do."

"No, honey. You don't. Not in me, or in yourself."

11

"What are you doing here?" Charlie opened the door to his condo but did not usher Spence inside.

"I need to talk with you."

Charlie pointed to his bruised jaw. "You can talk to my lawyer."

"We are lawyers, you dumb-ass."

"What do you want?" Charlie lifted his chin, then groaned in pain. "Shit, man. You got quite a punch."

"Think of how it would hurt if I hadn't raced down fourteen flights of stairs first."

Charlie hesitated for a second, then stepped back. "Come in."

Spence walked into the sterile black-and-white living room, and sat down on one of the leather chairs near the balcony doors. There he could see the condo from every angle. No tree. No decorations. No warmth. He could not imagine Natalie in the room for two seconds.

He also took a minute to check around for the tape or boxes of case files while they talked. Did not see those, either.

"You haven't been here in a while," Charlie said, as he

slouched down into the modern white couch and picked up the beer bottle in front of him.

"We haven't exactly been on friendly terms for months, now. Socializing was impossible. Probably always was." He always respected Charlie's legal skills. His people skills were another matter.

"Does Natalie know she's the reason for our partnership dissolution?"

They had fought this battle a hundred times. Spence tried one more time to explain. "She's not the reason. She was symbolic of our differences."

"Sounds like lawyer-speak to me."

"How about this: She was not the *only* reason." Spence realized that was the truth.

"Unless I'm remembering this wrong, and I'm not, you told me I treated her like shit and should let her go."

"I was right about that."

Charlie stared down at the top of his beer. "She left soon after."

"We have different ways of dealing with people. Different styles. The partnership wasn't working long before we disagreed about Natalie."

"We made money."

For a time, that was good enough. "We fought every day. There has to be something more to life than that. We both deserve to walk into work and want to be there."

"Is that why you're here now? To fight about work?"

"No." Spence tapped his fingers together. For once, he was at a loss for words. He was the guy who could stand in front of the jury and, off the top of his head, find the right phrase to make any point. When it came to Natalie, words failed him. It was as if words were not good enough.

Which was why he was here. To make a sacrifice. To show her that she deserved to be put first. That she mattered. That thin or chubby, he wanted to build a life with her. He was falling, and falling hard. If she did not give him a chance . . . well, he could not think of that possibility.

"I have a proposition." Spence glanced around one last time.

"I'm listening."

"I'll give you the perfect deal. One you will never get in court or from an arbitrator or from me again if I walk out that door without your agreement now."

"Why? You have the advantage in our dissolution, or so you keep telling. So, why negotiate now?"

"We're not negotiating."

"Excuse me?"

"I'm putting a one-time offer on the table."

Charlie did not move but his body held a new awareness. Charlie was a lot of things. A bad businessman was not one of them.

"What are the terms?" he asked.

"We both know you can't afford to buy me out." Spence held up his hand when Charlie started to object. "It's not a statement on your lawyering skills. I brought you on as a partner and I did that for a reason. But you haven't been practicing as long as I have."

"That just makes you older." Charlie chuckled at his joke.

Spence was not in the mood for humor. "I have more money and more clout. It's a fact."

"Not that I agree, but what kind of deal are we talking about here?"

"I'll sell you my interest in the condo suite for a steep discount. Instead of coming up with all of the money now to buy me out of the property, you can put up a small down payment and pay over time."

Charlie's eyes widened in surprise. "I get the office?"

"Yeah."

"Even though you had it before our partnership?"

That part stung a bit, but Natalie mattered more than a bunch of rooms. "That's the good part of the deal."

Charlie tried to hide his satisfaction but his eyes gave him away. "It's fair."

"Yeah, well, don't get too excited. It will be a bigger down payment than you want to pay. One that will hurt but be doable."

"I can work with that."

"And we'll divide the clients and split the accounts payable fifty-fifty, even though we haven't brought in money and clients on a fifty-fifty basis."

Charlie stared for a few seconds before speaking up. "Why are you doing this?"

Spence only had one answer to that: Because he was an idiot falling for a woman who did not trust him.

"I need something in return," Spence said.

"Name it."

"A look through the Watson case boxes. You have them here, right?"

The confusion on Charlie's face proved he had not stumbled across Nat's masterpiece. "Yeah, but why?"

"I'm looking for something."

"It's my case." Anger strained Charlie's voice.

Spence knew he had to defuse the situation or risk losing everything. "I don't want the appeal. The case is yours."

"Then what?"

"There's a tape in there."

"There're a bunch in there. Crime scene tapes and—"

"This tape is unrelated to the case."

"Huh?"

Nat would kill him, but there was no other way. Charlie was too curious to let the comment slide and Spence had no intention of stealing the damn thing. "You picked up one of Nat's tapes when you left her house. One she wants back."

"Which one?"

"I'll find it."

Charlie was smart enough to know this was important. To try to work an angle. "What the hell is on it?"

"It doesn't matter."

Charlie grinned. "Maybe it does."

Spence balled his hands into fists to keep from knocking Charlie on his ass a second time. "You don't get to look at the tape, keep a copy, or know anything about it."

"What's in it for me?"

Leave it to Charlie to look for an even better deal. Frustration boiled in Spence's gut at the thought. "An office suite you can't afford and a law practice you did not work to build."

"And what's in it for you?"

"I owe her. Hell, Charlie, you owe her."

Charlie scoffed. "I treated her fine."

"You made her feel worthless."

Charlie's face fell. He actually looked hurt and offended by the suggestion. "That's not true."

If Spence had the time and inclination he might have given Charlie a lecture on how to treat women. Since he had neither, he got to the point. "She needs the tape. I'm getting it for her. You're giving it to me."

"I don't know anyone who negotiates blind. I want to see this tape."

"You don't even get to talk about it."

"You're planning on monitoring my discussions now?"

"You're going to sign a confidentiality agreement regarding the dissolution of our partnership. There will be a clause in there about Nat. You talk about her or the tape, say anything derogatory or come near her again, and you lose the office suite."

Charlie rolled his beer bottle between his palms. "No way."

"That's how it's got to be."

"Now that I know what you want, what's to stop me from upping the ante? You leave here, I look at the tape. You stay, I'm going to need something else." Charlie took a long swig.

"How about being a man for once?"

"Your negotiating skills need work, partner. Insulting the other party is a bad strategy."

"I'm handing you a perfect professional situation. You get a new start, nothing but public goodwill from me, and an office that will impress clients." Spence balanced his elbows on his knees. "Compare that to what you can afford without this deal."

"You don't give me enough credit."

"I gave you too much." He stood up. "So, do we have a deal?"

Charlie glanced in the direction of his kitchen. "One tape."

"I get the one I want and the rest of the file stays with you." There was a beat of silence, but Spence knew he had won. Charlie was too savvy to let his curiosity kill the deal. Something Spence had counted on before he stepped in the condo.

Charlie tipped his beer in a salute. "Deal."

Spence walked into the kitchen with Charlie trailing behind. Two boxes and stacks of paperwork sat on the table. Spence did not waste any time. He fingered the thick black boxes and located the one with Nat's handwriting. After a quick check inside, he grabbed it and tucked it under his arm.

"I hope she's worth it," Charlie said, from the doorway.

"You know she is."

"What if it doesn't matter? If you do this grand gesture and she dumps you anyway?"

"That's the difference between us, Charlie. I'm not expecting anything in return."

12

Natalie dragged her fork through her frozen diet dinner entrée. Spence said he would be back. About twenty-four hours had passed, and nothing. She had even called the office and talked with Sue in the hope of getting some inside information, but Sue did not spill a thing.

Nat pushed out her chair and went into the kitchen. There had to be something with taste in her refrigerator. Just a little piece of—

The doorbell rang.

Her hand dropped from the fridge, and every bone in her body shuddered to a halt. She refused to run to the front door or get excited. It could be a neighbor.

"Open the door." Spence's voice carried above the second round of dinging from the doorbell.

She did not run. It was more of a jog with a short stop by the mirror in the living room to make sure she did not look as messy as she felt in her battered blue jeans and gray sweatshirt.

She opened the door to find Spence agitated and pacing in the hall. He wore his suit and had his winter coat slung over his arm.

"What the hell took you so long?" he asked, in the least welcoming voice ever.

"And good evening to you."

He glanced at his watch. "It's six o'clock."

"You came all the way over here to give me the time? How thoughtful."

Odd was the right word. The cool, calm Spence she saw every day had disappeared to be replaced by this fidgeting one. Something had happened or he had something very bad to say. Either way, she wanted to know and get it over with so she could move on to mourning whatever they might have had.

"It's not evening." He pushed past her and into the apartment. "Have you eaten yet?"

"I was munching on that tray."

He peeked at the entrée. "That doesn't even look like food."

"It's actually okay—" Now there was a lie.

"I have your Christmas gifts."

The abrupt change in conversation caught her off guard. "Plural?"

"Here's the first." He handed her the videotape. More like threw it at her.

That explained the harried state. He probably just stole it and was wracked with guilt.

She should have been thrilled. She could set aside all the worry and embarrassment. Charlie did not have her tape. She could destroy that horrible mistake and pretend it never happened. But all she could muster was concern for Spence. "How did you get it?"

His unease started to settle. Instead of walking around in circles as he had been doing, he sat down on the arm of her couch. "I traded for it."

Not the answer she'd expected. "Charlie watched it?"

"He didn't even know he had it."

That did not make any sense. "Then how did you trade?"

"I told him I wanted a tape."

"So you did tell Charlie all about it. Great. Now I'll never hear the end of this."

"Yes, you will."

Spence's assured reaction stopped her tirade. "What did you do?"

"Nothing."

"Something, I think." Knew. She knew it. Could feel it.

"I made Charlie an offer he could not refuse."

"Tell me."

A huge smile broke across Spence's face. "And in other good news, we settled our partnership issues."

She knew what that meant. How could he smile? "You used the tape to make a deal, didn't you?"

"Charlie got what he wanted. So did I." Spence slapped his gloves against his thigh.

"That's not possible. Charlie wanted your office and clients and all of this money." As usual, Charlie wanted the most with the least amount of work.

"He's satisfied. I'm pleased. It all worked out fine."

"Spence."

He got up from the couch and stood in front of her. "You were right."

More like dizzy with confusion. "About?"

"I didn't notice you before. Not as anything other than Charlie's put-upon girlfriend. I want to say you were taken and that explains my reaction and why I didn't go there, but maybe you're right. Maybe I just did not notice you as a woman."

Tears rushed to the back of her eyes. His honest delivery softened the blow. She wanted to know the truth. Needed him to say the words and not just feed her pretty lines.

She kept reminding herself of the fact, and that she had the tape back, which was the point in going to Spence in the first place. The *only* reason she went to Spence.

"I see you now, Nat."

Looking like a dishrag. "And I'm so lovely at the moment."

"Chubby, thin or whatever. I don't care." He cupped her chin in his hand. "The woman I care about, the one I'm falling for, is smart and funny, tough and beautiful."

His words refused to go into her brain. "You're what?"

"Gaining weight is not going to change how I feel about you or how much I want you."

On the scale of great speeches in history, this one ranked pretty high. The sincerity behind his words, the tender look in his eyes; she knew from all of his words and gestures, he meant what he said. He was making a vow. Pledging something more than a few dates.

"What did you give Charlie?" She had to know. Had to figure out if the price paid was too high before they went any further.

Spence wrapped his arms around her waist and pulled her close. "I would have given him everything if that's what it took to get that tape and make you happy. You're worth it. Worth all of it."

She melted into a pile of goo. A happy, bursting with excitement, pile of goo.

He was not the only one who'd learned something. So had she. The extra ten pounds would always bug her, but the woman who made love with Spence, who did not worry about extra skin on her thighs or how her stomach looked, had turned a corner. And Spence deserved to know the role he'd played in that change.

"I want you to keep it." She pushed the tape against his chest.

"What?"

"The tape."

"The tape you made for another man? He made a face that suggested he found the idea disgusting. No, thanks, hon." He tossed the tape on the couch.

"I actually made it for me." Since he looked skeptical, she continued explaining. "Charlie was the excuse, but I made it to try to see myself differently. Now, I don't need it."

Spence's arms tightened around her. "Why?"

"Because a few pounds here or there will not change who I am as a person. I don't need a video to see that." She finally "got" it. It all seemed simple now.

He kissed her jaw. "About time you figured that out."

"After all, you could gain a few pounds and that would not change my feelings for you."

His eyebrows lifted. "How many pounds?"

If someone had told her even a week ago that she would be standing in a room, secure in Spence's arms and joking about weight, she would have had the person committed. Now she knew the freedom that came with being with someone who cared about her for her.

"How many do you plan to gain?" she asked.

"I suggest we concentrate on more interesting things than weight."

Sounded like a perfect idea to her. "Agreed. But the tape still is yours. Watch it or don't watch it. It doesn't matter to me."

"I thought you wanted to destroy it."

"I'd rather keep it as a reminder of a time when my priorities got confused." The time before she figured out how to appreciate her body.

"And I'd rather explore and enjoy the live version of you than watch you on tape."

His words made her stomach flip over. "The only thing I need to make me happy is you."

"I was hoping you'd say that."

She skimmed her hands up his torso to rest on his shoulders. "On that 'falling for' thing?"

His skin took on a bit of a green cast. "Yeah?"

"The feeling is mutual."

"Well, I wasn't quite honest about that." He kissed her then. A short, sweet pop on the lips. "I should have said fallen. Past tense. I know it's only been a short time, but I'm about an inch away from being stupid in love with you."

Something broke loose inside her, filling her with a giddiness and satisfaction she had never known before. "That's mutual, too."

She did not wait for him to make a move. She knew where she stood and that he would not slap her down.

She licked his lips and watched the heat move into his eyes. "How about a kiss?"

His smile wiped away all of her doubts. "Happy to oblige."

His lips covered hers, sending warmth spilling through her body. Everything shifted back into place. All those years of doubts fled as fast as it had come.

She lifted her head and threw him her best seductive grin. "Did you say something about 'gifts'?"

"Women," he said, with exaggerated exasperation.

"Well?"

"We're invited to dinner at my sister's house."

Nat pulled back in his arms. "What? Now?"

"Yeah."

"You could give a woman some warning."

"I just did."

"I'd like some *advance* warning. Some time to make a good first impression. You know, actually comb my hair and wear clean clothing."

"Why are you wearing dirty clothes?" He actually sounded confused by her worries.

"I'm not, but this is your family, Spence."

"I want to show you off."

"Scare them off is more like it."

He tugged her back into his embrace. "They will love you just the way you are. Just like I do."

"They will, once I explain how I didn't know about this dinner until the last minute. Your sister will side with me. You'll see."

"You don't even know her."

"She's a woman, isn't she? She'll agree."

"Two women bossing me around. Just what I need." He clearly tried to sound exasperated but sounded amused instead.

"You're the one who made the plans without telling me. That's what you get."

"And you're perfect exactly the way you are."

She stopped torturing him and kissed him. When she lifted her head, the idea of going anywhere but the bedroom made her a little testy . . . but she could not be angry. Not now. Not at him.

"This is turning out to be a great holiday season," she said, as she loosened his tie.

"The first of many, babe. Merry Christmas."

Looking for more sexy holiday stories? Try
I'M YOUR SANTA,
available now in mass market
paperback from Brava.
Turn the page for a preview of
Lori Foster's story, "The Christmas Present."

With each step he took, Levi pondered what to say to Beth. She needed to understand that she'd disappointed him.

Infuriated him.

Befuddled him and inflamed him.

In order to get a handle on things, he had to get a handle on her. He had to convince Beth to admit to her feelings.

He needed time and space to accomplish that.

Thanks to Ben's directions, Levi carried her through the kitchen toward the back storage unit, where interruptions were less likely to occur.

The moment he reached the dark, private area, Levi paused. Time to give Beth a piece of his mind. Time to be firm, to insist that she stop denying the truth.

Time to set her straight.

But then he looked at her, and he forgot about his important intentions. He forgot everything but his need for this one particular woman.

God, she took him apart without even trying.

Among the shelves of pots and pans, canned goods, and bags of foodstuff, Levi slowly lowered Beth to her feet.

He couldn't seem to do more than stare at her.

Worse, she stared back, all big dark eyes, damp lips, and barely banked desire. Denial might come from her mouth, but the truth was there in her expression.

When she let out a shuddering little breath, Levi lost the battle, the war . . . he lost his heart all over again.

Crushing her close, he freed all the restraints he'd imposed while she was his best friend's fiancée. He gave free reign to his need to consume her. Physically. Emotionally. Forever and always.

Moving his hands over her, absorbing the feel of her, he tucked her closer still and took her mouth. How could he have forgotten how perfectly she tasted? How delicious she smelled and how indescribable it felt to hold her?

Even after their long weekend together, he hadn't been sated. He'd never be sated.

Levi knew if he lived to be a hundred and ten, he'd still be madly in love with Beth Monroe.

The fates had done him in the moment he'd first met her. She smiled and his world lit up. She laughed and he felt like Zeus, mythical and powerful. She talked about marrying Brandon and the pain was more than anything he'd ever experienced in his twenty-nine years.

Helpless, that's what he'd been.

So helpless that it ate at him day and night.

Then, by being unfaithful, Brandon had proved that he didn't really love Beth after all—and all bets were off.

When Beth came to him that night, hurt and angry, and looking to him for help, Levi threw caution to the wind and gave her all she requested, and all she didn't know to ask for.

He gave her everything he could, and prayed she'd recognize it for the deep unshakable love he offered, not just a sexual fling meant for retaliation.

But . . . she hadn't.

She'd been too shaken by her own free response, a response she gave every time he touched her.

A response she gave right now.

They thumped into the wall, and Levi recovered from his tortured memories, brought back to the here and now.

He had Beth.

She wanted him.

Until she grasped the enormity of their connection, he'd continue pursuing her.

Lured by the sensuality of the moment, Levi levered himself against her, and loved it. As busy as his hands might be, Beth's were more so. Small, cool palms coasted over his nape, into his hair, then down to his shoulders. Burning him through the layers of his flannel shirt and tee, her touch taunted him and spurred his lust.

Wanting her, right here and right now, Levi pressed his erection against her belly and then cradled her body as she shuddered in reaction, doing her best to crawl into him.

His mouth against hers, he whispered, "I need you, Beth."

There's nothing more irresistible than
EVERLASTING BAD BOYS.
This sexy anthology from Shelly Laurenston,
Cynthia Eden, and Noelle Mack is
available now from Brava.
Check out Shelly's story, "Can't Get Enough."

"Ailean," she somehow managed to squeak out. "Good morn to you."

"And to you, Shalin. You look awfully beautiful today."

The fact he could say that and sound like he meant it was probably why so many females fell under his spell. Yet Shalin couldn't be fooled. She had mirrors, did she not?

"Thank you. So why are you—"

"Och!" he cut in as he always did. The dragon rarely took a breath, it seemed. "You won't believe my morning, Shalin. You truly won't. Mind if I sit?"

"Uh—"

"Good. Thanks." He dropped down beside her. All that dragon as naked human male. It took every ounce of her strength not to reach out and touch him. Like that solid thigh brushing against her robe-covered leg, to see how it felt under her human hands. She'd never been with a male as human. She'd heard it could be . . . entertaining.

"So there I am, taking a bath, as she said I could, when suddenly her father comes in."

"Oh, that must have been—"

"Horrible, right. Because she told me that we were alone in

that house. But apparently not. I think she wanted me to claim her or marry her or whatever they call it."

"Even though you're—"

"A dragon, right. She doesn't know that bit, you see. Best to keep her in the dark about that, don't you think?"

"Well—"

"Especially for just a night of entertainment. Why she'd want me as a mate, I have no idea. So what are you reading?"

It took her a moment to realize he'd asked her a question he expected her to answer. "*Alchemic Formulas from the Nol- wenn Witches of Alsandair.*"

"Is it interesting?"

"A—"

"I don't know how you can read so many books. I get bored after a few pages."

"So," Shalin found the courage to ask, "you've never read the books about yourself?"

Ailean groaned, rested his elbows on his raised knees, and dropped his head in his hands. "Tell me you haven't read those."

Read them? She'd devoured them.

"Well—"

"Because I didn't authorize those to be written."

The books had begun to show up among humans and drag- ons nearly ten years before. She'd only just finished reading volume three the previous night and word of volume four being available soon had her nearly breathless. Each volume had two editions. One for humans and one for dragons writ- ten in the ancient language of their people. A language the hu- mans of this world could never hope to learn with their much weaker minds, ensuring the fact that the dragons that roamed among them freely remained a well-kept secret.

"The books aren't true, then?"

Based on his wince, she knew they were as true as they could be.

"I never said those things didn't happen. I just said I never authorized them being written about." He turned his head and looked at her, those silver eyes hot on her face. "I don't want you to think I run around telling tales about my relationships, Shalin. I can keep a secret quite well."

And how tempted she was to take him up on his unspoken offer, but that would be cutting her own throat. She'd officially be an enemy of Adienna then, and she simply wouldn't risk her life for any male.

"I—"

"Perhaps I could tempt you away from your interesting book with a promise of a delicious meal at one of the nearby taverns?"

Shocked, Shalin gripped the book in her lap tightly. He wanted to take her out? In public?

What should she say? *I'd love to? How about dinner in my room? Forget that, let's go for it right here, right now?*

Instead what she heard herself stuttering was, "I . . . I can't."

"Can't or won't?"

"Both." She shot to her feet, the book still in her hands. "I have to go."

He stood and towered over her as no human could. "Don't go, Shalin. Spend the night with me."

She should be insulted. He'd just left another female's bed and now, still naked and wet from the woman's bath, he'd asked Shalin to warm his bed. But this was Ailean the Whore. He wasn't doing anything out of character. She actually felt kind of proud he'd asked her at all. Although she knew that to be pathetic. And she'd never admit it out loud.

Shalin focused on the book in her hands. "That's very kind of you, but . . . but I . . . I—"

Big fingers lightly gripped her chin and tilted her face up to his.

"Gods, Shalin. You do so tempt me."

She nearly melted at his words. Melted right into a big puddle at his feet.

"Ailean, I—"

Shalin stopped talking when she realized guards stood behind him.

"There you are," one of them said, slapping his hand down on Ailean's shoulder.

Ailean gave a short snort. "And such a good job finding me, since I've been standing here for the last twenty minutes."

With a snarl, the guard motioned to the others and large steel manacles were locked onto Ailean's wrists.

"Don't look so, Shalin." Ailean grinned. "I have every intention of coming back for you."

Shalin opened her mouth to say something, but no words would come out. He'd rendered her completely speechless. But since he really didn't let her get a word in edgewise, this wasn't exactly an incredible feat. Holding the book close to her chest and pulling the hood of her acolyte robe down over her face, she nodded, turned, and fled.

Here's a sneak peek at Kathy Love's
I WANT YOU TO WANT ME,
available now from Brava . . .

Just as she raised her hand to knock again, the door jerked open, her fisted hand coming close to bopping him in the nose. In the dim light, Vittorio grimaced at her through sleep-heavy eyes. His long hair was tangled and shoved haphazardly back from his face. A bare muscled chest and flat stomach appeared over sweatpants slung low on his narrow hips.

"I'm sorry," Erika immediately said, even as her heart skipped wildly. An image of him lying in bed filled her mind, quickly morphing to a picture of her in bed with him. "I—I didn't think you'd be sleeping," she managed to mumble.

He frowned, blinking, then peered over her shoulder at the evening sky, which now nearly left them in darkness.

"I keep weird hours." His tone was flat, yet his voice still lent the words a beauty with its deep baritone timbre.

Erika stared at him, unable to keep from studying the shadows emphasizing the muscles of his chest and stomach. Chiseled and perfect. She immediately wanted to capture that perfection with her art.

But she managed to stop gaping and move her gaze up to his face, which was also a study in shadows and beauty.

Clearing her throat, she managed a smile. "I keep odd hours too."

He lifted an eyebrow, but didn't say anything. Instead he leaned on the door frame, crossing his arms over his chest. The movement caused his muscles to come to life. Erika's fingers twitched with the longing to move her hand over them like she would the smooth clay of one of her sculptures.

"I'm guessing you didn't come up here to discuss our sleep habits."

Erika's eyes returned to his, as did the sense of dread she'd been experiencing at the bottom of the stairs. Cool disdain— that was what she was getting. Crap.

"No." She offered him another small smile. "No, I came up to see how your head is." She reached forward to brush aside his hair to see the wound, but he caught her wrist, stopping her. His fingers cool, curled a tad too tightly on her skin.

"It's fine."

Erika nodded at the clipped response that didn't invite further questioning. Yet she didn't move, nor did he release her. Although his hold loosened and she could have sworn his thumb slid on the outside of her wrist like the briefest, faintest caress.

Crazy. She made a small noise in the back of her throat at the silly notion. The soft sound seemed to make Vittorio aware that he still held her, because he promptly dropped his fingers away from her.

Erika fought the urge to touch the place where his hand had been. Instead she stepped back from him. She should leave.

"Okay," she said feeling disoriented. "I just wanted to check." Check Philippe's theory, but as before she seemed to be the only one affected by Vittorio's nearness. Vittorio's expression was still remote, hardly filled with overwhelming attraction.

"I guess I should go, then," she added. She took another step backwards, then remembered the plate of treats she still held.

"Oh, and I made you these," she said, shoving the plate toward him. "You know, as a peace offering."

He stared down at the plastic wrap—covered squares as if he expected them to crawl off the plate and attack, perhaps sticking in his beautiful long hair.

Her fingers held the plate, tightening with the desire to touch the silky-looking locks. Was she utterly mad? This man was not interested in her—in the least—and she was fantasizing about touching his hair.

"I—" He still regarded the cookies with consternation. "I don't eat—sweets."

"Oh." She pulled the plate away from him. "Okay. Well, I did just want to say I'm sorry."

He nodded, saying nothing.

"About last night, I mean," she said, watching his expression.

A muscle in his jaw worked as if he was clenching his teeth. "As you've already said," he stated.

Erika nodded, not sure what else to say. It certainly didn't appear he was any more willing to forgive her tonight than he was last night.

Suddenly that uncharacteristic feeling of irritation swelled inside her again. Why did he dislike her so much? Okay, she had hit him with a cell phone, but it had been in an unusual circumstance. And she did feel truly awful about it.

But instead of just accepting that he wasn't going to warm up to her, she heard herself saying, "I know this is going to sound weird, but I'm actually trying to figure out if you are someone that my psychic told me I'd meet."

Vittorio straightened, and the remote look in his eyes shifted, but it wasn't to an expression she liked any better. His eyes widened with amused disbelief.

"Your psychic?"

Erika had had this reaction before. More than once. And she immediately regretted her honesty.

"I'm sure this sounds a little strange to you."

He tilted his head. "What did this psychic say?"

She hesitated. Was he genuinely curious, or did he intend to mock her?

"He's been predicting that I would meet someone who at least physically fits your description."

He nodded, his gaze leaving hers as if he was considering the idea. She still couldn't quite decipher what he might be thinking.

"And what else did this psychic say?"

Erika again debated what to tell him. But the lopsided, not altogether kind, slant of his lips made her stop. He just thought she was nuts. And he didn't appear to like her any better for her nuttiness.

"Forget it." She raised a hand in a gesture of defeat. "I just wanted to be sure your head was all right."

She started to leave, when his voice stopped her. "Thanks."